"You kids ever milked a cow before?" she asked, her hands on her hips, her elbows sticking out. Then she turned and walked back to the barn.

Somehow we knew that we were supposed to follow her, though following Nora was the last thing in the world I wanted to do.

I know that no one should expect someone like me—who grew up in the suburbs drinking milk out of a carton—to know anything about milking a real cow. But still, I couldn't come up with a single way to admit that to Nora without feeling like she was winning some kind of game.

So when we got inside the barn, where Nora had led the cow and she repeated her question, I said, "Sure, I've done it before."

Little Blog on the Prairie

CATHLEEN DAVITT BELL

BLOOMSBURY

NEW YORK BERLIN LONDON SYDNEY

First published in the United States of America in May 2010
by Bloomsbury Books for Young Readers
Paperback edition published in May 2011
www.bloomsburyteens.com

For information about permission to reproduce selections from this book, write to
Permissions, Bloomsbury BFYR, 175 Fifth Avenue, New York, New York 10010

The Library of Congress has cataloged the hardcover edition as follows:
Bell, Cathleen Davitt.
Little blog on the prairie / by Cathleen Davitt Bell. — 1st U.S. ed.
p.   cm.
Summary: Thirteen-year-old Genevieve's summer at a frontier family history camp in Laramie,
Wyoming, with her parents and brother is filled with surprises, which she reports to friends
back home on the cell phone she sneaked in, and which they turn into a blog.
ISBN 978-1-59990-286-9 (hardcover)
[1. Frontier and pioneer life—Wyoming—Fiction. 2. Camps—Fiction. 3. Family life—
Wyoming—Fiction. 4. Blogs—Fiction. 5. Wyoming—Fiction.] I. Title.
PZ7.B38891526Lit 2010   [Fic]—dc22   2009046897

ISBN 978-1-59990-677-5 (paperback)

Book design by Nicole Gastonguay
Typeset by Westchester Book Composition
Printed in the U.S.A. by Quad/Graphics, Fairfield, Pennsylvania
2 4 6 8 10 9 7 5 3 1

To Mom and Sophie, who witnessed my *Little House on the Prairie* obsession, and to Eliza, whom I hope may someday develop one of her own

Little
Blog
on the
Prairie

« 1 »

At first, it felt like a normal family vacation. There was the late-night packing, the airport breakfast, the fighting with my little brother over the window seat, the chewing of three pieces of gum as the plane took off so my ears wouldn't pop.

But there was nothing normal about the camp director, Ron, who met us at the baggage claim area in Laramie, Wyoming. Tall and gaunt, he was wearing a black felt hat, a roughly woven shirt, and boots he could have borrowed from his cousin Frankenstein. Back in sixth grade, I had to do a report on the Amish, and Ron looked like one of them, except the Amish usually drive buggies and make pretzels, and Ron was holding a sign that said "The Welsh Family"—that's us—as if he were some kind of celebrity limo driver gone wrong.

Two hours and one bumpy ride down an endless dirt road later, we met Ron's wife, Betsy. As we were tumbling out of the van she was standing on the porch of their house, and we could see right away that she was no Frankenstein. Instead, she looked like the Pillsbury Doughboy. Or woman. Or whatever. There were blond curls poking out from beneath her bonnet, her cheeks were red like they'd been scrubbed, and in her long, light brown dress and flowery apron, she could have been one of those women who work at the historic places you go to on field trips—you know, they show you all about spinning wool or baking bread, but you can see that underneath their dresses they're wearing sneakers and sweatpants.

"Welcome," Betsy called down from the porch, "to the year 1890."

And that's when it hit me. Those women who work at the historic field trip places? Betsy wasn't one of them. These weren't costumes she and Ron were wearing. Their clothes were for real. And in about five minutes, all of this would be real for me too.

My mom and I had the biggest fight of my life when she told me we'd be going to frontier family history camp—this place in the middle of nowhere, where you live with your family in a one-room cabin, you work all the time doing housework and farm stuff, girls have to wear dresses, there's nothing for kids to do, and anything you'd want to bring is not allowed—no iPods, no phones, no computers, no sports, no friends, no games. We'd be pretending to live in the time before even Monopoly was invented, not that I like that game.

At the end of the argument, which I guess it's pretty obvious I lost, I stood at the top of the stairs, looked down at my mom over the banister, and shouted, "It's not fair. You can't make me go!"

My mom shouted right back, "Genevieve, you will thank me later."

Have you ever noticed that when people say you will thank them later, you never do?

In the van, Ron had explained that we were the last of the four families to arrive—the others had come in the day before. We'd get our camp clothes, and then meet everyone at a picnic before going to our cabin. "Come," Ron said to my brother, Gavin, and my dad now. "I'll show you the barn while the ladies here get all feminized."

My dad turned off his BlackBerry for the first time all day. I don't think he had any idea what we were getting into—I doubt he'd even read the camp brochure. You see, my dad generally likes it that my mom makes all the dinners and most of the decisions, and he can go to work, come home, and then just roll around on the floor with Gavin or come stand on the sidelines at my soccer games. He always says "Ask your mother" when we're bugging him to bend some of her rules—like, whole-wheat bagels instead of regular, soup before candy on Halloween, no cell phones until college. But I know—I can just tell—that if my dad were our only parent, life would be much less complicated. For example, I'm pretty sure that if my dad had planned this vacation, we'd be back at Club Med, where we went last year and had hands down the best time ever because when you get bored, the counselors will take you windsurfing and you can eat anything you want.

As my dad and Gavin trotted off with Ron, my mom almost broke into a run going over to meet Betsy on the porch. The fringes on Mom's suede cowgirl jacket brushed against her jeans and her long hair swung in the same happy beat. This vacation— frontier history family camp—is my mom's dream.

Or one of them. She has a lot of dreams—to be a marathon runner, to build her own furniture, to visit the Galapagos Islands, to have children who perform in school plays (ugh). She was a *Little House on the Prairie* addict as a kid, and you could tell from the way she was walking, the way she was holding out her hand, the way she was smiling, that she couldn't wait for our family's very own *Little House* adventure to begin.

When my mom finished shaking hands with Betsy, Betsy turned to me. "You must be Genevieve," she said, and my mom gave a little gush of appreciation that Betsy had learned my name in advance. "You're about the same age as my daughter, Nora. I'm sure you two will get acquainted as soon as she's back from the milking," Betsy said.

"The milking?" I repeated, on the outside chance that if Betsy heard how absurd she sounded she'd take it back. My best friends, Kristin and Ashley? They would be choking with laughter about now.

But Kristin and Ashley weren't here. They were in school for three more weeks of eighth grade, and then they'd start the routine of mornings at soccer camp and afternoons at the rec-center pool that has defined our last few summers. I should have been with them.

Betsy held open the door and motioned for us to enter the house. "We'll get you dressed," she said, "then you'll get to meet everybody at the picnic." Her smile was contagious, like a yawn. My mom smiled back, and even I caught myself mimicking Betsy's grin—I could tell because my jaw hurt.

But after we entered the house, I felt my smile fade. For a second, I could only stand there and stare, forgetting that I was being rude.

I've always thought of our own house as ordinary. Gavin and I each have a bedroom; there is a room called the living room that no one goes in; there is a family room where we spend most of our time; there's also the basement, where we watch TV; in all of these rooms there are regular-size windows. That let in light, which is the whole point of windows, right?

But Betsy's house? It was tiny. Downstairs, it basically consisted of one room—the kitchen. And the windows were so few and so small, it was dark inside though it was the middle of the day.

At least it was warm, I thought, and then I noticed how great it smelled—like a bakery. It smelled even better than the Cinnabon at the mall. We hadn't eaten anything since our Au Bon Pain muffins on the plane, and now it was well past lunch. I was starving. "Whatever you're cooking smells awesome," I hinted.

My mom turned to me and smiled her isn't-this-fun? smile. I think she was excited that I had made a positive comment, so I quickly flashed back my don't-kid-yourself frown.

"I'm baking pies for the picnic," Betsy explained. "Strawberry-rhubarb and dried apple." She took a big whiff. "It does smell wonderful, doesn't it?" Again: big smile. "Oh, Genevieve, I just know you are about to have the experience of a lifetime," she said. "Don't you feel it? You should thank your mom right now."

"Yeah, right," I mumbled. I slung my knapsack over my shoulder and followed Betsy up the stairs.

What I wanted to tell her was that instead of feeling grateful, I felt a little bit sick. That all during the bumpy van ride, I'd been trying really, really hard not to cry.

I *had* cried the night before, when I was packing. After

putting all my summer stuff away—the tank tops and T-shirts there was no point in bringing, the ribbons Ashley and I had been talking about braiding into our hair, my Eugenia V. Crebs Middle School Soccer sweatshirt, signed in indelible marker by every single girl on the team at the end-of-the-season pizza party—I burst into the kitchen in tears and told my mom that as much as I'd hated the idea of Camp Frontier from the outset, I'd only now felt the full depths of the horror. I told her that I flat out wasn't going to go, that I would live with Grandma in Florida and eat peanut butter and jelly sandwiches and go to the science museum every day if I had to.

It was then that my mom let me open the present she'd planned to save until we returned. And once I opened it I was like, "Wow."

Because inside the organically composted Native American wrapping paper (my mom is totally into all that stuff) was my very own cell phone, something that she has forbidden since I started asking for one around age ten. I started to gush, but before I could even open the box she took it out of my hands. She laid it on the kitchen counter and said, "If you cooperate, this"—she paused as if to swallow her personal distaste for technology—"this thing will be waiting for you when we get back. It's linked up to our service plan. It's ready and waiting to go. But if you don't cooperate, I'm selling it on eDay."

"You mean eBay," I grumbled, but she wasn't listening. Because as usual, my mom would get what she wanted. She was right. I wanted that phone more than I wanted to cancel our plans. Ashley and Kristin are always calling and texting each other, and I wanted to be able to do that too. I wanted it in the way I'd wanted a bike when I was five, or to be friends with Ashley when we were eight and her family had just moved to town.

But did I want it *this* badly? As I trudged up the stairs after Betsy, I wasn't so sure.

« 2 »

First of all, young lady, we'll do you," Betsy said. I was standing in her bedroom, taking in the tiny room's sloped ceiling, dormer window, a dresser with big round knobs, and a four-poster bed that was high off the ground and covered with a quilt. A twin bed was pushed off to one side. Did their daughter sleep in their room? With them?

Betsy put her hands on her hips, looking at me up and down. "So tall," she said. "Lucky."

I didn't say anything because I guessed Betsy didn't know what it was like to be taller than all the boys in your grade, to be known as the girl who hung Robby Brainerd upside down by his ankles after she found him throwing frogs against the playground slide. To be the girl who always plays fullback on the soccer team, the one who has never been asked out by a boy.

Betsy gestured to the big bed, where she'd laid out some clothes. There was something dark brown, something blue with flowers, and other things that were all white and fluffy. Betsy ran her palm underneath the leg of what looked like pants—only they were white, with ruffles at the bottom and a pink ribbon at the waist. "I have a girl come out from town to run these up for me," she said. "We used the measurements you all sent in and I think they ought to fit you pretty well. Have you ever worn clothes that were made just for you instead of fabricated in China and sold in mass quantity at the G-A-P?" Her big blue eyes were sparkling, like it was Christmas morning, and she was Santa. And yes, she spelled "Gap" like it was a dirty word.

My mom rubbed the fabric between her fingers. She took in a deep and reverent breath, as if she were meeting someone holy. "They're just lovely," she said. "And so simple."

Now, I know from simple. I am the kind of person who wears jeans every single day in the winter, and shorts with good pockets every day in the summer. My mom always wants me to keep my hair long, and I do, but I brush it in the morning, put it in a ponytail, and don't think about it again all day. These clothes—there was nothing simple about them.

And speaking of hair, just then Betsy looked into my face—she actually leaned in so she could see all the way under the bill of my baseball cap. "Darling," she said, "shall I put your lovely long hair into braids?"

"Umm . . . ," I said, thinking, "Cell phone, cell phone." Before I knew it, she had whisked off the cap and begun brushing and pulling and tugging and otherwise making my scalp burn, wrestling my hair into two braids. My friend Ashley wears braids sometimes. It's part of her prep look—you know, a short plaid skirt, kneesocks, oxfords, glasses? It's cute. When I wear braids, it doesn't look cute. It looks like I have a fat face.

"There," Betsy said, smiling—she was like the Cheshire cat, this woman—and turning me so I could face my mom.

"So sweet!" my mom gushed. I turned away. It was hard to see her this happy when I was feeling like a trussed turkey.

Next, Betsy had me out of my jean shorts, my Chucks, and the Yosemite T-shirt I'd bought at Urban Outfitters, and into more clothes than I would normally wear in a week. There was a tank-top thing she called a bib; a petticoat, which is a kind of skirt you wear underneath your other skirt; pantaloons, which are pants you wear instead of underwear—they are open in the back so you can go to the bathroom without pulling them down; and wool stockings, which are actually very long socks that button onto straps hanging down from your bib. Over everything, you wear a long wool dress that weighs as much as ten algebra textbooks. Betsy lovingly pointed out the double stitching on the seams, the rickrack bib work, the puffs at the sleeves. "This was the fashion in 1890," she said. "A girl your age would already be considered a young lady, so I was careful to pick styles for you that are more sophisticated than what the little girls are wearing."

"Sophisticated," I repeated as I strapped on boots with twenty different hooks you had to wrap the laces around, and Betsy showed my mom the clothes she'd laid out for her. "So what year did you say you're pretending it is?" I asked. "1890?"

"Oh, no," said Betsy. "We're not pretending. 1890 is the year it *is*."

How I wished Kristin or Ashley were here so I could catch their eyes and whisper, "Crazy!" Desperate, I stole a glance up at my mom, but her back was turned as she struggled to attach her stocking to the straps.

Betsy brought out a mirror. It was about the size of a small book, but I could move it up and down my whole body to see what I looked like.

And let me tell you: it was worse than I had expected.

I think that even as I'd been dreading the idea of wearing all this stuff, deep down, I secretly hoped that my mom would be right and that inside these long dresses and frilly clothes, I'd look pretty. Wait, I take that back. It sounds so lame.

Let me try again. When I look in the mirror at home or in the locker room, or just walking by a storefront, I'm always surprised. And kind of horrified. How come I have such big cheeks and not enough forehead? How can I be so ordinary and also ugly at the same time? Wouldn't one of those be bad enough?

But even shock is not the right word to describe what I saw now. In my dress and braids, I didn't look plain and ordinary, disappointing, or simply ugly. I looked like a freak. I looked like someone I had never seen before in my life. I had to remind myself that I was actually still there, inside what I was wearing. I pulled a few strips of hair out from the braids so my face had a little something covering it, but that just made me look like a freak who'd been caught in a windstorm.

Betsy and my mom couldn't get enough of me though. "Oh, Genevieve," my mom cooed, and there were actual tears in her eyes. "This is amazing. Don't you feel like we're genuinely traveling back in time?"

I tried very hard to get her to stop being ridiculous just by staring at her. "I look like I'm in the Thanksgiving play," I said. "I look like I'm six."

Betsy smiled and then she was back to business, pulling a burlap sack down from a hook on the wall. "Everything you brought with you goes in here," she said. "Your toothbrushes, your socks and underwear. I lock it up and we don't get it out again until you go. This experiment won't work—it isn't good for you, it doesn't change you—unless you leave behind every aspect of the modern world."

"Um . . . ," I said. "Everything?"

"Everything," Betsy answered, and she dumped the contents of my knapsack out onto the bed. "This gadget," she said, holding my iPod, "has no place in this world." She fingered the lip gloss I'd packed even though I don't wear it—I was just seeing what would happen. "No, dearie, sorry." One by one everything I'd decided to bring was thrown in the burlap bag.

But when her hand closed around my boxed set of travel-size Clearasil products, I grabbed it back.

"No," I said.

"Genevieve," my mom counseled. "We talked about this." Horrible enough to recall, we had. That conversation—about how at Camp Frontier they didn't brush their teeth, no one wore deodorant, and bathing was a weekly (maybe), not a daily, event—that conversation goes down in history as one of the worst talks my mom and I have ever had.

So I knew. No Clearasil.

But I was looking at my mom now, not Betsy. I mean, let's cut to the chase—Betsy could giggle away in her bonnet and dress and believe that it was any year she wanted, but it was my mom who had written the check and I'm sure no one would have cashed it if it had been dated 1890. "I will cry every night," I said in a low voice. "I will walk all the way home." I could see on her face that she was close to giving in. "It's just this one thing,"

I said. "I'm giving up my whole summer, and all I want in return is to start high school not covered in acne scars." She was deciding, I could tell, and then she frowned, which told me I'd won. She turned to Betsy.

"We're asking an awful lot of a thirteen-year-old here," she said. "I think we'll still get the bulk of the experience even if we make this one exception."

Betsy raised her eyebrows. "All right," she said, "though my personal opinion is that clean water and proper nutrition—"

My mom cut her off. "Let's drop it," she said. She turned toward the stairs, her back straight and tall in her black dress that looked so much like mine. I was reminded for a horrific moment of the matching mother-daughter dresses she tried to force me to wear on Christmas when I was ten and already way too old for it.

I couldn't help but wonder now: if I'd just sucked it up about the mother–daughter dress back then, would my mom have gotten this kind of thing out of her system, and let me spend the summer hanging out at the rec-center pool where I belonged?

The thought was enough to make me want to cry all over again.

« 3 »

When it was my dad and Gavin's turn to change, Betsy smiled at me some more and said, "If you step outside, you'll find some kids running around. They're probably getting ready for the picnic. Introduce yourself!"

"Um . . . okay," I said, although I had no intention of introducing myself to anyone while I was dressed up like Strawberry Shortcake. "Can you tell me where I can find a bathroom?" I asked.

Betsy flung open the front door and pointed.

Now, I'd known what the bathroom was going to be. I'd read the word "outhouse" in the brochure. And yet I hadn't completely believed it. I'd thought, okay, there will be a secret, *real* bathroom—maybe just a small one—inside the house. Like the kind they have in old gas stations where they tell you they don't have a bathroom but if you look nice and helpless they'll let you in. Employees Only. For Emergencies. For me.

But no. Betsy was pointing toward the woods, where I could see a shape I recognized from TV shows and Road Runner cartoons—a tall shack with a narrow door and a crescent moon carved out under the roofline. "It's not as bad as it looks. You'll get used to it," Betsy said.

I didn't see how I could get used to that. Or any of this. Have I mentioned that I could barely breathe in what I was wearing? Betsy had explained that, for health and liability reasons, wearing corsets was optional, and both my mom and I had said no, but even without one, the dress felt like a straitjacket. Especially now that I had to pee.

Stepping out of the door, I ran.

But not toward the outhouse. I didn't have to pee that badly. I headed to the barn and then went around the back of it and into the edge of the woods. I was conscious of people in the yard, but I ignored them, and once I was alone, I stopped. I pulled the box of Clearasil from my pocket, unstuck the lid where I'd glued it shut the night before, pulled out the actual Clearasil tube, and dug through some cotton balls to find my new phone.

Here's the thing: after my mom and dad had gone to bed the night before, I'd snuck down to the kitchen and taken the phone from where my mom had left it on the counter. I'd only wanted to look at it, but when I saw that the box was sealed with nothing but a clear sticker I could easily peel away with my fingernail, I got the phone out, thinking, "No one will ever know."

I swear I just wanted to turn it on and check it out. But after I charged the battery and changed the wallpaper and set it up with my name, returning it to the box for the summer seemed like such a waste. I tried to convince myself I shouldn't sneak it in my suitcase. The battery wouldn't last for very long, I argued. I wouldn't have privacy, and it's not like I'd be able to get calls. I mean—I'd waited for a cell phone my whole life. I could wait two and a half more months. If I got caught with it at Camp Frontier, I'd probably never see it again. Bringing it made no sense.

But obviously, I hadn't listened to myself. And now—here it was! And I was glad. Just the feel of the cool plastic helped me to remember that there was a world out there where people dressed in normal, comfortable clothes, and could pee in sanitary, indoor bathrooms. Without really thinking about what I was doing, I turned the phone on. I watched the picture of a sunset morph into a sailboat. I checked the service signal, and almost couldn't believe my luck. There were three bars. I thought about making a call, but I didn't want anyone to hear. Who knew how close we were to the other people? I had to be very careful. So I texted Ashley and Kristin—the only numbers I'd programmed into the phone the night before.

```
Week 1 - Sunday
2:27 pm
Help! I'm dressed up like an American Girl
Doll minus the fashion sense. My sleeves
are so tight I can't lift my arms above
my head. Is this the new me?
```

I pressed send.

Watching the envelope icon spin as the text went zipping out into the world, I felt like someone who has just tossed a message in a bottle into the ocean.

« 4 »

As Betsy placed the last basket onto a table that had been set up behind a row of benches, a girl with red hair approached with a napkin-covered tin bucket that she placed next to it. The redhead appeared to be a card-carrying member of what I was already thinking of as the Doll Club: half of the kids milling around seemed to be nine-year-old girls carrying little dolls. "They're muffins," the girl whispered to Betsy. "My mom made them."

"Bryn!" Betsy exclaimed. "Your mom didn't have to bring anything today." She looked over the girl's head and waved at a woman who was standing next to a man with hair so red, I knew the couple had to be the girl's mom and dad. "I can't believe she even figured out how to use the stove."

The girl's—Bryn's—pale skin was covered in freckles. "We've been cooking on the woodstove in the yurt my dad built on my grandparents' farm. Erik, Anja, and I helped." The girl pointed into the crowd at the only other kids whose hair looked just like hers. One was a little girl, maybe seven or so, and the other was a boy who was walking back and forth on a bench like it was a balance beam. He looked older. "They'd done this before?" I thought. And then: "What the heck is a yurt?"

Soon, Ron started talking in that voice teachers use when it's time to start a class. "Okay, okay," he said. "Let's all sit down and we'll get started. Sit with your kinfolk. One family per bench." He looked over at Betsy and she nodded and smiled back at him.

"Now that you're all here and relatively well settled in," he said, "I'm going to explain our setup." I guess he was forgetting that we hadn't seen our cabin yet. Not that I wanted to, except that I was kind of holding out hope—unfounded, I know—that it might have a bathroom. There were so many buttons and layers to what I was wearing, I didn't really know where to begin, but at least it would be private.

"Some people say that they don't think the camp should have a competitive spirit," Ron said. "That it's pitting people against each other in a way that doesn't reflect well on the spirit of community life.

"So let me explain. Giving the camp a bit of a competitive edge re-creates the sense of urgency frontier people experienced on a day-to-day basis. For them, there were no modern-day conveniences to turn to. There was only the long cold winter that was fast approaching and the matter of survival. If a family didn't have enough seasoned wood to make it through the winter, they might freeze to death."

We were sitting right behind the family with the red-haired kids—Anja, Bryn, and Erik, the ones with the yurt, whatever that is. Across from us was a family I'd seen earlier, a woman whose short, no-nonsense haircut had been transformed into an 1890s style with the addition of a hair bow that looked like the kind they put on dogs after they visit the groomer. The dad was chewing on a stalk of hay and I elbowed Gavin and whispered, "Really? He's that much of a farmer already?" Their little girl was cradling her doll in both arms like she was holding a sleeping baby. I noticed its hair, which was made from strips of rags, was braided just like the girl's.

The boy was older. My age? It was hard to tell. He was still wearing his felt hat, though most of the men had taken theirs off. I wondered if the boy *liked* hats. Then I noticed that he'd pulled the hat all the way down to his nose and angled it to the side in a way that made him look like he should be in some black-and-white detective movie, wearing a trench coat and standing in the fog. Or maybe he didn't like hats after all. Maybe he thought this was a big joke too. Now, *that* would be cool.

In front of the straw-chewing, bow-wearing, hat-boy family was a group I immediately labeled the Happy Blond People. The parents could have been twins—they were both freckled and had blond hair cut short in a way no hair bow could possibly make look like an 1890s style. Their kids were happy, blond, and sporty too, except one girl whose long hair must have been dyed, it was so solidly jet black. She had her face in her hands but when she moved them, it hit me. Some of it had rubbed off, but you could still tell that she was wearing a lot of black and white makeup. A goth girl, out here?

When she caught me looking at her, I turned quickly back to Ron. "If they did not put aside enough food," he was saying, "people on the frontier might starve. What Betsy and I found so valuable in our experiments living on the land was the starkness of this contrast, the idea that you couldn't just open up a new line of credit on your house to pay for the things you needed. You truly had to rely on yourself.

"We want you to have this experience as well. So we'll meet up every Sunday as people would have done on the frontier if they were lucky enough to have established a church, and we'll share our progress and our frustrations. I'll make an assessment of how you're doing, which doesn't really matter in any way, but year after year, people tend to take pretty seriously."

"Oh, my God," I whispered to my dad. "We get grades?"

"Shh, Gen," he said, but the look on his face was the same one he gets when he's been stumped by a clue in the Sunday crossword.

"It's a simple system," Ron explained. "Each week I'll visit your farm and see what you're up to. I'll assign you a grade for the week based on overall preparation and the efficiency of your execution of what you set out to do. I use a scale of one to ten, and at the end of the summer, we add it all up to get your score. It gives you a goal, and it keeps us honest while we're out here. This is real. You won't get anything out of this experience if you don't feel that way. It's not a vacation."

My dad leaned over to whisper, "I thought this *was* a vacation."

"I gave you the brochure to read," my mom hissed.

"It sure is priced like a vacation," he grumbled.

"A few final words," Ron said, "about the actual work on your farm. Each of you has been assigned a cash crop that you will be raising on the bulk of your acreage. In addition, you'll be tending an extensive kitchen garden. This late in the season, all of the major planting has been done, and in the case of the gardens, we've even been bringing some things in. We do this before our families arrive. My daughter, Nora"—he pointed to a girl I'd seen helping him move benches earlier—"has been a great help with the work in the fields. Betsy has been magnificent in tending the gardens, and we've used some hired workers as we always do off-season. You'll be responsible for taking it over now, though. Thinning, weeding, watering to whatever extent that's feasible, and before the end of camp, we'll start pulling in the harvest, though most of that will happen after you have left.

"Each family will also take on a significant farm improvement project. We have some at the ready for you, or you can feel free to suggest one that speaks to your talents or desires. Just keep in mind that I'm talking about barn raising and road building—not fixing a door or screening a window."

"This sounds like sharecropping," my dad whispered to my mom, loud enough so the man with the red hair turned around to stare. My dad rubbed his hands over his forehead, scratching at his hair and then under his collar. "We do the work and live in unimproved cabins on the farmer's land. He keeps the harvest?"

My mom turned up the corners of her mouth in an if-you-insist-on-looking-at-it-that-way-you-deserve-to-be-miserable look. Just as she started to speak, the dad from the red-haired family leaned back toward us again. "Shh," he said, like someone was talking on their cell phone in a movie theater. My mom's face turned bright red. My dad rolled his eyes. I tried to draw my knees up to my chest, which is something I do when I'm embarrassed, but it's a lot harder when five yards of skirt, a petticoat, and bloomers are involved. Let's just say I almost fell flat on my face in front of the bench.

Gavin caught me, and as he was pulling me back to an upright position, he said, "Let the fun begin."

« 5 »

I'm guessing Ron used to be a mortician, but he couldn't keep a job for more than a year because the corpses he worked on never looked happy. I heard Betsy thought up the idea of this camp to save their family from financial ruin."

It was the goth girl. She was next to me in the food line, but her hair was hanging around her face in sheets, so I couldn't say for sure if she was talking to me. But when I laughed, she looked up and kind of quasi-smiled, though her eyes held that same, mournful I'm-trying-to-stay-goth-even-though-I'm-in-this-ridiculous-costume expression I'd noticed before.

"Okay," she said. "I made that up. But doesn't it sound right?"

"People are already baking muffins," I said, gesturing with my chin to the pail the red-haired girl had delivered, but keeping my voice low, as if we were spies.

"I'll tell you something, " she said. "The first time I find myself alone, I'm feeding this petticoat to a bear."

I giggled. "How about the wool stockings?"

"Already toasted," she said. "My mom was practicing lighting a fire in the stove and when they weren't looking, I shoved them in. Smelled kind of funny. Almost put the fire out. If they make me wear the other pair I'll bury them somewhere far away."

She stabbed a piece of ham with an enormous fork as she spoke, for emphasis, but it made a loud scratching noise against the plate and I was a little bit like, *whoa*. I mean, I didn't want to be here, but this girl was taking camp rebellion to a new level.

"Did you puke before?" she asked me.

I just stared at her.

"I saw you run out of the house and disappear behind the barn," she prompted. "I thought maybe you were puking. 'Cause of the monkey suit and all." She pointed to her own dress, which looked just like mine except her sleeves were not puffy at the shoulder, and the bib was covered in ruffles. According to Betsy's system of making different dresses based on your age, I guessed this meant she was younger than me.

"I wasn't," I said. "But I could have been."

"Maybe Ron was in a motorcycle accident so bad, he had to have half his body parts replaced and is basically an android now. Maybe Betsy was his physical therapist when they fell in love—he's her greatest success story."

"I'm Gen," I said.

"My name's Kate," she said back. "But my friends call me Ka. Rhymes with *Saw*, as in that movie, which by the way totally rocked." I didn't tell her I was too scared to see it. "You're not into this whole frontier idea thing, are you?" she asked.

I shook my head.

"Good, because there's this kid with red hair who is totally into it and I can't really let him get too near me." She was talking about the boy from the muffin family, the one who'd been walking on the bench like it was a balance beam. Now he was whittling, carving something Gavin later told me were homemade fishhooks.

"I love the twenty-first century," I reassured her.

"It's not even that for me," she said. "My mom?" She gestured with her plate to her happy, wholesome blond parents, who looked so sporty I was surprised they weren't carrying kayaks on their backs. "That's a guy she married just two days ago. This is his idea of a *honeymoon*. Those kids . . ." She gestured to the boy who'd been throwing the rock, and two Doll Club girls in matching dresses. "They're my new stepsiblings."

"Wow," I said. "Is that true?"

"Yes," she said. "Everyone is making all these Brady Bunch jokes, but seriously, it's awful."

"Have you known your dad—I mean stepdad—very long?" I asked.

"Like, six months," Ka said. "They're both gym teachers. They met at a gym-teacher convention. My mom and I live in San Francisco and they're from some conformist suburban dystopia near LA, but they have a big house, so we're leaving to move in with them."

Just then, her stepdad leaned down, kissed her mom on the lips, and then nuzzled her ear. I wasn't sure what dystopia meant exactly, but imagining moving in with a bunch of strangers while your mom macked it up with their dad—I think I got the drift.

"Wow," I said.

"Yeah," she agreed, looking on in disgust. "I don't know how

I'm going to get out of the move, but I am." She took a bite from a slice of bread on her plate. "Maybe when I unearth the truth about the experiments Ron was conducting for the government at Area 51, and about how Betsy is an alien from the planet of smiling extraterrestrials, my mom will see the light and we can bail."

I looked back over at my own parents. Speaking of smiling extraterrestrials. My mom was talking to the woman with the bow in her hair. You could hear their squeals and exclamations even from where Ka and I were standing. They were both trying way too hard. Gavin was walking on the benches in imitation of the red-haired boy. My dad was staring out into the woods like someone who's been hit by a blast from a stun gun. "I don't know," I said. "Sometimes I wouldn't mind swapping my family for a bunch of strangers."

"Trust me," she said. "My new older brother—boy jock wonder—is constantly throwing things at me and saying 'Think fast.' His sister is my age and we're supposed to be instant friends but we have nothing—we're talking zero—in common. Her name's Katie. I mean, we have the same name. How can we possibly be sisters, right? And you know what her nickname is? It's Kater-tot. Her little sister, Cara—they call her Cara-tot. They like these names. Their older brother, Matt, made them up. They both think he walks on water. It's nauseating. They're such . . . girls."

"Good luck," I said.

She nodded, but didn't say thanks. And I thought that was pretty cool.

I didn't talk to any of the other kids. Hat Boy was playing catch with the guy Ka had pointed out as her new older brother, Matt.

Ron and Betsy's daughter was talking to them like they were old friends. Everyone else seemed really young. I sat down with my plate of food next to my dad, and we both listened as my mom and the woman with the bow in her hair compared woodstove trivia.

"I heard you can put a piece of paper in the oven and if it bursts into flames, it's too hot to bake bread," the woman said. She brushed her hair up on her forehead as if she was swatting at a fly, but it was actually the bow that was bothering her. Instead of pulling it out, which is what I would have done, or burning it, which is I guess what Ka would have done, she gave it a little friendly pat.

"I read online that if you can keep your hand in the oven for a count of five but not more than eight, it's the right temperature to bake," my mom said.

"That sounds a little hard on your hand," the woman said, and then added, "Frankly, it's usually my husband who cooks. When he's too busy I just pick something up. This is a chance for me to reconnect to cooking. Or I guess I should say connect to it. I used to boil water in law school, but that was about it."

My mom nodded and smiled, looking smug. Maybe she'd never baked muffins in a woodstove—and she'd never gone to law school—but she took a lot of pride in cooking dinner for us every night.

Before I'd even had a chance to finish eating, Betsy was back, shooing us along. "Your family will want to get started on the walk to your cabin," she said. "We're running a little behind and it will be dark before you know it. You've got provisions in the place to get you started. Just the basics—flour, cornmeal, salt pork, lard, coffee, some dry staples. But you'll want to get cooking as soon as you can and eating fresh out of the garden. I'll pack you up a supper for your first night. Gen, follow me to the kitchen."

In the kitchen, I watched Betsy fill a basket with food for our dinner, including a loaf of fresh bread she pulled out of the oven.

Betsy's daughter came into the kitchen carrying a pail of milk. Her bonnet was hanging down her back in a way I caught myself thinking looked kind of cool. She was tall like me, with her long hair done in a thick blond braid. She looked like I imagined Betsy must have when she was a girl—with rosy red cheeks, big eyes, and a pretty mouth, though there was something funny about it, like she'd just eaten something sour. I wondered if she played sports, if I would like her, what kinds of bands she liked to listen to when she wasn't wearing this crazy dress-up costume, but then I remembered that all that was impossible. Nora wasn't visiting. She lived here. My mom had told me on the plane Nora was homeschooled and raised pigs. It was likely she didn't listen to music at all, unless someone actually played it on the piano.

"Nora's a whiz as a milker," Betsy said. "And she helped me make up all the dolls for the great crop of little girls we have in this year."

"You made all those dolls?" I said. Before I could stop myself, I started to laugh. I knew it was rude, but sometimes you just can't hold it in.

"Oh, yes," Betsy answered, as if my laughter was to be expected. Maybe Nora wouldn't be offended either?

But Nora was staring at me, her mouth hanging open.

"I had to," she hissed, and I pursed my lips hard, took a deep breath through my nose, and got myself mostly under control except for one last little snort.

Just then there was a knock at the door. Betsy answered it and in walked Hat Boy. As soon as he stepped into the room, he took off his hat, and seeing him without it, I realized I hadn't taken a good look at him before. He had dark blond hair, almond-shaped brown eyes, and though he was dressed in clothes like Ron's, he looked more normal in them—maybe because his shirt was open at the collar and I could see a braided leather necklace resting against the hollow of his throat.

He smiled at me and for half a second, I forgot all about Camp Frontier. I forgot how tired I was, and how stupid I looked in my dress, about how I still needed to pee but was too freaked by the outhouse and the thought of undoing all the buttons.

I looked away from him and down at my hands, which I buried in the folds of the dress. I didn't smile back. I always do this around cute guys—Ashley teased me that I acted like they were from another species or something. I've never told her that on some level, I suspected that was true. What would a cute guy want from a girl like me?

"My mom is wondering if you could pack a supper for us too," the boy said to Betsy. "She said for me to tell you she didn't have time this morning to figure out the cooking stuff and we're going to be hungry tonight if we don't bring something back." His voice was deep and a little raspy and he was asking in a way that made me think he was really nice—and also used to getting what he wants. I glanced up again just long enough to note that his shirtsleeves were rolled up at the wrists. I found myself think-ing: "Sexy," which took me completely by surprise. "Sexy" is a word I never use except when I'm making a joke about how someone's fly is down or they have food on their face.

"Now, Caleb," Betsy said. "Your mother knows very well that each family is entitled to one picnic supper when they first arrive. Your family had yours last night. You're on your own." She smiled, but it wasn't the beaming, approving smile of before.

I wondered what it was like for Ron to come home to Betsy's disapproval after he lost one mortician job after another. Or was learning to use his brand-new fake hands. I giggled, and then realized in horror that maybe Caleb thought I was laughing at him for asking for food he wasn't supposed to have.

"Well," Caleb said. "It couldn't hurt to ask."

He smiled at me again, quickly, and I looked down. As soon as he was gone, I wished I'd smiled back at him. I wished I'd said something. But then again, what I really wished was that I hadn't been dressed in a historical costume with my hair in braids.

Suddenly, I had an idea.

Outside, I reached into our basket, ripped off a hunk of the loaf of bread Betsy had packed for us, and found Caleb where he was standing by the benches.

"Here," I said, passing him the bread.

"Thanks!" he answered. I couldn't look at him. I couldn't say you're welcome. I didn't even register that it was kind of gross that he put the piece of bread directly in his pocket.

The only person who did seem to have the ability to speak was Nora, who had stepped onto the porch in time to see me pass the bread to Caleb.

"That's cheating," she said. She wasn't talking to me, though.

She was talking to Caleb. She was actually winking at him. *Winking?* And smiling. She had a great smile. I wished for a second I hadn't laughed at her inside. I wished I'd done something so that she'd want to be my friend too. I laughed now, to let her know I was willing to be part of the joke. But she didn't move or look at me. It was as if I wasn't even there.

« 6 »

Here we are," Ron said when we broke out of the woods on the path he'd been leading us through to our cabin. In the clearing in front of us, I could see a small building. Was it a shed? The outhouse?

"That's home," Ron said.

"That?" I said out loud. "That's a house?" It was even smaller than Ron and Betsy's. It looked—honestly—exactly like the shed our neighbors the Ostrakazis use to store their lawnmower. And the giant snowblower that Mr. Ostrakazi never offers to loan us for our driveway, even when he sees me up to my waist shoveling. My mom thinks shoveling is good for you.

"And there's the barn," Ron continued, pointing again. Get this: the barn was actually bigger than the house.

To the left of the house was a garden surrounded by a post and rail fence, and beyond that a field that looked like a meadow. "We've already plowed and planted corn," Ron explained.

"It doesn't look like corn," my dad said.

"That's because all you can see right now are weeds. You've got your work cut out for you, I guess."

"Ah," said my dad.

"There's a nice kitchen garden too," Ron went on. "As we are committed to 1890 farming practices, we don't use any chemical pesticides. We're actually classified as an organic farm. That lets us sell our stuff for more on the market.

"Hey ya, Daisy. Hey ya, Pumpkin," Ron called to a pair of chickens that were pecking at the ground near the house. And then, when we still didn't say anything he asked, "What do you think?"

None of us, not even my mom, moved. I was trying to take in the whole expanse of it—the bigness of the woods, the bigness of the mountains that you could see beyond the field, the smallness of the house, how cool the air was now that the sun had started to set.

Then we went inside.

"Sweet home Alabama," I muttered. The cabin was dark and creepy, and smelled kind of funky—like old bacon mixed with mildew and mold.

All the time I'd been fighting with my mom back home, at least we'd been doing it, well, at home. With carpeting, wallboard instead of rough planks, and with lights on in all the rooms. Even Ron and Betsy's tiny house felt like a palace compared to the cabin we'd just walked into. Their place had a real upstairs. All we had here was a loft with a ladder.

It was so much worse than what I'd been imagining that the horror canceled out my ability to feel anger. I even forgot for a second how badly I needed to pee—and trust me, I had to pee pretty badly by now. "This," I said out loud, not caring if I was being rude to Ron, "is it?"

Ron set a lantern on the table and showed my dad how to light it. It had kerosene in it, so you held a match to a wick and turned a little key to make it burn brighter or dimmer. It wasn't a lot of light even on the brightest setting.

My dad looked at Gavin and me. "You can never do this," he said. "It's not safe for kids."

"We can never turn on the lights?" Gavin asked. I think he meant it to be a sarcastic question, but his voice cracked. He sounded as freaked out as I felt.

I noticed bugs swarming around the lamp. A lot of bugs. A mosquito whined in my ear and I swatted at it. "Is there a hole in a screen or something?" I said.

"Screens?" Ron said. "Frontier cabins in 1890 didn't have screens. Mosquitoes were a part of life. If they're really bad, you can run a smoky fire or close the windows."

"There's no screens?" my dad said. He started to scratch at his neck.

My mom put the basket down on the table and went to the counter that ran along the back wall. There were a couple of barrels underneath it and a few shelves above that held dishes. There was a pump mounted to one end of the counter with a basin underneath the spout—not even a real sink. "This is the kitchen," she said, like she was speaking more to herself than to us. "Amazing. It's so simple. Think about our convection oven, our lettuce washer, our stand mixer—even the toaster—and then look at this," she said. "We have more counter space on the grill!"

"You've got wood for the stove in the lean-to next to the

house," Ron announced. "You can try for a fire tonight, or just wait until the morning, though it does get cold. I'll send Nora over tomorrow to make sure you are getting along okay, and next week we'll set you up with a milk cow." He was almost out the door before he remembered something. It was strange, he had looked so creepy in the airport and driving the van, but out here, he blended in, just like one more enormous and silent tree. I kind of wished he would stay. "You might want to clear a little bit of the forest growth from around the house," he said to my dad. "It will help with the bear problem this place always seems to have." He spoke casually, like he was talking about a rainstorm coming or a beautiful sunset.

"Bear problem?" my dad echoed.

Now, remember how I said my dad is really laid-back and lets my mom make all the rules? Well, here's something else to know about my dad. He is totally brave and a totally great guy, but he is really scared of animals. He crosses the street if he sees a dachshund coming. He makes my aunt send her cat to the kennel when we visit, claiming allergies everyone knows he doesn't have. We had a raccoon in the neighborhood for a while last year, and if you so much as put a paper plate on the ground during a cookout, my dad would be after you about how it would lead to exploding raccoon populations and everyone we know dying of rabies. I once saw him cower when a deer crossed the trail when we were on a hike. He has never taken us to a zoo.

So, bears.

"What do you mean, *problem*?" my dad asked. "They come into the yard?"

"Sometimes," said Ron. "One time we had a big teenager cub

try to get into the house. I think most of them aren't so dumb though."

"One tried to get into the house," my dad repeated quietly. He wasn't asking a question. Merely stating what Ron had said as if he were translating from a foreign language. As in, I'm sorry, I don't speak Crazy, I must have heard you wrong . . .

"Just the one time," Ron said, and then, as if it wasn't really worth explaining further, he changed the subject. "If one of you kids can toss some scraps to the chickens and lock them up in the coop before you go in for the night, I'm sure they'd be much obliged."

"Is that wise?" my dad said. "To let the chickens run around loose during the day with a bear on the prowl?"

Ron smiled—was he laughing at my dad? "It's full summer. The bears aren't hungry now," he said. "There's plenty for them to eat out in the woods."

And then he was gone, and it was just my dad, Gavin, and me, sitting in hard-backed chairs around a rough wooden table with a (smoking) lamp on it. As soon as my mom finished running her hands along the surface of everything, saying, "See how useful every piece of furniture has to be to merit being built at all? Ron made everything by hand!" She joined us at the table. It was freezing in the cabin.

"So!" Mom said. And it was clear we were all supposed to be as excited about this as she was.

"So," my dad answered. "I thought this was going to be a resort?"

"A resort would teach us nothing," my mom said firmly.

My dad looked up at the ceiling, where you could see a lot

of spiderwebs. And also, after your eyes adjusted to the dark, spiders.

"I feel like our family's closer already," I said. It didn't even come out funny, and no one laughed.

Meanwhile, Gavin started to look around. My mom began to unpack Betsy's food. My dad covered one of my hands with his.

"I think I found the TV!" Gavin shouted, and when I turned my head with a jerk, he was like, "Just kidding."

I didn't move from the table as my mom found a knife and sliced up the bread. There was butter shaped in a ball and wrapped in a cloth, and she spread some on each slice. The milk in the jug was still kind of warm and way thicker than I am used to. After a few sips I didn't want any more. But the bread and butter were amazing. The butter tasted richer than normal, and also, in a strange way, cleaner. It melted onto the soft, still-warm bread. We each got a piece of ham too.

"That's it?" my dad said when he'd finished his serving. He had his face buried in the bucket. "No leftover apple pie? I only had one piece at the picnic."

I didn't mention that I'd given half the bread to the cute guy. "Well, tomorrow, we'll make more food," my mom said. She was already paging through a cookbook she'd found next to an enormous Bible, the only pieces of reading material in the place. "Look at this!" Mom said. She flipped to the front of the book, and pushed it into the glow of the lamp. "This was published in 1882."

"Whatever," I said, standing up. I couldn't take it anymore. Not just the cabin, but the by-now-pretty-overwhelming need to pee. My grandma once said that when you hold it too long, your eyes turn yellow. If that was true, my eyes must look like two lemons popping out of their sockets.

The sky was still lighter than the dark mass of trees when I crossed through the yard, but inside the outhouse, it was pitch-black. I couldn't see if there was a bench or just a hole in the ground like my mom said they had when she studied abroad in France.

The darkness did nothing to interfere with my olfactory perception, however. I was almost rocked backward by the smell. Immediately I slammed the door shut and took deep breaths of uncontaminated air. Even the worst Porta Potties do not compare.

But when I say I had to pee, I'm not being casual. I'd been holding it now for four hours and it wasn't lost on me that Betsy had said I would only have one change of clothes. I took another deep breath and opened the outhouse door.

I groped forward, reaching for where I expected the bench to be. It was there, but it was also . . . wet. Wet? Wet!! Why? Because it was covered in black mold scum? It was too dark to say what I was touching. But there was one thing I could say for sure. I was not going to sit down on any slimy, wet, smelly wooden toilet seat I couldn't see. I planted one thick-soled boot up on the bench and felt around with my toe for the opening. Once I had located it, I hauled the rest of my body into a standing position over the spot where I took the hole to be.

That's when I came to terms with the fact that I had absolutely no idea what to do with my clothes. Feeling around the layers for all the buttons and bows and clasps Betsy had so expertly fastened earlier, it occurred to me that I was trapped. I might as well be in a straitjacket. I started to panic. My body was sending clear signals that clothing or no, I had to go *now*, so I hiked up my skirts, and while keeping them pinned to my sides, I managed to pull apart the bloomers at the—okay, I admit it, pretty darn convenient—slit down the middle and let go.

You know how good the first bite of a peanut butter and chocolate sundae tastes on the way home from a hot and sticky early September soccer game? Or the sight of presents under the tree on Christmas morning? That was *nothing* compared to the joy I felt just then. Even with pee splashing on my stockings, and also, I suspected, my shoe.

I felt so good that for a one crazy second I even thought, "Hey, I can get used to it here."

The yard certainly did smell good after I left the outhouse. The stars were coming out bright and clear in the sky. I stumbled past the chickens on my way back into the house and in a spirit of magnanimity muttered, "Shouldn't you be fed?" before realizing we had eaten every single crumb of food except flour and lard.

My period of positive thinking came to an abrupt end when, back inside, Gavin called down from the sleeping loft, "How come there's only two beds?" and my mom said, "Kids, family life was a lot less private back then. You two will need to share."

In those *Little House* books, Laura slept with her big sister— you got the feeling all the kids in a family would get just one bed to share. But here? No way. No one could possibly expect me to sleep with Gavin. He's a boy. He's ten. At home, he isn't allowed in my room. He isn't even allowed in the space outside my bedroom door.

There was simply no way I was going to accept this.

My mom said, "Betsy explained the sleeping arrangements. On the frontier, there wouldn't have been the resources to build you each your own bed. You'd have slept in the same one until Gavin was older."

I crossed my arms. "I'm not sleeping in a bed with Gavin."

"But that's what's going to make this whole thing so great," Mom went on. "Don't you see? That you're going to learn so much here? You're going to learn about how little you really need to be happy?"

"But I'm not going to be happy," I said. "I'm going to hate this. I refuse. I refuse to sleep with Gavin."

« 7 »

Week 1 - Monday
3:12 am
This is what it's like to sleep with Gavin:
I am up texting you guys at 3 am because
his pillow is soaked in drool and he mouth
breathes and I can smell his nasty breath.

Week 1 - Monday
3:13 am
Not to mention he tosses around all the
time and has pulled the quilt we are
sharing onto the floor.

Week 1 - Monday
3:14 am
And that the mattress is hard and thin
and laid on top of a hammock woven from

```
rope as thick as a pencil that digs into
me every time I move.
```

The worst part of all of this had been the moment we first climbed into bed—Mom, Dad, Gavin, and me in two beds in the same room two feet away from each other on our thin mattresses, with our thin pillows. It was like this old TV show I sometimes see in reruns where a big family that lives in the country all go to bed at the same time and you see the outside of the house and hear them all calling good night to each other— "Night, Mom," "Night, Dad," "Night, John Boy." It was just like that—except the only thing you would have heard coming from *our* cabin was the bickering:

"You're pulling the covers off me."

"You're pulling them off *me*."

"Gen, don't push."

"There's not enough room."

"Stop fighting."

"I want my own bed."

"Your feet are like icicles."

"I thought this was going to be a vacation."

"You didn't even read the brochure, did you?"

"Gavin, I have, like, no covers now."

"Go to sleep."

Eventually, I guess, we did.

I woke up to a banging noise. Or rather, I'd been awake trying to pretend I was still sleeping for what felt like hours, and the banging finally made me open my eyes. I was shivering, as Gavin had stolen the quilt away from me. Again.

"You are disgusting," I said. "You drool."

"Why do you smell like pee?" he said, and rolled over, wrapping himself up like a burrito, leaving my bare toes exposed.

"Hey," I said, pulling at the quilt. "That's not fair."

He grumbled something but didn't give the quilt back until I pushed him over.

"Genevieve," my mom called from downstairs. I realized now that the banging sound was her opening and closing the doors on the woodstove. "Since you're awake, can you run out to the woodpile and get more logs? I just can't get this one to fit in the door."

I pulled myself out of bed, but the second I put my feet on the floor, I yanked them right back in. "It's too cold!" I shouted down from the loft.

"How do you expect to get warm without a fire?" my mother shouted up again. When I looked over the edge of the sleeping loft, I could see her trying to slam in a log that was too big. "The longer it takes to get this stove lit, the longer it will be before I can make something hot to drink or eat. You too, Gavin."

"Where's Dad?" I asked as I started shimmying into my pantaloons—I couldn't believe I was wearing something called pantaloons. "Turn around," I said to Gavin as I lifted my other dress off the hook on the wall and laid it out on the bed. Next I ripped my flannel nightgown over my head and threw the dress on as fast as I could. The dress I wore today was blue with yellow flowers—not exactly my style. But it was way too cold to be naked.

"Dad's getting water from the stream," my mom explained. "If there is a stream. We don't have any idea where you're supposed to get water. There's a pump here in the kitchen, but it doesn't work."

"I'm going to look for Dad!" Gavin shouted as he clambered down the ladder. His clothes were so much less complicated, he was ready to go while I was still trying to figure out which ribbons on my petticoat held the thing up, which were for the stockings, and which ones were just for show.

Gavin opened the front door, and the room was suddenly flooded with light. I could see colors outside: a bright blue sky, the intense green of the woods, the packed-down dirt in front of the house, and some yellow weeds poking up through it. It looked cold—you can always tell—like at early Saturday soccer games in the fall, when the field is almost silver-colored with dew, and you get clumps of grass clippings stuck in your cleats when you run.

"Don't go out to explore yet," Mom called before Gavin crossed the threshold. "First wood! You too, Genevieve," she said. "We need a lot to keep this fire going."

I called back, "How am I supposed to button this dress?" I couldn't reach behind my back to get it fastened.

My mom took a break from the stove to come help, gathering her skirts in one hand and using the other to hold herself steady as she climbed the ladder.

"You mean in 1890 you couldn't even get dressed without someone to help you with your buttons?" I said.

"I guess not," my mom answered. "Your dad got a little impatient this morning helping me with mine." And when she turned I noticed he'd missed every other one.

"Here," I said, but just as I was slipping the last button through its hand-sewn hole, we heard shrieking coming from outside. Before we could even start to wonder what it was, Gavin burst in.

"You won't believe the chickens," he said, breathless, wild eyed, his fingers splayed—he was shaking them out like they were wet. "Oh, my God."

"Gavin?" my mom said. "What happened?"

"They tried to kill me," he said.

"Who?" answered my mom, making her way down the ladder as fast as she could.

"Gavin!" she exclaimed once she was standing on the floor again and could focus on what he was saying. "Where's the wood you went to get?"

"I got too scared," he said.

"Scared?"

"Of the chickens." He was mumbling now, like he was a little embarrassed. And he should have been. Who's afraid of a couple of chickens? Well, besides Dad.

"Look," my mom said. "You can't all be phobic. Farm kids need to be tough, and you two are farm kids now. Those chickens are more afraid of you than you are of them." She pointed to a box next to the woodstove. "This is the wood box. In 1890, kids would have kept this box filled to the top all day long, without ever having to be reminded. I know you are hungry and cold right now, but let's get off on a good footing. If you can take this on as a project, we'll all be warm and fed very soon."

"But—," Gavin started.

"Oh, fine," I said. "I'll get the wood." I was thinking that if I could get out of the house, I'd warm up in the sunshine.

But from the moment I took a step off the porch, I was pretty much attacked. Wings flapping, feathers flying, clawed feet leaping so high I was afraid for my face. There were screeches and squeals. I covered my eyes, tripping backward onto the porch, scrambling to stand up again, reaching blindly behind me for the door.

It was the chickens.

Gavin was right. They were going to poke out my eyes or peck off my toes. They would stop at nothing.

"I think they're hungry," said Gavin when I was safely inside, panting, untangling my skirt from my legs. I swore my dress had been in on the attack, whipping this way and that, trapping me. "It took them a minute to find me," he continued. "They came from over by the barn. But now they know where we are, they're just waiting for us to come out again. They're guarding the door."

"I don't think it's hunger," I said. "I think they *hate* us."

"Here," said my mom. "Give them this." She was holding some cornmeal in a tin cup.

"You give it to them," I said. "I'm not going back out there."

"Do chickens eat that?" asked Gavin. "What if that isn't something they even like? What if it makes them angrier?"

"It does look a little thin," Mom said. "I'm not sure how they'd be able to peck it up off the ground."

"Can I try a pinch?" asked Gavin.

"You want it raw?" said my mom.

Gavin just shrugged. "I'm hungry."

"I'll try to light the fire with what we have inside," my mom said.

"What time is it anyway?" I said. I was starting to get the feeling that it was really early in the morning. Like, bus-stop early.

"I don't know," my mom confessed, kind of laughing. "I don't know how you tell time out here. Ron gave your dad a watch yesterday, but he forgot to wind it, and now it's off. It's funny, all these little things, isn't it?"

"Ha," I said in a way that I hoped communicated that "funny" was dead last in the list of words describing all these little things—with "annoying," "unnecessary," and "unfair" coming closer to the top.

Just then my dad approached the cabin. I could tell because I heard the chickens start screaming and squealing followed by Dad letting out a surprised "Oh!" Then he must have started to run, because the screaming and screeching got louder and I could hear wings flapping. My dad burst through the door, out of breath, feathers floating in a cloud around his legs. He slammed the door behind him.

"They're just chickens," my mom said. "I don't know why you all are so afraid."

My dad didn't answer her. His face was white. "I think one of them was foaming at the mouth," he said.

"Beak," my mom corrected.

"Birds carry disease," he said. He placed the bucket of water on the table and held out his hand to examine it. "I guess it didn't break the skin." My mom rolled her eyes, reaching behind herself to straighten her bun, then peering into the bucket of water.

"It's only half filled," she said.

"Some of it spilled while I was running the gauntlet just now," he said. "I hope there's enough for coffee."

"I was going to make grits," my mom said. "It's fast, and we have cornmeal."

"Do I like grits?" Gavin asked.

"What *are* grits?" I said.

"You're going to make coffee first," my dad said. "Because I need coffee before I can take on one more thing today." His teeth were chattering. He pointed to the cookbook from 1882. "Does that show you how to make coffee? Do we even have coffee?"

My mom lifted the lid on a trunk. There were some bags and a few tins in it. She pulled out a wooden box with a crank on the top and a tin box with a lid. "Coffee!" she said brightly. It was pathetic how she was trying to act like she was in a good mood and trick the rest of us into agreeing with her.

"Is there orange juice?" Gavin asked.

"How can there be orange juice if there isn't even a refrigerator?" I said.

"How can there be no refrigerator?" Gavin asked.

"We've got to light this fire," my mom said.

"We've got to get me some coffee," said my dad.

My mom had put a match to the fire in the stove and after a few smoke-filled attempts finally got it going when we had our first visitor. Those hungry chickens were like a doorbell, squealing and squawking. I knew somebody was in the yard.

My mom was too busy flapping air into the stove with the bellows to notice, but I opened the door a crack to peek out.

It was Nora.

I watched her, wanting to see how an experienced farm person managed around killer fowl. A muzzle? A shotgun? But the thing is, when the chickens saw it was Nora, they didn't even attack.

"Hey, Pumpkin," I watched her say to one of the chickens. Just the sound of her voice seemed to calm them down. "Hey,

Daisy." She pulled a handful of something out of her pocket and tossed it on the ground. Daisy and Pumpkin scrambled to peck at it. It didn't look like cornmeal.

I would have stepped into the yard and asked her what she was giving them, but when she looked up, there was a glimmer of something in her eyes that made me afraid to talk to her.

Instead of saying hi to me or anything like that, Nora shook her head like I wasn't there and said, "The new folks never feed those poor chickens. And if you'd fed them and shut them in the coop like my dad told you to last night," she added, meeting my gaze, "you'd be eating eggs for breakfast this morning, instead of what all it is you're planning to make without milk or eggs."

With that, she stepped inside and walked around the cabin like she owned it, which I guess, technically, she did, but still. She pulled the drawer out of the coffee grinder and looked inside, nodding briefly to show my dad that she approved. My mom had finally closed the door to the stove, and Nora opened it again, inspected the fire, added two pieces of kindling, then closed the door and changed the vents in the door and the side of the stove until they met her approval.

"Breakfast plans?" she asked my mom, not even bothering to expand that thought into a full sentence.

"Grits," my mom said, and Nora nodded, neither approving nor disapproving.

"Better with a little salt pork if you can spare it," she said. Then she jutted her chin toward a shelf where all the dishes were stacked—tin plates, a stack of tin cups. Nora said, "Coffeepot's up there."

I looked over at my dad, hoping to get some kind of a

reading from him on Nora. He didn't disappoint. He had a kind of sarcastic expression on his face. Nora turned to me like a teacher who hears a kid talking in the middle of class.

"You're Genevieve, right?" she said. "How old are you?"

"I'm thirteen," I said. "But I turn fourteen in September. I'll be in high school." I don't know why I needed to tell her that, other than the fact that the term "high school" felt comforting. It was nice to remind myself that Nora or no Nora, at some point all of this would be over and I'd be back with Kristin and Ashley in the world where I belonged.

"I'm fourteen," Nora said. "But I'll be fifteen in October. So I guess that makes me a full year older than you."

"Almost," I said.

"What?"

"Almost a full year," I said. I knew I was being picky about it, but she was wrong and that should count for something when you're acting like you are the biggest expert on everything in someone else's house. "My birthday's in September. So we're actually eleven months apart."

As if I hadn't said a word at all, Nora reached up to the dish shelf, pulled down a tin cup, and used it to scoop water from the bucket and pour it into the pump mounted on the counter. She pumped vigorously and poured more water into the pump, until water started flowing out of the pump on its own. "You've got to prime the pump in the mornings," she said. "Especially when the place stands empty a few days."

Meanwhile, my mom had put the coffee grounds in the pot, and was starting to heat up the water for the grits. "Will you stay for breakfast?" she asked Nora.

"Nah." Nora shook her head. "I've got chores and lessons, and shoot, we get up at 4:30 in the summer. For me, it's closer to dinnertime than it is to breakfast."

"It's almost nighttime?" Gavin asked.

"Did you really just say *shoot*?" I asked.

Nora ignored my question. "No, dinner's what you eat at the noon meal," she said. "And we're having chicken and dumplings."

I wish I had been stronger. I wish we all had. But at the mention of chicken and dumplings—and I didn't even know what that was, except something they had for dinner in the song "She'll Be Comin' Round the Mountain"—I felt my spine go limp. It was as if all the bones in my body had been replaced by longing for whatever chicken and dumplings were. One look at Gavin, Mom, and Dad told me they were feeling exactly the same way. We were all leaning toward Nora as if we might smell the hot food coming off her.

"I'm sure you'll be having stuff like that in no time," she said, and I knew that what she really meant was that we probably wouldn't have a meal like that until we got home and drove straight from the airport to a Boston Market.

Grits, which we sat down to eat as soon as Nora was gone, taste exactly like what they are—cornmeal mixed with water. I don't think they're supposed to be crunchy, or have a smoky flavor, but these did.

"Why did we come here again?" I said after taking my first bite.

My mom said, "They're better with butter."

My dad said, "And when they're not burnt."

My mom pushed her dish away and stood up to pump water

in a bowl to do the dishes, and my dad said, "You're going to boil some for that washing, right? The only thing that would make it worse out here is if one of us got dysentery."

My mom said, "Don't you have some work to do outside?" and Dad stood, took one more bite, then left the cabin. My mom turned to me. "Genevieve," she said. "It will be your job to clear the table, scrape the food off the plates into a bowl for the animals, and clean the dishes after the meal. You can also make the beds, and I'll expect you to set the table and sweep out the house after every meal. When you're done you can help your dad in the fields."

I stood there and stared at her. There's such a thing as realizing that you truly are in hell.

Week 1 - Monday
11:16 am
I am standing in the middle of a cornfield.
I am holding a hoe. As my mom said when
we were setting off to work in the field,
we are farmers now.

Week 1 - Monday
11:17 am
Here's the thing: being a farmer is BORING.
I am halfway down one row, there are ten
rows to go, and it's already taken TWO
HOURS.

I turned the phone off and slipped it into my pocket. I did this every time I sent a text, promising myself I wouldn't get it out again until much later. I didn't want to get caught. And I didn't want to run down the battery. But then two seconds would pass and I'd find myself reaching for it again. I couldn't help it. It was like the way Gavin sneaks his Halloween candy from the jar on top of the fridge where my mom makes him keep it.

I had to have some weeding done when my dad got back, though, so I swore that this time I'd keep the phone in my pocket. My dad had gone to get us water, taking Gavin along with him.

Before we'd headed out to the cornfield, my dad sat Gavin, my mom, and me down on the edge of the porch to tell us what we needed to know about bears.

"I assume you're not talking about the Chicago football team," my mom had said.

"They could be anywhere," my dad replied.

When Gavin said, "Seeing a bear would be so cool," my dad hunched his shoulders up toward his ears, drew his bushy eyebrows together, and stood over him.

"Bears are no joke," he growled. "You have to be careful. Especially in the woods."

Gavin had been swinging his legs, but now he stopped.

"You're scaring him," said my mom.

"You kind of look like a bear right now," Gavin said.

"You should be scared," Dad said to Gavin, but he backed away. "If you want to avoid a bear, the best thing to do is make sure they know where you are. Call out to them as you walk. Call out 'Bear, bear.'"

"They speak English?" I asked.

"Do you know what you do if you see a bear?" my dad asked.

"Run?" I said.

"Never run. I'm telling you . . ." He looked at each one of us hard. "If you see a bear, stay put. Wave your hands above your head. It will make the bear think you're bigger than you are, that you're not worth attacking." He was demonstrating, but with the sun behind him, he looked like he was performing a rain dance. "And if they come for you anyway, what you do is you crouch down on the ground." He showed us this too, his forehead in the dirt, his knees tucked under his chest, his arms covering the back of his head. His voice was muffled, but he still managed to shout out, "The idea here is that you're using your body to protect your vital organs. Better to have the bear rip some meat off your back than to puncture your lungs or heart."

Now, all alone in the cornfield, I thought, "Ugh. Meat."

```
Week 1 - Monday
11:41 am
ARE there really bears out here? My dad
said if you're all by yourself you should
sing to keep them away.

Week 1 - Monday
11:42 am
But the way I sing, a bear might attack
me just to make me stop.
```

I heard something rustling behind me and I jumped. I stashed the phone thinking it must be my dad. But then when I called out "Dad?" and the sound of my voice died unanswered in the great openness of the field, with the mountains beyond, I started to get a little freaked out.

"They told him don't you ever come around here," I started,

my voice warbly and small. "Beat It" was the only song I knew all the words to because my sixth-grade gym teacher had made us learn a dance to it. I went on a little bit louder. I wanted to be sure a bear could hear.

And by the time I got to "So beat it, just beat it," I was singing in a regular voice.

Holding the hoe in two hands, I brought the blade down on a clump of weeds growing up around a cornstalk. You have to hit them at the root and it's not always easy to figure out where they are. This time I took down the corn plant as well. I'd been doing that a lot.

The next time, I didn't hit the corn. I started doing a little dance in time to the song, hacking away at the weeds. "So beat it," I sang, whacking at a root. "Just beat it." I was belting it out, but who cared? Except for the bears, I was completely alone.

I was already on the third verse when I noticed Gavin and my dad ten feet away, listening. Gavin said, "Yeah, the '80s!" and I felt my face go hot. I went back to my weeding in silence.

```
Week 1 - Monday
1:24 pm
You know what's worse than being caught
by your little brother singing "Beat It"
at the top of your lungs while you do a
little corn-weeding dance? Having him
follow you down the row singing, "Showin'
how funky and strong is your fight. It
doesn't matter who's wrong or right,"
doing a little dance of his own, and
```

```
stopping only to say, "Come on, Gen, you
know you're feeling it." All morning long.

Week 1 - Monday
1:29 pm
My one consolation is that last night
Gavin got a mosquito bite on his eyelid,
and it's swollen so bad he can't open
that eye. Actually, it kind of makes me
feel bad for him.
```

After lunch that day—grits again, because my mom hadn't figured out how to cook anything else—we went back into the field. I was able to text again when it was my turn to fetch water, and that's how it went over the next few days—heinous chores, stolen moments to text, lots of singing and calling out to bears who may or may not have been listening.

```
Week 1 - Tuesday
7:17 am
Grits for breakfast.

Week 1 - Tuesday
12:06 pm
Grits for lunch.

Week 1 - Tuesday
5:49 pm
Grits for dinner.
```

Kristin wrote that night to say she was using my texts to start a blog for the computer class her mom was making her take. Then she texted:

```
I am sending you an imaginary box. Inside
the box is bubble wrap. Inside the bubble
wrap is a bag. Inside the bag are Cheetos.
Mental Cheetos. Go ahead, take a bite.
Good, no?
```

Wednesday my mom figured out how to make beans and we ate them three meals in a row. At least it wasn't grits.

Kristin texted:

```
Three times? LOL.
```

I texted back:

```
Week 1 - Thursday
9:02 pm
Listen to this: Mom said there's a barrel
of salted beef in the pantry but it could
be rancid. We could get sick. We could
even die. So all summer, for dinner, we
can choose between beans, grits, and ...
death.
```

Ashley texted a lot too, telling me about the guy she picked up while standing in line for a roller coaster. He was cuter than the new lifeguard at the pool, although the lifeguard was from Europe and had a foreign accent.

Her questions to me were always basically the same:

What's up with cute Hat/Necklace Boy?

The fact is I didn't know. Not that I wasn't curious. All during our first week, as I got used to the routine of working in the field, sweeping out the smelly cabin, washing the dishes after every meal, our only visitors were Ron—who seemed to come over exclusively for the purpose of pointing out the number of corn plants I was killing instead of weeds—and Betsy, who gave my mom a lot of pointers in the kitchen.

I wondered if we'd see any kids before the next picnic on Sunday. Would Ka still be funny? Would Nora still be mad at me? Would I have the nerve to talk to Caleb the next time we met?

Friday after lunch, Gavin and my dad were back out in the cornfield, my mom was in the garden, and I was cleaning up after lunch when I saw the red-haired boy from the yurt-loving family come out of the woods.

"I'm Erik," he said after he'd knocked on the cabin door. "Matt and Caleb are getting a game of kick the can together. You and your brother want to play?"

"Sure," I said. I used to play at camp.

"We're meeting at Ron and Betsy's," he said. "At eight or whenever it's starting to get dark." He turned and started to walk back away. Just before he was out of hearing range, he shouted, "Grown-ups aren't allowed to play."

Week 1 — Friday
2:27 pm
There's a game of "no grown-up" kick the
can on for tonight. What kind of grown-up
would want to play kick the can anyhow?

Apparently, the kind of grown-up who wants to play kick the can is . . . all of them.

Starting with my parents. As soon as they heard there was a gathering, they insisted on bolting down their dinner and coming along with us. Maybe they were starved for non-family human contact as much as we were.

"You cannot play," I said to them on the way over.

"Of course not," my mom demurred. But I could tell she expected me to change my mind.

When we arrived in the clearing, Ka's mom and stepdad were already there, looking trim and crisp. Even in their costumes, you could imagine coach whistles hanging from strings around their necks.

Caleb's mom was holding his little sister's hand, and his dad—who had been chewing on straw before—was now swinging a big walking stick. The grown-ups immediately started chatting—my mother and Caleb's mom, the red-haired family's mom and Betsy, plus the red-haired dad and the blond gym teachers.

It was funny to see them acting like old friends. Even the kids were doing it. The posse of nine-year-old doll fanatics were jumping up and down with excitement, telling stories.

"I sewed a handkerchief!"

"Our chicken bit me!"

"My dad got lost in the woods!"

I tried very hard *not* to look for Caleb, but, of course, I did. And then when I saw him, I had to groan. He was sitting with Nora, and for the first time, I was like, *Are they a couple?* He'd lost the hat permanently now, and the full force of his cuteness hit me. His crooked smile. The way he reached out a hand to confidently high-five Ka's older brother, Matt—the jock he'd played catch with the week before.

Nora laughed at something and leaned against Caleb's arm. He leaned down to pick up a stick from the ground and I saw that his hair was streaked with blond from the sun. Also, he looked really tan. Or maybe that was dirt? After two days in the cornfield, Gavin and I had noticed that when we washed our hands we'd have dirt lines at our wrists that were like suntans, only in reverse. Gross on me, but on Caleb it didn't matter. Dirt looked good on him.

I spotted Ka's goth black hair in the sea of happy gym-teacher blond that was her stepsisters and I crossed the lawn to her.

"Oh, my God, I cannot believe I survived this last week," she said when she saw me.

"I'm sharing a bed with my little brother," I said.

"Matt gets his own bed because he's fifteen," she said. "I have to sleep with Katie." She pointed to her wholesome-looking stepsister. "She's already a cheerleader. In middle school! And she totally wants to play with the dolls. I'm like, 'Go ahead, Kater-tot. I don't care what you do.' And then she cries to her dad that I think she's dumb, and my mom yells at me, and I'm like"—she threw her arms up in the air—"'It wasn't my idea to come here.'"

It was a good thing Ka couldn't see how she looked in a mirror. Blond roots were starting to show in her hair. Her white makeup was completely gone and in its absence I could see that, like it or not, she had a spray of adorable freckles just like her mom's across her nose. There wasn't much goth going on anymore.

I laughed. "My mom can't cook out here," I said. "All we've had are beans and grits."

"What's your crop? We got millet. I don't even know what that is."

"We have corn," I said. "Do you have eggs yet?"

"Yeah, but we only have three chickens, so it's like everyone gets a half an egg at a time."

"We only have two. One's a rooster, so he doesn't lay eggs." I didn't tell her how, since it's my brother's job to feed them, the chickens followed him around the barn. Once when I was hiding out in the hayloft, I heard him talking baby talk to them.

"My mom's freaking about milk because we don't have our cow yet. She's really into strong bones. Betsy sent some milk over."

"She hasn't sent us anything," I said. "Did Nora come over?"

"Totally harshed on us," Ka said.

"I know," I agreed, and felt immediately better. It's always nice to dislike someone together.

When Matt called us over to start the game, the red-haired dad—Anders—ambled over to join us. In the course of a week, his pale skin had turned lobster red. A girl in my class got sunburned like that on our eighth-grade class trip to Washington DC, and a teacher had to take her to the hospital.

"No grown-ups," Erik said as soon as he saw him. "Go sit

with Mom." He looked over at his mother, who was sitting on the porch, knitting. Knitting? I noticed none of the other moms were talking to her.

"But I love kick the can," Anders argued.

Erik rolled his eyes. "You cheat, Dad. And you play too rough for the other kids."

Anders didn't look like he was going to back down, until my dad slapped him on the shoulder. Between his animal phobias and his coffee withdrawal, I'd forgotten there are things my dad is actually good at—making people feel comfortable while getting them to do what he wants them to do is one of them. "I guess this is the time when we dads would be kicking back with a couple of pipes now, wouldn't it?" my dad said.

Anders went with him, but he looked back over his shoulder at us as he walked to join the grown-ups. He reminded me of a little boy I used to babysit who would play this jumping game on his bed after lights-out. His mom said it was okay, but I don't think she realized he would jump for, like, an hour before going to sleep. I think eventually they got him some meds.

Anyway, to start the game, Matt made us all say our names. We were standing in a rough circle, with Caleb and Nora on one side of Matt along with Caleb's sister, Stephanie, red-haired Erik, and his equally red-haired sisters, Anja and Bryn. Gavin and I stood on the other side of Matt with Ka and her stepsisters, Katie and Cara.

"How old is everyone?" Matt asked and quickly took a count. "Okay," he said. "You guys"—he pointed to Katie, Erik, and Ka, who were all twelve, and to me, Caleb, and Nora—"you guys have to pull off some jail breaks." He looked at the younger kids—which consisted of Gavin and the Doll Club, who were all ten or younger. "We're coming for you," Matt said. "If you get captured, just hold tight. I'll be It first. This tree's the base. Caleb, you want to kick?" Typical, I thought, to assume a boy could kick it the farthest.

But then Caleb wound up and gave a huge kick to the can—a biscuit tin Betsy had donated that looked officially 1890. With a hollow *clunk* the can went careening through the air and Matt was after it, catching it on the fly and racing back to the tree. Meanwhile, everyone else had started to run.

As I crashed through the brambles, breathing hard and looking for a hiding place that was safe but not too far from the can, I felt like I was in some kind of a horror movie, like there was a camera and a madman following me. I swung myself behind a bush just in time to hear Matt yell out, "Cara trying to crawl under the porch!" I heard a shriek and I peeked to see Cara streaking across the lawn. If you get spotted, you can avoid going to jail if you kick the can before It does, but Matt was guarding the can and she didn't have a chance.

Matt waited until Cara seemed to have a shot at making contact, then gave the can the slightest of taps to show that he didn't even have to try.

"Matt!" she whined, but he just pointed to the jail tree and she sulked over.

"Stephanie," Matt called to Caleb's sister. "I just saw your skirt in that bush by the barn." She giggled. "Last time I checked, bushes didn't giggle." And there was another mad dash, but she was laughing too hard to even run for real. Matt gave the can another obligatory kick.

Pretty soon Gavin was in jail, followed by Bryn. Anja ran for the can when Matt had his back turned, but he sensed her and sprinted to beat her to it. Matt was good, I thought. I guess that's what having a gym teacher for a dad will get you.

As Anja was dragging her skinny self off to jail, I felt a body colliding with mine. It was Ka. "We need a plan," she whispered, out of breath from running. She pressed herself up against the tree. "I'm going to sneak around. I'll make a distraction and pull Matt away from the can."

"Okay," I said. "And I'll run in and kick."

"Don't mess it up."

"Okay," I said.

Just then Erik made a run for the can—Matt had headed off in the opposite direction. Ka put her hand on my arm and we both watched. It looked like Erik was going to make it.

"Matt sees him," Ka whispered.

"He can't," I said.

"Trust me."

And she was right, because the second Erik got close to the can, Matt started to sprint and kicked it out from under him at the last second. "Jail for you, Red," he said, and Erik slunk off to join his sisters. If Matt was a kick-the-can expert because his dad taught gym, Ka, with her gym teacher mom, had probably also acquired some serious skills.

When I turned to say something about this to Ka, she was already gone. I could see her crouched-down form sneaking from one tree to another, but I doubted that anyone else could. She kept low to the ground and was perfectly silent. She was patient too, waiting before each move for Matt to turn away.

She reached the opposite side of the yard and started to make noises that I wouldn't have thought were intentional if I hadn't seen how perfectly silent she'd been before. Matt heard all of them, standing still each time to listen. I knew it was risky, but I reached for my phone anyway.

```
Week 1 - Friday
8:54 pm
Matt and Ka play kick the can like a
couple of covert military operatives. My
training at Camp Sunshine doesn't even
remotely measure up.
```

Pretty soon, the noises seemed to move from where I knew Ka was hiding to about twenty feet away. Ka must have been throwing sticks or maybe rocks. When Matt headed over to the spot where the rocks were hitting, I even saw her arm flash out from behind a tree. She was brilliant—she'd tricked him into following a nonexistent target.

Matt took a few steps, then a few more, keeping one hand back behind him, pointing to the can as if he were maintaining some kind of invisible hold on it, prepping his body to run fast.

While he was looking away, I followed Ka's example, running to a tree closer in to the can. I checked to see if Matt had seen me. I knew I had to hurry because soon, he was going to be close enough to see her.

The can lay in the shadow of a tree, next to all those eight-, nine-, and ten-year-olds who had started to play patty-cake games like they were on the bus on a field trip to Great Adventure. Matt was just far enough into the woods that he might not beat me to the can in a sprint. I started to move.

I was holding my skirts in my hands, wishing the lace-up boots had better traction. Actually, I would have settled for any traction. People didn't start wearing sneakers until the 1920s or something, and I slipped on every piece of crushed grass or spot of mud I touched. Still, I was booking. I could feel my skirts flowing out behind me and my knees pumping up toward my chest. The can was close. It was impossible for me not to get it and then—

I did it. I kicked the can.

The entire pack of Doll Club girls cheered. Running and screaming, they disappeared back into the woods, their braids flying out behind their heads. I hate to admit it, but they looked cute, their boots kicking up behind their skirts as they ran.

"Aargh!" Matt screamed in mock anguish. I was already on the run by the time he made it back into the clearing, but I heard him shout, "Whoever did this to me, I won't forget you!" He sounded like he was half laughing, half imitating a villain in a superhero movie.

"It was Gen!" Anja shouted out, even though that meant she gave away her hiding place and was recaptured ten seconds later. To avoid Matt's seeing me next, I stopped myself in midsprint and swung around a tree trunk, where I thought I'd be out of sight.

What I didn't realize is that there was already someone hiding there. It was Caleb. I nearly sat on him.

"Ooh," I said, pulling myself back up to standing. But he grabbed my hand and pulled me down so I was right next to him, my skirt landing in a pouf, some of it even covering his legs. Reaching over to pull it back onto my lap, I could smell the still-new wool of his rough shirt and pants.

"Stay down," Caleb said. "He'll see you."

Our faces were so close I could see that his wide eyes were flecked with darker and lighter colors—they looked gray from a distance, but really they were half green. I felt delicious and warm and tingly inside. "Have you been here all the time?" I said. I didn't really care where he'd been. I was mostly just glad to have him here now.

"I've been moving around," he said. "I saw your kick." He lifted up a hand for a high five, and when I hit it, he closed his fingers around my palm. For a second, I didn't understand. We were totally still. Then I realized that Caleb must have been listening to some rustling in the woods that I was too distracted to hear. Matt called out, "Cara and Stephanie!" putting them in jail again.

Caleb pulled me to my feet. He whispered, "We've got to get moving." He was still holding my hand and I was paying no attention to the game, I was so amazed by the feeling as he led me deeper into the woods.

It was dark now and we didn't see Nora until we were almost on top of her. "Look who I found," Caleb said to her, then explained to me, "We've been holed up back here, and I was on a can-kicking scouting mission when you beat me to it."

Nora looked from my face down to Caleb's and my hands. I let go.

"Three's too many for a stealth team," she said, speaking to Caleb only, ignoring me. "We'll get caught."

And then she stormed off.

"Is she mad?" I said.

Caleb shrugged, and I couldn't tell if his shrug meant "Hey, I don't care." Or if he was shrugging because he didn't want to tell me.

But then, a few minutes later, Nora was back. She smiled at both of us, put her finger to her lips, and said, "We have to stake out a perimeter. My dad taught me this. For hunting. Gen, you stay here, and Caleb and I will find spots on either side of you. Move a few feet forward every minute or so, okay?"

What I didn't realize is that the animal being hunted was me. Shortly after Caleb and Nora disappeared in different directions, Matt shouted from about two feet away, "Gen behind the tree!" And even as I sprinted toward the can—he beat me to it— my brain was busy realizing that Nora must have alerted Matt to where I was. A minute later, Caleb was captured too—he surrendered so easily I wondered if maybe he'd let himself get caught just to hang out in jail with me. And then when Nora straggled in a second after him I wondered if she'd let *herself* get caught to keep tabs on him.

The three of us watched from jail as Ka came in, then Gavin, and finally Katie, ambushed during a heroic last-ditch attempt to set us all free. The game was over and it was dark, so instead of picking a new It, we just stood around talking in little groups, waiting for the parents to finish chatting as well.

While we were standing around, Nora kept herself glued to Caleb's side. She laughed at everything he said, and played with the strings on her bonnet. At one point she even grabbed folds of her skirts and jiggled them a little, showing off her ankle. I think maybe it was supposed to be flirty, but to me she looked like a wannabe cancan dancer.

I caught myself thinking, "Does my ankle look cute sticking out from under my long skirt?"

And then I immediately crushed that question with a command: "Have some dignity, Gen."

At the end of the night, as my family trudged back through the woods to our cabin and cornfield and kitchen garden and so-far-eggless chickens, Gavin said, "All I did was hide behind a tree and get caught before I even made a run on the can, but still, it was fun." I thought about how Caleb and I had sat at the base of the tree, him holding my hand, and Nora or no Nora, I knew exactly how Gavin felt.

```
Week 1 - Saturday
6:23 am
Last night, Gavin told me my butt was
keeping him from sleeping so I pushed him
out of the bed and then I got in trouble.
Typical.


Week 1 - Saturday
7:37 am
Gavin hunted around for forty minutes
this morning and he finally found it. An
egg! For breakfast!


Week 1 - Saturday
2:24 pm
Gavin and me lying on our backs in the
shade.
Gavin: Do you think that watching clouds
in 1890 was what they did instead of
watching TV?
Me: I don't know but the idea that they
```

considered cloud watching entertainment
is maybe even more pathetic than the
fact that they always had to eat beans.
Gavin: I think the beans part is just us.

« 9 »

```
Week 2 - Sunday
9:43 am
One of Gavin's jobs is to carry ashes
from the stove to a big bin in the out-
house. We all pour some ashes down the
hole when we're done. Everyone has ashes
under their nails. Ew. Getting ready for
the Sunday picnic--that's this morning--my
mom made us all scrub our nails clean.
```

On Sunday, while I cleaned up the breakfast dishes and made the beds, Gavin hauled a new bucket of ashes to the outhouse and brought in a load of wood. My mom packed up the picnic basket, and my dad made sure that the doors and windows were locked up tight in case the bears came while we were gone.

As we passed Ron and Betsy's house, I pointed. "Imagine!" I said to Gavin. "A bedroom with a door!" I was being sarcastic, and talking a little like our grandma, but I was also kind of serious. My mom heard me and smiled, which immediately made me wish I'd kept quiet. If I sounded too cheerful, she might get the idea that I liked it here.

After the game of kick the can two nights before, kids kind of smiled at each other as we took our seats on the family benches. Ka sat with us since there was barely enough space on her bench for her mom and stepdad, Matt, Katie, and Cara.

"I bet Matt was really impressed with himself after he shut us all down the other night," I said.

Ka rolled her eyes. "They gave him the Hinchey Hooray."

"What's the Hinchey Hooray?"

She performed a mute clapping routine, sticking her fists into the air, chanting and ending with "Ouga ouga Hinchey."

I let my mouth drop open in an obvious, silent groan.

"I know," she said. "They do it all the time. They keep asking me if I want one. And I'm like 'Ouga this.'" She made an obscene gesture.

Once the meeting got started, Ron made the "leader" from every family stand up and report on what was happening at their farm.

Caleb's dad, Peter, went first. He was chewing on straw again, and while all the other men had changed into shirts with collars and long pants, he was wearing an undershirt and work pants—you got the feeling he was the kind of dad who was always in sweatpants at home. Caleb's mom, I noticed, looked wrinkly—or maybe it was just the dirt caked on her face that made her wrinkles stand out. By Friday's kick the can game, she had lost her bow, and now she had a piece of string tying her hair back that looked like the twine you'd use to bind newspapers at the curb.

In his slow Southern accent Caleb's dad described all the different potatoes they were growing, and then announced his farm improvement project. "We notice that there's nowhere for kids—or adults for that matter—to swim. So I was thinking that Caleb and I would take a crack at damming up a spot we checked out on the creek to make a swimming hole. I remember one at my grandparents' when I was a kid and I thought it would be good for the family and the farm to have a place to wash and play."

"That's your farm improvement?" asked Ron, leaning on the word "farm" as if maybe Peter needed reminding of what that word meant.

I'd never seen someone nod with a Southern accent before, but Peter did just that—a low-chin, exaggerated bow. "Yes, sir," he said, and he sat down.

Ron shook his head, laughing a little. Betsy smiled and said, "I think a washing hole sounds nice. And it's lovely to see a man thinking of his woman's ease."

Ka elbowed me in the ribs. "Thinking about a woman's what?" she asked.

"Clark?" Ron said next, pointing to Ka's stepdad, who besides looking sporty, blond, and healthy, also looked young. He had clear skin and very little facial hair. When he spoke, he kept his voice intentionally low, and I wondered if he was compensating.

"We've spent this week working on jelling as a team," Clark began, running a hand through his hair—he probably had no idea that because it was dirty, it stood on end when he did that, making him look even younger. He cleared his throat. "A teen, two tweens, and a nine-year-old is tough. But Ron, I'd say we're really bonding!"

"Uh . . . no," Ka whispered. "All we ever do is fight."

"Any improvements you're thinking about?" Ron asked.

"Yes, Ron," said Clark. "We'd like to build some extra beds, and maybe a partition in our downstairs, or maybe an extra room."

"Or maybe a planet where they can send me to live all by myself," Ka muttered.

Clark plowed forward, his light eyebrows furrowed. "As you know, Ron—" I guess Clark was also one of those grown-ups who think people will take them more seriously if they address the person they're talking to by their first name. "We're a recently blended family and it's pretty tough on the kids to be sharing space. We were thinking Matt could sleep downstairs—maybe we'd rig up a room for him off the side of the house, and the girls could have their own beds with us upstairs, or maybe even separate, with some sleeping downstairs in the kitchen."

"He's totally freaking out about the fighting," Ka whispered. "And the other day, I thought my mom was going to cry."

"That sounds like an admirable project," Ron said. "And typical of an 1890 frontier. Settlers would begin with a need for basic shelter, and build onto the original structure as the years progressed."

He turned to the Puchinski bench. Red-haired, red-faced Anders was squirming in his seat like a kid who knows the answer, waiting to be called on by the teacher.

"Our week has been full, that's for sure," Anders began. "On Monday, first thing I divided the kids into work teams, and then established a grid for weeding the field. I decided to incentivize the weeding by assigning a number value to each quadrant of the field . . ."

"Have you noticed that every sentence out of his mouth begins with 'I'?" Ka whispered when he was a long three minutes in—the man talked and talked and talked. And Ka was right. Anders took credit personally for every single activity on his farm that week—and that was a lot to take credit for, as the Puchinskis were doing about three times as much as the rest of us combined. They'd dug a secondary well and small-scale irrigation system for their garden, weeded their entire wheat field, expanded the chicken coop, killed a chicken and rendered its fat, built a shade pavilion by the field so they could eat their noon meal out there and save the time of coming in, and Disa—the muffin-baking mom—had sewn curtains for all the windows in the house out of the bolt of calico fabric each cabin had been rationed—I was using ours as an extra pillow.

"Is he going to stop soon?" I whispered to Ka.

"Or ever?"

"Whew!" said Ron when Anders was finished. Actually, technically, Anders hadn't finished. Ron had cut him off. "That's impressive. Sounds like there's a lot going on. Have you thought about what you would like to do for your farm improvement project?"

"Oh, yes," Anders said, the look of irritation that had crossed his sunburned face the second Ron had cut him off replaced by a new interest in his own idea. "I've been thinking about our wheat crop. I know you sell it and in 1890 that's historically appropriate—with access to trains, major markets commodity farming had already become the name of the game—but what about milling some for use here? It could be kept in cold storage and would last through the winter. I've been improvising with some plans for jerry-rigging a millstone, or going back to some hand-milling techniques. If anyone has any ideas, please come talk to me after the meeting." He laid a hand on his wife's head. "And I hope you all get a chance to note Disa's corn biscuits, because she's been experimenting all week to get them just right. The ones we've brought for our picnic today look mighty fine."

My stomach literally growled. Ka giggled.

Ron looked over at my dad. "Doug?" he said. "Your turn. You want to say something?"

My dad looked surprised. I guess he'd been assuming my mom would do the talking. I know I had.

"That's okay," my dad said. "We're not really doing very much on the farm this week. Just settling in."

"Why don't you tell us about it?" Ron prompted. "Stand up, Doug," he added, like my dad was a fourth grader giving a book report.

My dad stood. "We haven't done anything on the order of the Puchinskis," he said.

"Own what you are doing," said Ron. "Even if you've been idle, this is the place for a reckoning."

At the word "idle," I saw my dad's chin duck back and his eyebrows shoot up. He's a big guy, with a big paunch, and when he squares his shoulders, it's impressive. "I certainly wouldn't describe the past week as idle, Ron," he said, and there was something so extra courteous in his tone that I could tell he was angry. Also, I think I was just noticing this for the first time, there was something leaner about my dad's face. Was he losing weight?

"All week we've been out in the cornfield," he went on. "Mean-while, the kids have done a bang-up job getting the hen to lay some eggs. But I have to say, what I feel should really be the first priority is keeping us safe from the bears. Bears are . . ." He paused. "Unacceptable." He sighed. He looked exhausted. It was weird—my dad wears a suit every day, with the ties Gavin and I give him for Christmas and his birthdays. On weekends he wears one of three sweatshirts and jeans. In his new clothes there were moments when he seemed to be a stranger.

"This camp . . ." He looked down at my mom and she smiled at him, kind of encouraging, kind of nervous, like she didn't know what he was going to say next. He didn't smile back. "This camp wasn't my idea," he said. "And I think this last week I've been figuring out what it's all about. For instance, I didn't know that I could eat only so many beans." He was joking then, trying to make up for saying too much when he'd meant to say so little, but no one smiled or even nodded.

I saw my dad's eyes get a little wider, and it was clear he didn't know how to be done talking, but he was afraid to confess anything more. When I tell you that this was worse than seeing his paunchy belly with no shirt on—which I did when he was working out in the field—you should know that it was really, really bad to see his belly.

"Why are the other families just staring at him?" I whispered to Ka.

"I don't know," she whispered back.

Meanwhile, my dad was looking around at everyone like he was deciding something. Finally he said, "I guess we're the camp underachievers this week. All we've done is weed and I barely feel like I'm making a dent. No mill plans in the works. No swimming holes. We're not building onto the cabin anytime soon." He sat down.

There was silence. I don't know what there was supposed to be—applause? Pats on the back? I had the feeling there should have been something, some response, and instead, it was just absolutely silent.

Finally, Ron prompted, "Maybe you'll come up with an idea over the course of the week." He clapped his hands. "Okay," he said. "I think the women are getting anxious to show off the dinners they've brought with them. If no one has anything else to add, I'll do the progress assessments. Starting with the Puchinskis.

"Anders, your early rising has helped you—and that's appropriate to farm life, where you had to be out in the fields as soon as the sun was up. You're the only family to complete the weeding of your crop in a week and Disa's improvisation in the kitchen is admirable. The cookies you shared with me on our visit were delicious. I'm giving you an eight."

Disa, who so rarely spoke, looked up from her knitting to smile and nod, her black hair slicked back neatly into a bun.

"Drivers—" That was Caleb's family. "You're doing all right with your farming, but your work in the house is below par. The chicken Peter cooked over an outdoor fire was a standout, but Betsy says you're lacking a regular kitchen routine. You need to keep the fire regular, the water on, the floor swept. I'm giving you a six.

"Meyer-Hincheys—" That was Ka's family. "You called it bonding, but when I visited your place last week all I saw your kids doing was fighting. And whatever you want to call it, it's getting in the way of work on your farm. On the frontier, a family was an economic unit, and putting together and pulling apart was less common because of that. You get a six as well.

"Welshes. Okay, you have problems inside and out. Betsy tells me you've been living on a diet of beans and cornmeal. Your weeding is quite slow, especially considering that half the time you seem to be pulling up corn plants instead of weeds. I'm giving you a four." He clapped his hands to show that the assessment was over and looked at Betsy. "Picnic time?" he said. Betsy nodded.

"A six?" Ka said as we stood up and reached for the baskets we'd stored under the benches. "I thought we did better than that."

"A four?" my mom said.

"At least we get to eat," said Gavin.

But "eat" wasn't exactly the right word for what we did after everyone laid out their blankets in the shade. Mostly we watched other people eat.

There were strawberries and salad. There were hard-boiled eggs and bread with jam. There was spinach and sweet potatoes. There was a raspberry rhubarb pie with a crumb topping.

And what had my mom brought? It was a dish she claimed to have invented. She unveiled it as if it were a big treat. "Onion sandwiches!"

They were exactly what they sound like—bread with cold fried onions in the middle. "I was looking at these chive thingies in the garden and I just had an inspiration to pull them up, and then when I saw that they were onions, I was thinking I'd do a focaccia. But I've been having trouble with bread and there's no olive oil. Aren't you glad we waited to assemble them until now?"

Mom valiantly pretended she couldn't see the Meyer-Hincheys' piles of fresh berries and the Drivers' fritatta. "Imagine if the onion goop had been soaking into the bread all morning during that meeting?" She lowered her voice. "Especially while Anders was going on and on."

"That meeting?" said my dad. "I don't know if it deserves to be called a meeting. It was more like a humiliation festival. And I think we should have gotten higher than a four."

"Well, it's only the beginning of the summer," my mom reasoned.

"Hmph," my dad said. His tone reminded me how he'd rail against the parents at my soccer games who stood on the sidelines and yelled at their kids, at the coaches, and at the ref. "No one is as concerned about the bears as they should be."

"Doug, please," my mom said. The Puchinskis were looking at us. "Try your sandwich." And then, "I'm not in love with this format either," she whispered. Her eyes strayed to Disa Puchinski, who was holding a biscuit so flaky all she had to do was grasp the edges and twist and it pulled exactly in half. "Those look incredible."

For a second, our family just stared, feeling depressed together, surrounded by everyone's lettuce and strawberries and flaking pastry. Our picnic blanket, which doubled as a tablecloth, wasn't even all that clean. Gavin had spilled a bowl of beans on it the night before.

Gavin was the first to take a bite of the onion sandwich. "Mom!" he said. "Hey! This sandwich is actually good."

"It's good?" said my mom. If he'd told her she was just elected president of the United States, I'm not sure she could have looked more pleased. "You like it?" She took a bite. "It *is* good," she said.

I took a small bite myself, and I have to say, it was pretty tasty. The bread was not as rock hard as her first couple of attempts had been. And the onions were sweet and rich and they sort of melted into the bread. "Okay," I said. "You're right. This is good."

But my dad couldn't be swayed. "I'm not coming to this meeting next week," he sulked.

"Well," said my mom with her mouth full. "I'm not either." At first I was like, "Does that mean we're quitting?"

But then she finished chewing. "I'm not coming back here until we have something more to show for ourselves. I think it's time to harvest Pumpkin."

Gavin nearly choked on his sandwich.

"Pumpkin?" he said. "The chicken?"

"By harvest," I said. "Do you mean kill?"

"Pumpkin's a rooster, guys," my mom said. "He doesn't produce eggs, so we have to eat him."

"But he's going to bleed if we kill him," Gavin said.

"Yes." My mom nodded. "That's true."

"What if we kill Daisy by accident," I said. "And then we don't have any more eggs? Do you even know which of them is which?"

"Daisy's the one with the brown patches," my mom said.

"No," Gavin said. "Daisy's the one with the orange dots on her wings."

"I thought the orange dots one was Pumpkin," my dad said.

Gavin handed his sandwich back to Mom.

"Why are you giving this to me?" she said.

"Because I can't eat another bite of it," he said. I wish I'd been principled enough to take the same stand, but I've always been a faster eater than Gavin, and my sandwich was long gone.

"Oh, Gavin," my mom said. "Come on."

He turned his back.

"Okay," she said. "What do you say to not doing it this week? We'll find something else to eat this week."

Gavin stuck his hand out from behind his back. My mom returned his sandwich.

I lay back on the blanket, staring up at the sky. The cruel, bright blue sky, twinkling at me through the trees. My family was the camp losers. Why were we even here? Why couldn't we spend our summer somewhere where there was food to eat?

I closed my eyes, wishing not for the first time that this whole place would just disappear, and that I'd wake up and find myself back at home, in my clean room. (Well, okay, it was never all that clean, but at least it was carpeted, warm, and dry.) Food should be something you just walked downstairs to the kitchen for, without having to argue over killing it or whether there was enough.

As I lay there, I felt a shadow fall across my face and I opened my eyes to see Caleb standing over me. I sat up. He was holding a plate of food. I noticed a slice of the fritatta his family had been eating before and a piece of chicken—it wasn't fried, like Nora's. It was a drumstick, coated in herbs.

"I thought I might broker a trade," he said, looking first at me, but also at my mom and dad. "We don't have very much bread—my mom hasn't figured out how to get it to rise more than an inch. Would you be interested in donating, say, half a loaf of bread to our picnic in exchange for this plate of food?"

My mom was blinking, as if she thought that Caleb might be teasing. It didn't help that he was standing right in front of the sun and it was shining behind him, like he was an angel who had just stepped out of the clouds. My mom laid a hand across her heart. My dad stood up. Gavin ducked his head. And after I kind of mumbled something—I mean, I was pretty much dying with embarrassment—Caleb unloaded the food he'd brought and took some of my mom's onion-sandwich bread back to his family. He didn't come back or say anything else. But Nora was looking over at me, glaring.

```
Week 2 - Sunday
8:49 pm
Caleb Driver's leather necklace is the
cutest thing I have ever seen.


Week 2 - Monday
9:35 am
When my mom said we had to get the
laundry done this week and I asked, "Do
we take it to Betsy's?" she laughed so
hard I was worried they'd have to call
some men in a van to take her away.
```

Week 2 - Tuesday

7:45 pm

Ron had told us that every family would be given a cow the second week of camp, but I'd forgotten all about it until this morning. Gavin and I were pulling up potatoes in the kitchen garden, and suddenly there was Nora, leading a cow by a rope. She looked like she'd marched right out of an illustration from a Mother Goose book, with her cap and her braid and her boots and her long dress that she wore like it wasn't driving her totally crazy the way mine was.

Week 2 - Tuesday

7:45 pm

Sometimes--and I know this is pathetic--I
have to force myself to remember that
Nora should not look normal to me, that
1890 should always cause a shock to the
senses, but it's hard sometimes to
remember.

When Nora looked up and saw us, she frowned, or at least I think she did. Her sunbonnet was casting a shadow over her face like she was some kind of gunslinger in a Western. She draped the cow's lead (that's a word I was about to learn) over a hook outside the barn, and took a few steps toward me and Gavin where we were on the fence, so we could hear her without her having to shout. "You kids ever milked a cow before?" she asked, her hands on her hips, her elbows sticking out. Then she turned and walked back to the barn.

Somehow we knew that we were supposed to follow her, though following Nora was the last thing in the world I wanted to do.

I know that no one should expect a girl like me—who grew up in the suburbs drinking milk out of a carton—to know anything about milking a real cow. But still, I couldn't come up with a single way to admit that to Nora without feeling like she was winning some kind of game.

So when we got inside the barn, where Nora had led the cow and she repeated her question, I said, "Sure, I've done it before," and I'm not sure whose glare hit me first, Nora's or Gavin's. The looks they were giving me were like searchlights crisscrossing over my body, looking for some evidence of a lie.

Immediately, I thought, "Should I take it back?" I could say I'd milked a fake cow at the petting zoo we used to go to that had wooden cutout cows with big fat rubber udders filled with water and hanging down so kids could practice squeezing out milk.

But I didn't say that. I shrugged and I said, "Tons of times. What's the big deal?" It was stupid, okay, I know that.

"Great," Nora said. "So you should be all set."

I was scrambling now, thinking, "What am I doing?" And "Why did I say that?" I was thinking that it would be ugly when it finally came time to try to get milk out of this animal. I was thinking that maybe my dad would know what to do with the cow, the way he'd known all about bears.

For now, though, this was about Nora and me. I had my fight face on, the mask I felt forming during soccer games, when I knew I couldn't let the other team get even one shot on goal.

My fight face worked. Nora maybe—at least for a second—believed me. Her expression changed. She's really pretty, or at least she could be—and while she was feeling surprised, she kind of forgot for a second to look mad.

In fact, she looked kind of impressed, and I found myself wishing I did know how to milk a cow because I liked the idea of Nora being impressed with something I could do. For a second I wished she was someone on my soccer team who I could hang out with and practice corner kicks or juggling. She could be pretty cool if she were a normal kid my age.

It was just a second before she pursed her lips right back into the sneer and said, "Okay, then. Jezebel here's ready to go, so get yourself a bucket."

"Now?" I asked, and I think it was the question—or maybe the desperation in my voice when I asked it—that gave me away. Nora's smile uncurled like a snake.

"What's going on?" my mom said when I burst into the kitchen. I tried not to look too panicked. I was thinking maybe I could figure out how to milk a cow just by trying. I was thinking that maybe all that experience at the petting zoo when I was—what? seven?—would somehow make me look like a pro. And while I was thinking all this I was standing dumbstruck inside the doorway, my hands clenched at my sides. It was all I could do not to put them on my head and pull at my hair and say, "Oh, God what have I done?"

"Gen?" my mom prompted.

I didn't answer her because just then I was realizing that I'd forgotten what I'd come in for.

As if she could read my mind, Nora called from outside, "Milk bucket's on a hook by the door!" Oh yeah, I thought, and I grabbed the tin bucket I hadn't even noticed before, hanging exactly where Nora had said it would be.

I gave myself a pep talk. "Be brave!" I said. I held my head high and carried the milk bucket like I'd been carrying one every day of my life. Actually, I held my head too high. I didn't see one of the chickens—I still didn't know if it was Daisy or Pumpkin, it was the one without the orange spots. When I stepped on it, it let out this huge squawk and I was like, "Sorry, sorry!" I kept walking and tried to look like, well, like someone who knew how to milk a cow.

Once I was inside the barn, up close and personal with the cow—Jezebel—I had a moment of intense doubt and I bet it showed.

Jezebel was a reddish brownish color with white spots and big haunches, but the main thing about her up close is that she is just simply very large. The top ridge of her bony back came up to my shoulder, and I'm not sure that Gavin was taller than she was.

I had to think. I had to make a plan. I had to find her udder. I looked down.

At the petting zoo, I think they had little stools for the kids to sit on, but I didn't see any of them around. Maybe there was some trick to milking cows on the frontier? Did people slide underneath them on a board on wheels like a mechanic working on a car? Did they squat?

I was getting ready to try that when Nora said, "Stool's over there." I followed her gaze to the far corner of the barn, where sure enough I found a three-legged stool. Okay, I thought. This is a good thing. I knew there was supposed to be a stool, and there it is. I can do this!

The first mistake I made was to put the little three-legged stool down behind Jezebel. Fortunately, she kicked it away before I was sitting on it. I quickly picked up the stool from where it had landed, as if I could keep Nora from seeing what had happened, but of course she did. When I glanced up, she was shaking her head like she should have known. I tried putting the stool more to the side of the cow this time, and then I lowered myself on top of it.

From this angle, Jezebel loomed even larger, and when she shifted on her feet a little bit, I jumped up. I'd thought for a second I was about to be crushed. "Easy, girl," Nora said, rubbing Jezebel on the shoulder, and talking to her so nicely Jezebel calmed right down.

I needed someone to talk that soothingly to me. All my life I'd heard about people milking cows—you think it's no big deal but with a cow this close I realized I was actually in danger.

When I looked up again, Nora had her eyebrows raised and her lips turned down in a sneer.

Gavin was taking a few steps back and had this kind of psycho smile on his face—like he was half thinking he should run, and half thinking that the entertainment experience of a lifetime was about to begin.

"Well?" said Nora.

I felt like I was in a dream. I adjusted the stool's position slightly and, even though my stomach felt like it wanted nothing more than for my entire body to collapse around the stool, to bring it nowhere near that cow—and what kind of name was Jezebel anyway? It made the cow sound so angry—I laid a hand on Jezebel's shoulder like Nora had, and lowered myself onto the stool for the second time.

I pulled the bucket up under the udder. I mean, I'm not totally dumb, I knew *where* you were supposed to put your hands, and that you needed to squeeze and the milk would come out.

What I didn't know is that you're not supposed to squeeze too hard. I guess in my desire to seem like I knew what I was doing, I really wrenched Jezebel the first time. She grunted and moved to the side, but I held on. I squeezed again. Jezebel grunted again, and tried to take a step away.

"You're supposed to push the milk out with your hands, not send it back up into the cow," said Nora. "It hurts her, don't know you that? You want me to show you?"

The only way to combat how humiliating this was was to

pretend I hadn't heard Nora. But when I squeezed again, I relaxed and also pulled down as I was squeezing, gliding along— I don't know how I knew to do that but maybe I'd seen it on TV or something—and a huge, I mean an enormous, squirt of milk splashed into the bucket. It was so much it actually sprayed my face. I had to wipe off my eye with the sleeve of my dress.

I didn't dare look up at Nora. I squeezed some more. "You going to milk one-handed?" I heard her say. "We'll be here all day." So with my other hand I took another teat and milked that one too. And as I pulled on first one and then the other, I felt like someone out of a movie, which must have meant I was doing it right.

I gave Nora a huge, sticky-sweet bubble-gum-ice cream-with-candy-worms-and-Sour-Patch-Kids-on-top smile. "Surprised that I can do this?" I said.

Nora turned around as if she were somehow bored of the whole thing now, like something about the view through the open barn door was fascinating.

I kept milking. Squirt, squirt—the sound made me want to laugh, like someone had just burped. Little by little, the bucket was filling up. The milk was warm, and the smell reminded me of a road trip when Gavin spilled milk from McDonald's in the car and we had to live with it all the way to my aunt and uncle's house in upstate New York. It wasn't a sour smell, but it was *really* heavy. We're talking intense milk.

Nora turned to Gavin. "Cow's going to be living here, you'll need to know how to muck out a stall." She might as well have said "I'm going to take you out back and beat you to a bloody pulp," her tone was so mean.

Gavin—who didn't yet know that mucking out a stall meant shoveling straw soaked in cow poo and pee—looked from me to Nora and back to me again. I nodded, to show him that it was okay, and also to show Nora that Gavin couldn't be bossed around by her—the only person who was going to be bossing him was *me*.

Before I'd faked my way into milking the cow, I don't think it would have occurred to Gavin to check with me about something he was going to do. Suddenly, Gavin and I, we were a team. Ouga, ouga, Welsh!

```
Week 2 - Tuesday
8:57 pm
For dessert we had warm milk with a few
spoonfuls of leftover coffee and this
tiny bit of brown sugar my mom's been
saving as a treat--café au lait.

Week 2 - Wednesday
7:56 am
I milked the cow again! I can milk a cow!
I've done it twice now--in the afternoon
yesterday and this morning. Take that,
Nora-know-it-all!
```

« 11 »

Just after breakfast on Wednesday, my mom called me into the house. "Don't work in the corn today," she said. "I need your help with the washing."

"The washing?" I said. I wasn't sure what she meant by that.

"Laundry," she clarified. "We need clean clothes." She took a whiff as if to confirm something she suspected. "Gen, is it you?" she said. "I smell old pee."

"No!" I said, but of course it was. My second pair of stockings were stiff with crusted dirt and sweat, so I'd switched to the ones that still had the evidence of my first adventure in the outhouse. My mom sniffed again, and I opened the door to try to bring fresh air into the room, hoping she wouldn't understand why I was doing it. I guess giving the tights a second chance had been a mistake.

```
Week 2 - Wednesday
5:24 pm
In theory, doing laundry doesn't sound
that bad. You heat up lots of water, add
```

soap, soak the clothes, scrub them, wring
out the dirty water, soak them again,
scrub them again, wring out the dirty
water--again--soak them, rinse them, wring
out the water, rinse them a second time,
and then wring out the water one more
time before hanging them out to dry.
Sounds easy, right?

Week 2 - Wednesday
5:27 pm
No.
It's not easy.
Doing laundry is a nightmare.

Week 2 - Wednesday
5:37 pm
Here's the main problem with laundry (if
you really want to know, and trust me,
you don't)--everything starts off about
ten times dirtier than normal laundry
at home. I mean, the white shirts, the
bibs and petticoats--they were brown.
And on top of that, washing them doesn't
really help. By the end of the day,
you're hoping to get things to a place
where they're maybe as dirty as the
stuff you would put in the hamper at
home.

"Ooh, laundry!" Betsy squealed when she came by and saw the ugly scene. Every pot we had was filled with water and heating up on the stove. There was a washtub on the floor overflowing with suds. My mom had taken out this thing called a washboard, which is made of wood covered in wrinkled tin and looks like something you'd use as a musical instrument in elementary school, but is actually something you're supposed to use to scrub out the dirt from clothes. You rub them up and down on the board, and then wring them out, soak them in the water, and do it again.

I think I rubbed more skin off my knuckles than dirt out of the clothes.

By the time Betsy arrived there were puddles of water on the floor. Our hands were red and chapped. My mom had sweat pouring down her face—God knows I could feel it dripping down mine. The muscles in my upper arms were burning and so weak from trying to wring out these enormously heavy shirts and petticoats that I could barely get them to move.

"This . . . is . . . awful," my mom panted from behind the tub of bubbles. She was trying to rinse a pair of bloomers and every time she wrung them out, there was still muddy water coming off them.

"Historical records show that any family with even the tiniest bit of disposable income sent their laundry out," Betsy chirped. "And something fairly sad to keep in mind is that for women who needed to earn money, doing laundry for other people was one of the few jobs they could count on. Can you imagine doing laundry not just for your household, but for someone else's as well?"

"They must have had a technique," my mom said.

"It gets easier over time," Betsy said. "But it's the worst chore. I think that's one of the reasons you get it out of the way on Mondays."

"Wash on Monday," my mom recited. "Iron on Tuesday. Mend on Wednesday. Churn on Thursday. Clean on Friday. Bake on Saturday. Rest on Sunday."

"Very good!" Betsy clapped. "I follow that myself."

"I remember it from *Little House on the Prairie*," my mom said.

"You wash *every* Monday?" I asked. "I was hoping we could get through the rest of the summer without doing laundry again. Wearing dirty clothes is so much better than this."

"Unless you smell like pee," my mom said.

"Oh, you two, you're funny." Betsy laughed. Neither my mom nor I explained that we hadn't been kidding.

When Gavin and my dad came in for lunch, which Betsy insisted on calling dinner, my mom and I just stared at them from behind the clouds of bubbles and steam. We were dripping by then. I don't know if it was water or sweat. Our hair was soaked. "Don't even think about eating right now," my mom said.

But the second she mentioned eating, I realized I was starved.

"We have to take a break," I said.

"You're right," she agreed. "*We* need to eat." She let the petticoat she'd been wringing out drop back into the dirty water, then realized what she'd done and slapped her hands on either side of her head. I once saw a woman in a movie react that way when she realized she'd left her stove on, and the next scene was of the house on fire.

Quickly, we assembled lunch. Cold beans spread on cold

grits, which can be sliced when they congeal. Totally foul, but no one was complaining because clearly my mom was not in a position to hear it.

When we looked over at the buckets again after lunch, I felt the blood draining down to my feet. "I can't do it," I said. "I can't wring out another shirt."

But my mom must have been revived by the meal. "Change of scene," she said, starting to drag the washtub out onto the porch. "Grab a handle." Though my arms were still as weak as Jell-O, I did.

She was right. It was better working outside. At one point, after a particularly painful bout of wringing—my dress had to be scrubbed three times because of the grass stains—my mom pointed out to the yard and said, "Look at that view."

I did. The sky was what the art teacher in my school calls a highly saturated shade of blue, dotted with white puffy clouds. The only noise I could hear was the wind moving in the tops of the trees way above us. They were everywhere, the trees, their trunks lost inside the green light filtering through the leaves. "It looks like something on a Hallmark card," I said.

Mom laughed out loud. Then she pinched the bridge of her nose and sighed. "You can take the girl out of the twenty-first century . . . ," she began.

Instead of saying "But you can't take the twenty-first century out of the girl," which is where I guessed she was going, I said, "But you *shouldn't* take the girl out of the twenty-first century, because the twenty-first century has washing machines."

My dad came back from the cornfield early and hammered a nail to the outside wall of the house, tied some rope to it, and then strung it to another nail he hammered into the side of the barn. "There," he said. "That ought to help."

It did. Pretty soon, we'd draped all the clothes we'd washed over the line to dry. After we dumped the last tub of dirty water over the side, I was resting on the porch, when my mom asked me to fill the wood bin.

"What are you doing now?" I said.

"Ironing," she answered, her face grim.

"Ironing what?" At home, anything that needed to be ironed got sent to the dry cleaners.

"Everything," Mom said.

"But it's still wet," I said.

"Not for long," she explained. "And if you let it dry all the way, the wrinkles are harder to remove."

I hauled myself up to a standing position and loaded my poor, aching arms with wood. My mom pulled two irons, which were actually flat metal triangles with handles, out from under the counter where the pump was.

She found a board leaning against the wall behind the door and laid it across the backs of two chairs. When the first iron was hot, she spread a petticoat across the board, took an iron off the stove, being careful to hold it with a folded-over rag in her hand, and laid the iron down on the petticoat.

Immediately, something didn't smell right, and when my mom lifted the iron away, there was a dark brown triangle-shaped print where the iron had been. The cotton was smoking.

"Is that supposed to happen?" I said.

My mom didn't answer. She put the iron down on the stove, closed the damper to shut down the fire, walked out the front door, put both hands on her hips, and stood on the porch, shaking her head.

"What?" I said.

"I'm done," she answered.

And I was afraid enough of the look on her face not to ask her done with what.

That night, after dinner, which was cold grits and beans again, my dad brought the clothes in from the line and my mom made an announcement. "Life on the frontier was more fun than this," she said.

The muscles in my arms were burning and I couldn't open and close my fist without skin splitting. "What about laundry isn't fun?" I said.

She ignored me. "In 1890, there would have been musicians in the family. Storytellers. Games. We would have done more than just stare out at the trees and think about home."

"I'm not staring at the trees," my dad said. "I'm looking for bears."

"Fine," said my mom. "But can't we sing while you're staring?"

"I don't sing," Gavin said.

"You used to," said my mom. "You and Gen used to sing all the time."

"When?" said Gavin, as if he didn't believe her.

"In your cribs," my mom explained, a dip in her voice acknowledging that, okay, she was going back pretty far in time. "Gavin, when you were two and Gen was in kindergarten, you would sing back and forth to each other across the hall as you were going to sleep."

The memory of when we were that small must have triggered some cooperative spirit in my dad—my parents love thinking about that time. In pictures they always look happy and healthier: hiking with Gavin in a backpack carrier and me totally psyched to have my own water bottle, or sitting out on the patio at Grandma's house eating muffins. Without taking his eyes off the tree line, Dad said, "Okay, we'll sing." Gavin started to complain and my dad said forcefully, "We will *all* sing."

And so we lined up in a row on the edge of the porch, and sang songs we all knew the words to. The list was pretty short. "Twinkle Twinkle," "ABC," "Erie Canal," "Feelings," "Somewhere Over the Rainbow." And "Jesus Christ, Superstar," which Gavin and I had been in the chorus of during my mom's my-children-will-perform-in-school-plays phase.

Our voices sounded really small and warbly against the big night sky.

```
Week 2 - Thursday
7:50 am
I am so tired that last night I fell
asleep sitting up on the porch at 8:30 pm.
```

« 12 »

I had to be careful about texting now. Every time I turned the phone on, I got a beep and a message telling me the battery was low. I didn't know how much longer I had.

But it was hard to resist. Sending a text made it seem like my friends were right next door.

```
Week 2 - Friday
9:17 pm
Ka snuck out tonight and came over after
dinner. We spent an hour coming up with
former lives for Ron and Betsy. I'm not
going to write them all because there
are too many.
```

```
Week 2 - Friday
9:17 pm
Okay, here's one: grizzly-bear wrestlers
in a circus sideshow.
```

Week 2 — Friday
9:19 pm
This one's pretty good too: identity
thieves (they're off the grid because
they're on the lam).

Week 2 — Friday
9:21 pm
Yoga instructors who had to leave the
business because Ron's so stiff he
couldn't touch his toes.

Week 2 — Friday
9:23 pm
Spies in a forgotten sleeper cell left
over from the Cold War.

Week 2 — Friday
9:25 pm
Cult leaders who are pretending this
is just a summer camp but really are
jump-starting a commune--just wait until
the fall when they won't let any of us
leave!

Week 2 — Friday
9:27 pm
Okay, I'll stop.

. . .

On Saturday morning, we were still finishing breakfast when Nora came by carrying two more chickens—Macduff and Macbeth. "You get six total," she said. "Cassandra and Romeo are coming next."

"Who names them?" my mom asked.

"My mom gave Pumpkin and Daisy their names, but when she's stumped my dad has this *Reader's Digest Abridged Shakespeare* set," Nora explained. "We just rotate through the names. This is the third Romeo we've had this year—all hens too."

"Do Macbeth and Macduff get along?" my dad asked. "You know, in the play, Macduff kills Macbeth?"

"Don't know and don't care," Nora said. "A name's a name. You gotta kill them all in the end, so it's better not to get attached." We'd followed her out to the barn, where she was holding open the door to the coop with her hip and shoving the chickens inside without letting Daisy get out. "Where's Pumpkin?" she said. "Did you finally get after him with the hatchet?"

Gavin winced. "He likes to sit in this one box in the barn," he explained.

"Weird rooster," Nora said. "You know you're going to have to get to him sooner or later." She squinted off to the fields like she was looking for something on the horizon. "Pumpkin's still young enough. He'll be good—tender."

Gavin made a face.

"I know you eat chicken at home, right?" Nora said. "Bet you buy them all cut and wrapped up nice in plastic in the grocery store, don't you?"

"It's different," Gavin said.

"Oh, please," Nora said. "Chickens are stupid, even for birds.

A lamb that comes when he's called—now that's hard for a kid to watch get killed. I know. I did it. And a pig? Forget it. Pigs are like dogs. You should never get to know your pigs too well."

"Did you have to learn that the hard way too?" my mom asked. She sounded like she was trying to use the voice she uses on Gavin's friends when she needs to remind them that she's in charge when they're at our house, her would-you-like-me-to-call-your-mother-and-see-if-you-get-to-eat-candy-before-dinner? voice. But it wasn't quite working—she sounded a little like she was begging Nora for something.

And whatever it was she was begging for, Nora wasn't giving it up. "I had to learn *everything* the hard way," she said.

Sunday, when we arrived at Ron and Betsy's for the third picnic, Anders Puchinski—whose sunburn was peeling so badly I half expected him to add discarding his skin like a snake to his list of many accomplishments—talked on and on about the wheat mill he was building, how he'd located a couple of grindstones and had been working on cutting them down to the right size. Disa had made her first pie crust. The Drivers had found the right section of the stream to dam up to make their swimming hole and had started hauling rocks over to it the day before. My dad talked about finishing weeding the cornfield, what a great feeling that was. The Meyer-Hincheys hadn't built an addition or even a new bed, but they'd moved Matt, Katie, and Cara downstairs, while Ka now slept upstairs with the parents. Every time anyone in the happy blond family mentioned Ka, they sighed. Even Cara, who was nine.

Then it was time for progress assessment numbers.

The Puchinskis had met all of their goals. They got another eight.

The Drivers hadn't done laundry. They got a six.

The Meyer-Hincheys hadn't finished weeding their millet. They got a six.

"And the Welshes," Ron concluded. "You have yet to kill one of your chickens, but more significantly, you haven't even selected a farm improvement project. I'm giving you a four."

My mom jumped out of her seat. "Wait," she said.

For a second, there was silence. Everyone on the benches looked up. Ron said, "Cheryl, women in 1890 weren't accustomed to speaking out in a forum like this."

"Sorry!" she said, smiling. But she didn't sound sorry. She cleared her throat. "I know enough about history to tell you that in 1890 women were already practicing law in the U.S. court system, being admitted to the American Medical Association, running for and holding political office, and in some states such as Wyoming, inside of whose borders I believe we stand right now, women had already fought for and received the right to vote."

"Hear, hear!" shouted Caleb's mom, who probably had no idea there was a huge streak of black grease on her forehead.

"That's true," Betsy chimed in. "Wyoming Territory. Women were voting here as of 1869. Almost cost Wyoming its statehood, but the people stayed firm."

Before Ron could close his mouth—it had been hanging open during my mother's and Betsy's speeches—my mom continued with a laugh, "What I started to say is that Doug has been working so hard clearing trees, it occurred to me that this is our farm improvement if anything is."

Dad stood. "Cheryl, I think you're right," he said.

"Oh?" said Ron.

My father coughed. "I'm clearing out the woods around the cabin."

"Well, that's what everyone's doing. Cutting trees and amassing firewood is part of your regular responsibility," Ron chided.

"I'm not sure most people are going to cut as many as I plan to," my dad said. He was speaking quietly, the way he does when he's angry.

"How many do you have in mind?"

"A four-acre parcel," he explained. "About the same size as our cornfield."

I could see the slight flush of pleasure on my dad's face when Anders Puchinski let out a whistle and Ron tucked his chin, like a turtle scooting into its shell. "You sure that isn't too much to take on?" Ron said.

"I'm not doing it to impress you," my dad said. "It's the only way I'm going to feel safe from the bears. I saw tracks when I was out in the woods this morning, and I don't like that. Not one bit."

"Very well," said Ron. "I'll upgrade you to a six, like the others."

At the picnic, my mom unveiled another surprise. It was butter.

She had made butter. All by herself.

We spread it on bread, on radishes (my mom said they do this in France), on cold sliced grits. It was so good I felt like I'd eaten an entire McDonald's supervalue meal.

And when I lay back this time on the picnic blanket, I didn't think the sky was cruel and that everyone had better food than us. The only thing in my mind was that finally, maybe, I was full.

Matt had found a biscuit-tin lid, and he and his dad, Clark, were getting a game of Ultimate Frisbee together. Ka's mom—Maureen—marked the end zones with people's sunbonnets, and Matt and Caleb elected themselves captains and started dividing the teams.

Matt picked Katie and Erik and Anders and Maureen. Caleb picked Nora and me and Ron and Ka and his dad. No one else wanted to play. And no one really seemed to know the rules. Did you have to throw the Frisbee before someone else could count to ten? Did your whole body have to be in the end zone when you caught the Frisbee for a score, or just your feet?

It didn't matter. At least to me. Caleb threw me the lid and said "Nice!" when I caught it, and Ka high-fived me after she'd made a score. A goth girl who high-fives? Unusual. Maybe this place was getting to her. I, for one, was pretty sure I was staying the same, even if today, I felt pretty good.

I had no idea that next week, everything would change.

« 13 »

Sunday night, just as I was composing a text up in the hayloft of the barn, the battery on the phone died. I'd known that this would happen sooner or later, but it still felt like a shock, and it took some time to register the full impact of the loss.

I left the barn in a daze that reminded me of a time when I took a soccer ball to the face during a game and couldn't feel my cheek for an hour.

Over the course of the next few days, all I thought about were the things I wanted to tell Kristin and Ashley. About how, after we'd weeded, the corn suddenly seemed to shoot up and sprout tassels. About how, one day, we saw minicobs forming in the crevice where the leaf met the stalk.

Not that I cared or anything. It was just interesting.

Without the phone, the routine of our days dragged. Every chore seemed to take twice as much time. While sweeping up ash from under the stove, I ended up having a coughing fit and I just sat down on the porch and stared out at the sky, wishing I were somewhere, anywhere, else.

On Wednesday, I milked Jezebel the way I always did, but for some reason she gave only half her usual amount. Gavin was supposed to clean out her stall, but he was nowhere to be found, so I had to take care of it—a nasty chore.

When I brought the milk bucket into the house, my mom was washing some tiny carrots she'd dug up from the garden—you pull the small ones so the others have room to get big. She looked tired. She was sitting at the table instead of standing at the counter, her bun had slipped down to her neck, and her eyes were drooping like she was having trouble staying awake. She used her arms to push back some hairs that were falling loose and when I put the bucket of milk down on the table, she gestured with her head toward the counter as if she didn't have energy to speak.

I poured half the milk into a jug for drinking—the rest went into a pail on the shelf where it would separate, the fatty parts rising to the surface—yuck. Mom managed to summon the energy to get a few words out. "Set the table?" she said, without looking up.

"Don't I get to rest?" I asked.

"Sure," she said. "After the dinner is served."

"But you're working at the table," I protested when I got the plates over to where she was—there was no room for them.

"Set it around me," she said. "I can't move." That's when I saw that she had her feet resting on the chair opposite. I took the lid off the pot that was on the stove top and started to dish out . . . yup, beans. Again.

"Is the butter all gone?" I asked. She'd made a second batch that morning and we'd had it at lunch.

"Yes," she said. "Took a day to set, an hour to churn, and about fifteen minutes to eat it all up."

My dad came in, pumped some water into a basin and washed off his hands and wet his face. Still, there was a line of dried, salty sweat at the edge of his hairline that reminded me of the tide mark on sand at the beach.

Gavin came in next. He'd been running. I could tell from the way he was breathing.

"Don't worry about Jezebel's stall," I said, laying on the sarcasm. "I took care of it for you."

"Thanks," he said, like I'd been sincere. And then, "Come here a sec."

My mom said, "Dinner's already on the table," but Gavin dragged me onto the porch anyway. "Look," he said, and I did, though I saw nothing but the wide-open door to the barn, the edge of the trees, the garden to the left, the field up the hill behind. "No. Here," he said.

And I saw that he was holding his hat—the newsboy cap he'd been given on the first day, which Mom made him wear to the picnics. Now it was upside down. He was using it as a bowl. "Look inside," he insisted, and that was kind of exciting because I was expecting maybe something good to eat. Berries? Walnuts? The Puchinskis and the Meyer-Hincheys were always finding food in the woods.

But the hat was filled with dirt. Except some of it wasn't dirt. Or rather, some of the dirt was moving. I saw more: some of the dirt definitely wasn't dirt. It was worms.

Gavin has always loved really disgusting pets. Chickens are just the most recent example. When he was seven, he had a pet snake and a pet iguana. That was when Ashley started making me line the crack at the bottom of my bedroom door with a towel when she slept over.

"I dug them up," he said.

"I thought maybe you had something good in there," I said. "Like you'd found berries in the woods."

"If you were starving, you'd eat worms," he pointed out.

"But couldn't you use a bucket?" I said. "You're going to have to wear that hat when Mom makes you get all authentic at the picnics."

"It's going to be worth it," he said.

"If you eat those worms your breath's going to be even more stinky than usual."

"I'm not going to *eat* them," he said.

Mom called from inside, "Dinner's getting cold." Gavin slid the hat back under the porch, covering it with a large piece of birch bark weighted down with a rock, I guess so the worms couldn't escape.

At dinner, my dad looked directly at my mom and said, "I want to get this out of my system, so I have to say it out loud: I hate it here."

When she didn't answer, he went on. "I chopped down four trees with an ax this afternoon and hauled them to the edge of our property using ropes attached to my body. All because we are spending two months of our lives and all my vacation time at a place with . . ." He paused here, and I imagined he was considering all the terrible things he could say about Camp Frontier. "With a *bear problem*," he finally ended. "I'm trying, okay? But my hands have been bleeding." He showed us his palms, pocked with blisters, some swollen, some already split open, pink or even bleeding.

There was something about the way he was looking at all of

us that kept us from jumping up and offering to get him something to put on—gloves, or whatever they had instead of Band-
Aids in 1890. He lowered his head and went back to shoveling
beans into his mouth.

"Okay," my mom said. "Gavin, I hate to say this, but we're
going to have to kill Pumpkin."

Gavin stared. "No way," he said.

My mom ignored him. She looked at my dad. "Don't you
think roast chicken and chicken soup would make a difference?
There's stuff I can make even just with the bone marrow."

"You can't!" Gavin said.

"I don't know," said my dad. He was looking at my mom
kind of strangely, like she was someone who had just walked into
our house and he was trying to figure out if he'd ever seen her
before. "It might help."

I haven't seen Gavin cry since—well, I don't know since
when, but maybe the last time was a year ago when my mom
accidentally (she said) put his Wii into the garbage and he had to
wait for four months until Christmas to get a new one. He
choked back a sob now.

After dinner, my dad went back out into the woods. Gavin disappeared down the path with his hat, going who knew where.
I had to help my mom wash dishes.

Washing dishes on the frontier is one of the most disgusting
parts of being here. You use a rag, right? Not even a sponge. And you
rub it on the dishes in greasy semisoapy water. In spite of the fact
that this water has floating bits of beans and onions in it, you're
still going to pull a plate out of it and be like, "There! All clean!"

"Is Dad okay?" I asked my mom as we were working.

She looked at me like she was going to tell the truth and then she waited one second and lied. "He's adjusting," she said.

He's *not* adjusting, I wanted to say.

Neither was I.

And killing Pumpkin was going to make Gavin cry.

I missed my friends. I felt like they'd been with me on this trip—they'd been just a text away—and now they were gone.

My mom and I hung the dishtowels on the clothesline, then my mom went into the garden to weed. I sat on the fence watching her until I couldn't take it anymore. With the vague idea of going to find Ka, I walked into the woods and headed down the path.

It was weird. Gavin disappeared by himself all the time, but I'd never left the farm like this. I guess because I'd had the phone, I had never needed to go looking for something to do.

As I reached Ron and Betsy's, I noticed a little path leading off before the opening to their clearing. I decided to see where it led. Eventually, I broke through some thickly growing trees and brambles to find myself standing in front of a shed that was bigger than an outhouse, but smaller than our cabin. It was made of rough logs, just like ours, but there was something different about it. The windows, I realized. They were made of aluminum, double-hung—and were those screens?

And what was that shiny thing on the top of the building's roof? Could that possibly be—? I got a better angle so I could see—and yes, it was: a solar panel.

I know they didn't have solar panels on the frontier back in 1890 and I'm pretty sure aluminum windows weren't part of the package either. I was pretty sure this was something I wasn't supposed to see, but I inched my way around to the back of the shed, and a window.

I peeked through it, into a room whose bright white walls, blue carpet, and electric lights almost blinded me after so many weeks of everything being wooden and dark and drab.

But I wasn't so blind I couldn't take in the computer. Yes, that's right: a full-on twenty-first-century desktop complete with a flat-screen monitor, wireless keyboard, and a mouse pad that I could see even from the window was a tribute to the Milwaukee Bruins.

I think I might have convinced myself I was dreaming if Nora—real, living, breathing Nora—hadn't been sitting at the computer, her back to me, typing away as if an 1890s girl with a secret computer habit was nothing but completely ordinary.

She was dressed in the red and black checked cotton dress she always wore. I could see the soles of her totally authentic 1890 boots where her feet were tucked behind her chair—I could see a hole in the bottom of one that was the size of a dime. She wasn't wearing her sunbonnet, and her fat braid was relaxing down the middle of her back like a boa constrictor getting some sun.

When she turned slightly I noticed a few details that were not totally authentic 1890: first, she was chewing gum. Second, she was writing with a pen that has a troll head on the top that you can spin until its bright pink tuft forms a kind of I-just-got-electrocuted hairstyle. Third, she was listening to an iPod—I saw the earbuds, and then when I recognized a lanyard that Ashley had made, I realized it was my iPod. *Mine!*

Lastly, she was drinking—she took a swig right as I was watching—a genuinely modern Diet Coke.

Oh. My. God.

So *this* is what goes on here.

Not even real Coke. Not even Classic Coke.

And not even her own iPod. Nora was listening to mine.

I reached for my phone, and for the hundredth time remembered that it was dead.

But not for long, I thought.

I ran, counting on the noise of the music piping into Nora's ears from *my* very own iPod to mask the sound of sticks breaking and leaves rustling as my skirt dragged along the bushes. When I reached our barn, I scrambled up to the top of the hayloft, grabbed the Clearasil box from its hiding place, pulled out the phone charger, shoved it deep into my pocket, scrambled back down the ladder, and then, making sure that no one could see me, jogged off into the woods, following the path that led back to Betsy and Ron's.

« 14 »

It was funny how places were starting to seem closer together the more I walked the distances between them. The first night, the trip from Ron and Betsy's to our cabin felt like it took forty-five minutes. When we went back for the picnic, in the light of day, it seemed to take more like ten. Now that I understood the lay-out of the place—our farm and the Puchinskis' were on one side of Ron and Betsy's house while Caleb's family's and Ka's were on the other, the trip felt even shorter. Tonight, I was so afraid I'd miss my chance to charge the phone, I ran the distance in a few minutes, reaching Nora's electricity shack before I'd figured out how to get inside.

I sneaked up from the back again and looked in the window. I couldn't believe my luck. Nora was gone. I opened the door and let myself into the tiny office room.

I took a second to look around. Everything about the space was so modern it looked like someone bought it five minutes ago at Staples. I checked out the minifridge—it was filled with bottles of Diet Coke lined up like good little children during a fire drill in elementary school.

Plugged into the power strip next to the line for the computer was my iPod. Sweet! I hooked my phone up to its charger, popped the earbuds from my very own iPod into my ears, closed my eyes, and felt how amazing it was to hear music after more than two weeks of nothing more than the noises of the chickens, the woods, my brother, my parents' fighting, and my mom going completely and utterly insane.

I picked the song my soccer team had been listening to on a boom box in the bus on the way back from our last game of the season—"Thunder Falls"—and for a minute just missed everything and everybody from home. I thought about how much I really, really liked the twenty-first century. I liked having friends, and things to do that were fun and hard, like soccer, instead of things that were just plain hard, like dishes and milking the cow. I missed clothes that were comfortable, sidewalks that ran in front of houses, Oreos, riding my bike, and swimming.

I felt so safe and clean and calm that when I opened my eyes, it took me a second to register that I was no longer alone in the shed. But I wasn't. And as soon as I figured it out, I was like: RUN.

But I couldn't. Because the same thing that made me want to run was also blocking my way.

It was Caleb. How long he had been there I didn't know, but it was obvious he had been waiting for me to open my eyes and see him there. Like an ax murderer standing at your kitchen window when you're home alone at night. Only cuter.

This isn't rational, but I started to scream, thinking Ron and

Betsy would probably hear me through the woods. But before I could get out much of anything, Caleb clamped a hand over my mouth and whispered, "Shut up, shut up" so many times that I was finally like, "Okay" and he was laughing so hard he eventually took his hand off my mouth anyway.

I scooted back a few feet away from him, but I didn't leave, because by now I had come to my senses. I felt myself blushing.

He said, "Hey," and then he drew his eyebrows together—he had nice strong eyebrows—and looked down, as if he had to check his legs and arms to make sure he was still there before he spoke. "Sorry," he said. "I didn't mean to scare you. I knew you'd be freaked out. Nora didn't tell me you would be here. She said I was the only one who knew about this place."

At the mention of Nora's name, I must have looked a little wary. He said, "Sorry, do you even know what I'm talking about?"

"Um," I said. "No?"

He immediately blushed, which made him seem flustered and off center. His shirt was open as usual to show the braided leather necklace and his tanned throat, which looked strong and finely cut all at the same time.

At last I said, "You scared the bejeezus out of me," and we were both laughing again like this was some kind of long-standing inside joke.

Even after we'd sort of stopped, I felt this happy kind of giggle climbing up through my throat and I was like, "Shut up, shut up, shut up" to myself.

You know how I said before that there are times when I feel like there's a happy, pretty girl inside me—someone like my mom—and I fully expect to see that happy, pretty person when

I catch my reflection in the mirror? And then did I mention how it's always surprising when I see it's just plain old me? Well, just now, in those first few seconds of meeting Caleb, I was sure I would look in the mirror the next time and see not the plain girl dressed like she was working in some crazy history theme park, but myself as I always wished everyone could see me.

It was Caleb making me feel this way. He did this thing with his eyes that made me feel like he was really listening. And then he started to tell me about himself as if he really wanted me to know.

He told me that his family was from Virginia, just outside Washington DC, and that his dad is from the South, just like my dad is.

"Did your parents force you to do this too?" I asked.

He nodded. "Absolutely. When he said family camp, I was thinking Club Med."

"Me too!" I said. I was so happy to hear someone else saying the same thing as me I had to look away. I didn't want to act like an idiot. "I'm missing soccer camp," I said. "And sleepaway camp, and tryouts for travel team are this fall. I'm going to have to try out after not having played in two months."

"This is the last summer before my parents make me get a job," Caleb said. "So it's also my last summer of freedom, and this is how I'm spending it."

I wondered what he would do—would he be a lifeguard? A busboy in a restaurant? A server in an ice cream parlor? He was older than me. What if he had a car? I didn't know anyone who could drive yet.

"I miss sandwiches," Caleb said.

I laughed. "We have sandwiches here," I said. "It's one of the only things we do have."

"No," he said. "I mean real sandwiches. Bologna and American cheese and bright yellow squeeze mustard."

"And bread that is the same size slice after slice."

"I even miss commercials."

"I miss carpet. I miss furniture that doesn't hurt to sit on."

"I can't believe how beautiful real swimming-pool water is," Caleb said. "Just thinking about it makes me want to . . . I don't know. Cry?"

"I miss swimming too," I said. "I love that feeling when you're out of the water and you're pretty much dried off but your wet suit is keeping you cool."

"I miss how sometimes when it's really hot my friends and I will go to some movie just for the air-conditioning, and when I walk in, I feel my whole body start to wake up. It's just so nice to be cold."

"You want to know why my family is here?" he asked.

I nodded. There was nothing about him I didn't want to know.

"American Girl dolls," he said. "My little sister is totally into them. My dad is too. He built Steph a dollhouse that goes all the way up to the ceiling in her room. My mom complains about the messages the dolls send, but she's always at work.

"Anyway, last spring, the case my mom's been slaving away on the last six years finally settled and she took a week off work to spend time with my little sister. I don't know what happened— there was a lot of shouting—but by the end of the week, my mom had stopped harping about how she wanted Steph to play more sports and she tracked down this camp. So here we are. I still haven't figured out if she's trying to make a point about how the dolls are unrealistic, or if she's trying to make my sister's dreams come true. All I know is I feel like our whole family has been shrunk down and we're trapped inside that big dollhouse in my sister's room."

"What about you? If your dad is busy with your sister and your mom's always at work?"

"Me? I just hang around the city center, lighting things on fire."

"Come on," I said. "In these costumes you can't tell who anyone is. What are you like at home?"

"I don't know," Caleb said. "I hang out with my friends. We go to the movies a lot. My buddy Fred's parents are never around and they have a big TV. I'm on the swim team." He blushed. "And dance choir, though that's not as lame as it sounds."

"Do you wear shiny costumes?"

He nodded.

"Jazz hands?" I said.

He waved them, a sarcastic smile on his face, then went stony. "No."

"My mom said your mom was the first woman to make partner in her law firm," I said.

Caleb smiled ruefully. "The third woman," he said. "But I always wished she was more like your mom. Into cooking and stuff.

I rolled my eyes. "All my mom knows how to cook these days is beans. And she makes me do all the dishes. She was so excited about learning how to use the stove, and cooking and all, but I guess it's harder than she thought."

"Her bread was great," Caleb said.

I said, "No, your chicken was great."

"My dad made the chicken," Caleb said. "And my mom actually got mad at him about how well it turned out. She said it makes her feel that much worse that she isn't this domestic goddess or whatever."

"You can't be in here" were the first words out of Nora's mouth when she came in and saw us. She spoke so fast it was as if she'd been waiting to say them to me for a long time and had just now found her excuse.

But I'd been waiting too. "Why?" I said, standing up to face her. "So you can listen to my iPod and drink beverages that are a little bit outside your time zone?"

"Coke was invented in 1886," she said.

"Well, I doubt you had twenty-ounce plastic bottles of it lying around the frontier," I said. "And you're drinking *Diet* Coke anyway. It is so not . . ." I knew that the word I was searching for was out there. It was a condemning word. It would finish the discussion about Coke, and make Nora feel as stupid and small as she always made me feel. But instead of saying something like "It is so not *authentic,*" the word I came out with was "fair."

"Nora," Caleb stage-whispered from the floor where he was sitting, watching us go back and forth. "I think you'd better give Genevieve a taste of some of that non-1890 beverage while her cell phone charges. Or she's going to let the cat out of the bag."

As if she had just realized Caleb was there, Nora turned, gave him a huge smile, and sat down right next to him. Suddenly, I felt really dumb. I mean, I didn't have to be an expert in human behavior to recognize what the situation was—they'd planned to meet here. What was going on? If Nora and Caleb weren't on some kind of date right now, why had she taken her hair down? She had, and out of the braid it was curly, reddish gold with blond streaks like she was a shampoo model.

"Okay, fine," Nora said. "Have a Diet Coke."

I didn't want a Diet Coke. I don't even like diet soda. But at that point, I knew that if I said no, I'd have to come up with some other reason to stay. And that's how I ended up passing a bottle of Diet Coke around with Caleb and Nora, who it turned out *had* been meeting in the cabin every night for a week to do just that. In other words, I was a gigantic third wheel.

But still, Caleb was talking to me. Maybe he was just being nice? "I like your music, Gen," he said. "We've been listening to your iPod all week."

"I don't care for it much," Nora said. "I prefer Matt's."

"But Ka's . . ." Caleb paused. "That girl listens to some seriously scary stuff."

I didn't say anything.

"I used to think she was goth," Caleb went on.

"She is goth," I said.

"What's goth?" Nora asked.

Caleb looked at me and I looked at him, and he said, "It's kind of hard to explain. But if you look at her playlist, Ka's emo."

Can I just say how great it felt to be saying words like "emo" and "goth" out loud?

"She listens to emo?" I said.

"What's emo?" Nora said.

"Emo's short for overemotional," Caleb explained.

"Like, crazy?" said Nora. "Ka doesn't seem crazy."

"More like sad," I said.

"Ka's sad?" Nora asked.

"No, *she's* not sad," Caleb said. He grinned at me and suddenly, we had another inside joke between us. "She's just emo."

"Emo sort of means sad," I explained. "But it's just kind of a sad style. Like, the way you dress. Black stuff. Leggings."

"But it's really your music that makes you emo, or goth, or whatever," Caleb said. "Ka has Dashboard Confessional, My Chemical Romance, Yellowcard."

"Those are band names," I explained.

"They're classic emo," said Caleb.

"I really wouldn't have thought that's what she was listening to," I said.

Nora put her head in her hands. "I hate this," she said. "I hate that there's all this stuff I don't know."

Caleb and I just stared. I mean, speaking of overemotional . . .

But then Caleb put a hand on Nora's shoulder. "It doesn't really matter," he said. "It's just a time and a place."

"Time and place is everything," Nora said.

"It's not that big a deal," Caleb reassured her.

I took another sip of Diet Coke and decided it was better not to say what I was thinking, which is that time and place meant more than Nora could even know. And also—that Diet Coke is *awesome*. Why had I never appreciated it before?

"You know, I can remember TV," Nora went on. "From before we came here. I remember watching *Sesame Street*. We had the movie of *Aladdin* when I was little. I had Disney Princess pajamas. We lived in a regular house."

"So what happened?" I said.

"They always say they hated it," Nora explained. "My mom and dad, they say we were lost in the modern world. My dad sold insurance. My mom was a secretary in a dentist's office, and she really wanted to be a stay-at-home mom.

"When my parents decided that living out here was what they wanted to do . . . ," she went on. "Well, it was my dad's idea at first. I was five and my mom said she wanted to home-school me, so Dad found this place and decided to try farming. My mom said fine, but there was one thing she couldn't give up, which is Diet Coke. She practically lives on it. This place— here—it started out as her Diet Coke storage unit. My dad gets it at Costco and brings it in by the case. And then my mom needed the Internet connection—it makes it so much easier to get lesson plans. But I know they sneak out here too. They e-mail their family. My dad plays solitaire. Sometimes I just think they come out here to avoid being surrounded by 1890 all the time. They want 1890 for me, but for themselves, some-times they want to take a break. I'm not supposed to be out here. Ever."

"They don't know you use this place?" Caleb asked.

"My mom must know. I mean, her soda's disappearing. But she doesn't say anything because if my dad found out he'd prob-ably tear the place down, and it would be 'good-bye Diet Coke' and 'good-bye Internet' forever."

"Why?" I asked. "I mean, why would anyone care that your parents sometimes take a break from their life? Doesn't everyone?"

"I don't know," Nora said. "My dad doesn't even use a Web site to promote the camp, something people have been telling him to do for years. He has this crazy fear that if too many people found out that he was using a computer, it would be worse than the year he sprayed Roundup on the wheat field. He lost his organic certification for a season and some of the camp families totally got angry about the non-1890 farming practice. They didn't care if we lost all our wheat."

"Roundup?" Caleb said. "What's Roundup?"

"You don't know what Roundup is?" Nora said, the kind of "duh" in her voice that Caleb and I had carefully kept out of ours when explaining what emo was. "You know all that weeding you guys did?"

"Yeah," I said. How could I forget? It was two weeks out of my life. I was still sunburned from the days I spent in the field.

"A few applications of Roundup—it's a weed killer—and you wouldn't have had to pull a single weed."

"Wow," Caleb and I said in unison.

"It's poison, basically," Nora said. "A pesticide." She took a swig of her Diet Coke. "But I don't care. Organic farming—1890 farming—it's stupid. If this were my farm, we'd be drinking Roundup in our milk."

"Wow," I said. "But I always thought you loved it here. You're so good at all that milking and farming stuff."

She looked at me like I was stupid. "Just because I'm good at something doesn't mean I like it," she sneered. "And I'm not telling you this because I want you to finally understand the real me." She stretched her arms up over her head like a cat, then poufed up her hair with her fingers. "I'm just explaining why you can't come here anymore, Genevieve."

I didn't register what she said, it came so out of the blue. I mean, hadn't we just been talking? Almost like—I hated to even think it—friends?

"It's one thing for Caleb," she went on. "But not you. And if you tell anyone you were in here, I'll tell my mom and dad I saw you using a cell phone, and your whole family will be asked to leave."

I was staring at her, absolutely staring. I felt myself sputtering.

This may sound ridiculous, but I felt tears in my eyes. I'd been so . . . comfortable.

I looked over at Caleb. His whole face had gone red. "Come on, Nora," he said.

"Stay out of it," she hissed.

I thought about telling Nora how stupid Camp Frontier was, about how she really *was* missing out on real life. I thought of saying, "All the stuff you know how to do—milking cows or whatever—it doesn't matter in the real world."

Why didn't Caleb saying anything more in my defense?

It took me a few tries to unplug the phone from the power cord and gather up the charger. I shoved it into my pocket, then put a hand on my iPod, where I'd put it down on the desk. At least I'd be able to listen to music now—I could hide the iPod in the Clearasil box in the barn with the phone charger.

"No," Nora said.

"Are you kidding?" I said. "It's mine."

"Camp rules," she said. "If you take that iPod out of this shed, you're going to have to explain to my mother why it's missing. I might get blamed, but more likely, they'll trace it to you."

"That's not fair!" I shouted.

"Don't worry," she said, and I couldn't believe how cold and calm her voice was. I couldn't even look at Caleb now, I was so embarrassed by what was happening. "You'll be out of here in six weeks and it'll be like you were never even here. It's what happens to everyone. You're not going to be any different."

She stood up and held the door open for me. I couldn't believe it. I could get up and leave, or stay and literally fight her for my stuff. It wasn't really the stuff I cared about, though. It was the feeling I'd had, so briefly, of being comfortable and clean and warm and liked. It was finally getting to talk to Caleb. And all of that was going to be gone.

"This is crazy," Caleb tried again, but Nora wasn't listening.

"Forget it," I said, salvaging a last tiny scrap of pride.

On the way home, I stomped through the woods, calling "Bear! Bear!" every few seconds, because as stupid as that made me feel, the woods at night were scary. I thought about Nora's last words to me, about how I would be gone in a month and a half and it would be like I'd never even been here. They were intended to make me feel like I didn't matter. Like I didn't even exist. And they did.

But I couldn't deny that it was also exactly what I'd been telling myself every minute since I'd arrived.

. . .

When I reached our cabin, my dad was still splitting wood even though it was dark. He didn't act surprised to see me. He didn't even seem to have noticed that I'd disappeared without telling anyone where I'd gone. He said, "Hi Gen." I waved. I remember thinking then for the first time that maybe he was losing his mind.

Inside the cabin, my mom was sleeping. Her hair was down and spread out across the pillow, hiding any view I might have had of her face. Gavin was nowhere to be seen.

I lay on my bed—and I know this will sound dumb, but I missed Gavin. Not his drool or his stinky mouth breathing. It was just that without him there, without my mom puttering around with some destined-to-fail frontier cooking project, the house felt empty. It was smaller than our garage, but now it felt like if I called out my own name into the rafters, I might hear an echo coming back at me.

There was only one thing I could do to make myself feel better, and with my mom asleep, I could do it in bed. I pulled out my phone, opened up a new message, and started to type.

```
Week 3 - Wednesday
10:12 pm
So...Nora? The poster child for Camp
Frontier? You won't believe what I found
her doing tonight...
```

It was a lot of typing, but I told them everything. And then, after I thought I was done, I sent one last missive.

```
Week 3 - Wednesday
10:30 pm
Is Ka right? Are Ron and Betsy a front
for some elaborate crime ring?
```

I couldn't resist another.

```
Week 3 - Wednesday
10:35 pm
That would be AWESOME.
```

« 15 »

Week 3 - Thursday

4:50 pm

I woke up this morning to the most
amazing smell. It was bacon--or salt pork,
which is a lot like bacon. There was a
coffee smell too, the stuff my dad calls
sludge and drinks up here with no sugar
because we don't have any. But there was
something else mixing all those smells
together that made my stomach start
gurgling immediately. And this is what it
was: fresh-caught fish.

Here's what happens to fish when you cook it over an open,
outdoor fire with some salt pork in the pan. It gets lacy on the
edges. Brown and crispy. It flakes apart and the grease from
the salt pork slips in between the flakes and the whole thing

melts on your tongue. You can even kind of taste the river inside the flesh of the fish because it is so clean and fresh.

I had still been sleeping when my mom and dad were awakened by Gavin and Erik Puchinski, who were shouting to them from the clearing in front of the porch. It was about five in the morning, and my mom said they were dancing around with twelve small silver fish hanging from a string that they were carrying between them.

By the time I saw the catch, it was filleted and frying in a pan. "You two caught these?" I said to Gavin and Erik, with my mouth full, unbelieving, kneeling on my skirts at the edge of the fire and licking fish juice and salt pork off my fingers. The Puchinskis were sitting around the fire too—Erik had run over to get them. Since there weren't enough plates or forks, I was sharing with my mom and dad and we were all eating with our fingers. Erik's mom, Disa—who must have been pulled out of bed like the rest of us—somehow managed to be perfectly dressed in clean, ironed clothing, her hair neatly pulled back and her daughters' hair braided as if they were ready for church.

"We made hooks out of nails," Gavin said.

"Whittling them from sticks didn't work," Erik added. "So I pulled the nails out of a feed box in the barn."

"We bent them by banging them with rocks."

"Gavin dug up the worms."

"We tied the nails to some string and weighted them with rocks."

Erik's little sisters were looking at him like he was some kind of superhero—and I have to say, I was also impressed.

"Corn cake?" Disa offered, and I happily took a second from her basket.

"What's in these?" said my mom.

"Just cornmeal, salt, and water," Disa said. "We've been eating them since we got here and are sick to death of them."

"But they look so much like real food," my mom said.

Disa laughed. "You could make these easily. Just keep a low oven. Put some in after you've cooked breakfast when the stove's cooling down, and they'll be ready by lunchtime. They're good, actually, with cheese."

"Just spending time with you makes me feel like I'm better at this than I am," my mom said. "It's like the way I always feel thinner around my thin friends."

Disa laughed. She laughed at everything my mom said—which made my mom want to keep talking, though I think Disa was laughing because she didn't always know how to respond. "I've been so amazed this summer," she said now, "that none of the other families have tried living like this before. I thought everyone would be more like us."

And then my mom was getting a lesson on how to make cheese, and I got up to play a game Erik and Gavin had invented with rocks.

Here's how the game went. Erik found a rock and scratched an X on a tree. Everyone who wanted to play gathered as many rocks as they could find and then we all took turns trying to hit the X with the rocks. Fun, right?

Actually, it was. I was really good at it, and so were Gavin and Erik, but Anja, who was only eight, needed a lot of do-overs. No one cared except Bryn, who stamped her feet and whined "It's not fair" while Erik rolled his eyes and made a big deal of being nice to Anja. You got the feeling Anja, Bryn, and Erik were getting a little sick of each other. But with fish in our bellies we all felt so good it was like a party. A six o'clock in the morning party. Pretty soon Anders looked up at the sky and said, "It's getting time to get to work."

"How's that mill going?" my dad asked as Disa packed up.

"Not too bad," Anders said. "But we need some mules or something to pull the grindstone. I'm thinking of harnessing the kids."

We all stared at him for a minute.

"You're kidding, right?" my mom was finally brave enough to ask.

Anders gave a huge belly laugh. His red hair seemed to stand up on end, he was shaking so hard. For the first time I thought maybe he had something resembling a sense of humor. Maybe, I caught myself thinking, he's actually kind of funny. Or maybe it was just that I was fish-drunk. There was a lot of sighing and licking of fingers, and then Jezebel was lowing at me from the barn, wanting to get milked, and it was time for Gavin to check on Daisy's eggs before he went inside and took a nap.

Pretty soon, though, he joined me in the cornfield, and my dad was back chopping down all the trees in the woods.

```
Week 3 - Friday
9:24 pm
The secret to Gavin's fish-catching zeal?
We were sitting on the garden fence
tonight and he told me. "Every single meal
that goes by with no protein, I'm expecting
Mom to serve up Pumpkin on a plate."
```

Week 3 - Friday

9:30 pm

For a second, the idea of Pumpkin on a plate made me hungry. And then I laughed really hard.

« 16 »

```
Week 4 - Sunday
9:15 pm
"You have a lot of emo on your iPod," I
said to Ka at the picnic on Sunday. It
was the Fourth of July and Betsy had
made each kid a cookie in the shape of
the flag, decorated with red, white, and
blue icing--she'd dyed it with berry juice.
We were digesting the cookies and also
our progress assessment scores--the
Drivers and Meyer-Hincheys got eights,
the Puchinskis got a ten, but we didn't
break six because we still hadn't eaten
Pumpkin.
```

Ka looked at me like she didn't know which end of my statement
she should take a bite of. And then her brain figured out the

most important part. "How did you get my iPod?" she said. "Do you have it? Can I see it?"

"Nora has it," I said, nodding in her direction. She was bringing a bucket of cold water out from the kitchen for people to take drinks from if they were thirsty.

"Nora?" Ka breathed. "I didn't think she even knew what an iPod is."

"Oh, she knows," I said.

And then I told her. About stumbling upon the electricity shack. About seeing Nora sitting at the computer inside. About going back when my cell-phone battery died.

"Wait," Ka said. "You have a cell phone? Here?"

"I haven't told anyone about it," I said. "I didn't even think I was going to use it." I explained how my mom gave it to me the night before we left, how I'd snuck it in, if only to be able to look at it. "I just text my friends," I said. "It makes it easier. To be able to tell someone else what's going on."

"Wow," Ka said. "So what happened when you went back?"

I told her about Caleb's being there and Nora's kicking me out and how Caleb only sort of stuck up for me. About the Diet Coke. "Oh!" I said. "And I finally know what Ron and Betsy were doing before they came here." I passed on everything Nora had told me about their past—their real past—and how I almost felt sorry for Nora, being stuck out here for the last ten years.

While Ka and I were talking, we were sitting on a log at the edge of the woods. The Doll Club girls were setting up some kind of a doll hospital or school—or maybe it was a school for very sick kids who sometimes had to be put in bed for a long time. Gavin, Bryn, and Erik were teaching Katie how to play the rock-throwing game. Ka had just finished telling me about how Katie and Matt got to go berry picking after dinner the night before while she'd had to say behind and finish the dishes. She and Katie alternated meals but Ka thought it always seemed like the nights when it was her turn to do the dishes, something conveniently fun came up for everyone else.

"And by the way," Ka said. "The Dashboard Confessional? The Yellowcard? That's Katie's music. She forgot her iPod for the plane ride and my mom made this big deal in the airport of making me download some albums for her to listen to. It was her way of trying to get Katie to like her."

"Oh, man," I said.

"I actually like a few of the Yellowcard songs," she said. "But not their new stuff."

"Yeah," I said, though I had no idea what she was talking about. Suddenly I wondered if I was even remotely cool enough to be Ka's friend outside Camp Frontier.

"So what do you think?" I said. "About the shack?"

"What do I think?" asked Ka. "I think let's go."

"Let's go?" I said. "But if I show my face there again, Nora will tell her parents about my phone."

Ka stared at me in disbelief. She waited a few seconds, as if what she had to say was so obvious, she was trying to give my brain a second to get there on its own and save her the effort of explaining. "Nora's not going to rat you out," she said. "She's bluffing. She can't."

"She sounded pretty convincing the other night."

"But if she tells on you, what's to keep you from telling on her?"

I was starting to see Ka's point.

"You're both holding knives to each other's throats," she added.

"Isn't that a little overdramatic?"

"Oh, my God, I can't wait to check my e-mail!" Ka squealed.

After the picnic, my parents, Gavin, and I were making our way home when I heard footsteps behind us. It was Caleb, running. I assumed he had somewhere he needed to get to fast, so I stepped off the trail to let him pass. I was still so embarrassed about what had happened in the electricity shack, I didn't want to talk to him. Sort of.

But then he came to a stop where I was standing. "Hey," he said, brushing his hair off his forehead. I could see the necklace he wore poking up over the buttoned collar of his shirt. "I didn't realize you were leaving."

"Yeah," I said.

"I was asleep," he said.

I said "Yeah" again. I didn't say how I'd seen him drift off while his sister, Stephanie, was putting tiny braid after tiny braid into his hair or how, after he'd fallen asleep, Stephanie slept too, using his arm as a pillow.

"Why do you have to go so early?" he asked. He still had corn-rows mixed into his hair.

"Jezebel gets really ornery if she isn't milked right at four thirty," I explained. I was being funny—I hope he got that—but I was also speaking the truth. If you don't milk a cow at the same time every day they start to make these funny noises, roll their eyes, paw the barn floor, and generally look angry.

"Good point," Caleb said. "I mean, think how you'd feel, if no one was letting you pee?"

"It's not *pee*." I laughed. "We're not drinking her *pee*." The second Caleb's eyes lit up into a smile, I felt my knees melt.

He said, "Look, about the other night. Nora's not that bad. I know she's a little rough around the edges, but she's a good kid."

"Yeah," I said, wondering why he was defending her to me. *Was* she his girlfriend? I didn't have the courage to ask.

"The swimming hole my dad and I have been working on is almost done," he said. "Maybe you can come out and swim in it with us sometime?"

"Okay," I said although I didn't know who "us" was. Him and Nora? Him and his dad—the guy chewing on straw and nodding with a Southern accent? I certainly didn't want to go swimming with Caleb's dad, but the idea of hanging out with Nora was worse. Maybe I'd get lucky, and Caleb and I would swim with the Loch Ness monster.

I must have been smiling at my own Loch Ness monster joke, because suddenly Caleb was smiling back at me, looking puzzled but happy. I didn't know what else to do but keep smiling, and we stood that way until Gavin yelled, "Gen, come on," and Caleb said, "Swimming, right?" and I turned around and kind of skipped down the path to where my family was waiting.

```
Week 4 - Sunday
3:45 pm
Skipped? I know. It's totally embarrassing,
and yet it is also true.
```

When my mom had finished her oatmeal the next morning, she stood up and dumped her bowl into the basin we used to wash dishes. She poured hot water from the kettle over it and, with our one knife, scraped flakes off a bar of soap. I felt my throat closing up. After seeing the food I was eating—the oatmeal—floating around in that gray hot water slop, I couldn't eat another bite.

My dad finished his, took a last swig of coffee, and stood. "I'll be getting out to the clearing," he said.

"What clearing?" my mom said

"I'm calling the woods the clearing now," he explained. "Because I've cut down nearly a hundred trees at this point. So as I see it, I have just as much right to call it a clearing as to call it the woods."

My mom laughed. "All right," she said. "Gen, can you work on the butter while I get the washing started?"

"Want me to pick some corn?" Gavin said. "There's real cobs now."

"They're not big enough," said my dad. "You can come with me and help carry wood."

Gavin groaned. He hated this job and had splinters up and down his arms.

But at least he didn't have to make butter. Next to laundry, making butter was the worst job the frontier had to offer.

Here's what you need to do to make butter. After you get a bucket of milk, you let it sit on the counter for a day. Before long, some stuff starts to collect on the top—a skin—and then if you leave it, it gets thicker. That's how you get cream. I know, totally foul, but you spoon that into this big wooden bucket with a paddle in it called a butter churn. Then you sit there using the paddle to mix up the cream stuff until your arm feels like it's about to fall off. You lift the lid on the churn, check to see if you've got butter, and see that no, it's not even close. So then you get really depressed. Being depressed is an enormously important part of the process; you can almost tell how thick the butter is just by how defeated and miserable you feel personally. But you keep stirring it some more anyway. It takes about five hundred million years before the stuff in the churn turns to butter, and by the time it has your arms are trembling, you have blisters on your hands, you hate your mom, and you promise that, to make it last longer, you will hardly eat any of this butter yourself. But it's so good, that's kind of a hard promise to keep, especially when everyone else is slathering it on everything like it's free.

My mom once went through this phase of making us all eat I Can't Believe It's Not Butter! I texted Kristin and Ashley:

```
Week 4 - Monday
11:56 am
I Can't Believe (I know how to make)
Butter!
```

I hoped they got the joke. In case they didn't, I sent a second post:

```
Week 4 - Monday
11:57 am
Making butter is the stupidest waste of
time in the world, considering you can go
buy butter in any grocery store in the
world any day you want. But stupid or
not, I know how to do it and in fact I'm
getting kind of good.
```

Tuesday night after dinner and chores, I found Ka waiting for me as we'd planned on the path that led from our house into the woods. I could hear my dad hacking away at the trees not too far from us—I'd watched him and knew that he was repeating the same cycle of motions over and over: pull back, swing, chop, dislodge the ax. Pull back, swing, chop, dislodge the ax. He was going fast too, chopping at a sprint. My mom rubbed grease on his hands every night now and he was wrapping them in rags while he worked, but still, they were blistered and sometimes even bleeding by the end of the day.

Ka whispered so my dad wouldn't hear. "I just went by Ron

and Betsy's and didn't see Nora anywhere around. I think she's going to be there."

"Okay," I said. "Are you scared?"

"A little," said Ka.

"Me too," I said. "Nora's so mean."

"There's nothing she can do to us," Ka reminded me. "She can't tell her parents about what you're doing without their finding out that she had a part in it too."

I didn't point out that if my parents found out I'd brought the phone out here, Nora's getting in trouble would do nothing to change what would happen to me.

When we reached the clearing, Ka and I snuck around the back of the electricity shack and looked in the window before trying the door. Nora was there, and so was Caleb. Ka raised her eyebrows, took a deep breath, and knocked. Ka, I was learning, is very brave.

"Hey, Nora," she said. She sounded as calm and unruffled as if she were talking to friends in the computer lab at school. "Mind if I check my e-mail? Hey, Caleb."

Although maybe "unruffled" is not the best word. Because Ka was still twelve, all her dresses looked like the ones the little girls wore, with ruffles up and down the front. Ka was totally ruffled.

Nora, who had been openly staring at Ka, not knowing what to make of her surprise visit, now focused her narrowed eyes on me. "You told her?" she said. "Didn't you hear what I said the other night?"

"Um," I said. I wished I had a snappy comeback, something a girl detective from a TV show might say. Instead, I came up with "I heard you say that you would get in trouble if anyone found out camp families are in here. So I'm pretty sure you're not going to breathe a word."

"Are you threatening me?"

I didn't answer her because just then Nora and I were both looking over at Caleb, who had started to laugh. "This isn't funny," Nora said to him. "I could get in a lot of trouble here. We all could."

"So don't say anything," Caleb said. "No one needs to know." I heard the slightest trace of his dad's Southern accent in his voice.

"They're gonna know," Nora sulked, but she had stopped looking at me and leaned back against the wall. "Five minutes," she said. "Check your e-mail and get out of here."

Ka sat down at the computer and started to type. "Oh, my gosh," she said after a few minutes had passed. "I have five hundred and sixty-two e-mails!"

Just then there was a knock on the door, and Ka's stepsister Katie poked her head in. "Ka?" she said. She saw Nora and Caleb. Then her eyes moved to the Diet Coke in Nora's hand and she was like, "Oh . . . ," her voice filled with undisguised longing. Caleb immediately started to laugh again. Matt peeked his head in behind Katie's.

"You told them?" I said to Ka.

"They must have followed me," she said.

"We did," Katie answered. "You keep sneaking off and we wanted to know where."

Ka threw up her hands. "You're spying on me now?" she said. "I don't believe this. You guys need to get lives."

"We have lives," Katie snapped. "We were trying to keep you from getting in trouble with your mom."

"Yeah, right," Ka scoffed.

"It's true," Matt said. "We're sick of your sad, angry rebel act. Get over it."

"You get over it," Ka said. "I'll take care of myself."

"So what is this place anyhow?" Matt asked, taking in the computer, the iPods, Nora's Diet Coke.

Nora looked at Caleb and I almost felt sorry for her, there was such clear panic in her wide eyes. "I'm going to get in so much trouble," she said.

That's when Erik Puchinski filed in behind Matt.

Nora wailed, "Did you have to invite everyone?" She didn't even seem angry now—she looked like she was going to cry. Before I could protest that I hadn't invited anyone but Ka, Nora stood up. "Everybody out!" she said. "Show's over. Yes, there's a computer here. Big deal. But this building is off-limits. Employees only."

No one was listening.

"Whose iPod is that?" Erik said.

"Where can I get a DC?" Katie asked, tucking her blond hair behind her ears and standing on tiptoes to see over Matt's head.

"Out!" Nora said. But Matt had already opened the mini-fridge.

"This is totally stocked!" he said.

"Caleb, help!" Nora said.

Caleb just smiled and shrugged. "Cat's out of the bag," he drawled.

And then Caleb gave Nora a big smile, turned to a cabinet behind him, pulled out a box with everyone's iPods in it, and said, "Okay, people, help yourselves." He put an arm around

Nora's shoulder. "Don't worry," he said. "Your folks are never going to find out."

I could see that she was too glad to have his arm around her to say anything. Not that it would have done any good.

Within minutes, it was clear no one was going anywhere. Diet Coke was flowing. Music was playing out of the computer's speakers. Katie was sitting on the desk next to the computer, swinging her legs so you could see past her boot lacings to her tights; Caleb was in the chair, playing videos of his favorite comedians on YouTube; Nora was draped across the back of his chair, watching them; and Ka, Matt, and I were on the floor, where Matt was dialing through Ka's iPod.

"Dude," he said to Ka. "You must have been so mad when your mom made you put all Katie's lame music on here."

"Your screamer garbage isn't any better," Ka said. "I hope I don't have to put up with it next year."

"Next year?" he said. "I thought you said you were going to find a way to get out of moving to our house."

"I am," Ka said. "Don't worry about it."

"So," Matt tried again. "You don't like screamer?"

"I like screamer," Ka said, and then, "Except when I don't. Which is, like, oh, yeah—always."

He laughed. "You're funny, Ka."

And I had a thought that I knew Ka would kill me if I ever voiced—she and Matt were starting to sound like actual siblings.

Katie took a swig of her soda. "Sorry your mom made you take stall cleaning for the rest of the week," she said to Ka. "I didn't tell her it was you who took the cheese."

"I don't care what you do," Ka said, but I wondered. Didn't she?

I felt too good to wonder for long about Ka, or about anything. Even Nora looked like she was having a good time.

```
Week 4 - Wednesday
8:47 am
I'm exhausted. I drank so much soda last
night that I lay in bed staring up at the
rafters. It must have been until at least
three o'clock.
```

I didn't go back to the electricity shack until a week later, when I needed to charge the phone. Ka had said she would meet me there after she finished her chores. I was nervous, but also excited, hoping I'd find Caleb again. Only this time, alone.

Unfortunately, when I got to the shack, it was just Nora and me.

I said "Hey" to her like I was going to be civil but not try to act like I was friends with her or anything. I was surprised she even let me in, so before she could tell me to go, I plugged in the phone so it could charge.

Nora looked up from the computer. "That's your own cell phone, right? You don't use your parents'?"

"Yes," I said. "This is a phone, but also a camera, and you can play music but I don't have any downloaded yet. You can go online on it."

"I already know that," she said. She was supersnippy about it too.

"Okay," I said. I thought the conversation would end there, but she kept going.

"I've been watching all the gadgets my mom collects from the people who come here changing over the years. They all have keyboards on them now."

"I guess that's right," I said. I showed her how you could type on mine.

"I always check what people put in those bags my mom collects," she went on. "When I don't know what they are, I look them up online. So if you're thinking I'm some bumpkin who doesn't know anything about the world you live in, you're wrong."

"Okay," I said, hoping that silence would do all the work of pointing out that I hadn't said she was a bumpkin. (I would never use the word "bumpkin." There is something so, well, bumpkin-y about it.)

Ka rushed in a few minutes later, and before long Caleb, Erik, Matt, Katie, and even Gavin—I guess news that Ka and I were braving the shack again had spread. "What is he doing here?" Nora complained when Gavin showed his face. "I told you guys, no one else can know."

"Sorry," Erik said, ducking his head. "We were supposed to go fishing, so I had to tell him where I was going instead."

"Okay, fine," Nora grumbled. "Have a Diet Coke."

Caleb came and sat next to me on the floor in front of the minifridge.

"I liked what your mom said at that meeting a while back, about women voting and stuff," he said.

"Really?" I asked. "She's not much of a women's libber at home or anything."

"I've been raised on it," he said. "But I think this place will bring that out of you."

"Yeah," I said. "It's not really fair that Gavin and I both do all the outdoor work, but whenever it's time for an inside chore, it's always, 'Gen, can you wash the dishes,' 'Gen, can you whip up some butter?'"

"You know how to make butter?" he said.

"It's no big deal."

"I wish you would teach my mom."

I laughed. "I mean, I love her and everything," Caleb went on. "But she is about to organize a feminist uprising, she's so sick of the kitchen, and still she won't admit she's no good at it. And the sad part is, she'd be good at organizing a feminist uprising. At her job, she's always holding everyone's feet to the fire making sure the women lawyers aren't getting shafted."

"She really can't cook at all?" I said.

Caleb shook his head. "The only thing she made that's been any good are pancakes. Once. But she didn't know how much batter to make, so we each only got one."

I laughed some more and then suddenly I was feeling nervous. I couldn't think of anything else to say. Ashley always knows what to do around boys, but I get tongue-tied.

If I didn't come up with a thought, a question—anything— he was going to talk to someone else. I looked at the walls, the windows, the carpet for inspiration. There was nothing.

Until I saw the computer. And I don't know what I was thinking except that I had to say something to Caleb to make him understand that I did indeed want to talk to him. So I blurted out, "Hey, want to see the blog my friend Kristin is making about my time here at Camp Frontier?"

"Blogs are cool," he said. "Especially funny ones. Is yours funny?"

"I don't know," I said, thinking back to all the texts. What had I written? Then I remembered one in particular and laughed.

"What?" he said.

I couldn't think of any way to make what I was laughing about sound less embarrassing, so I just said it. "One of my first posts was about peeing on my stockings."

He laughed too. "Seriously? Come on," he said. "I've got to check this out."

I typed in the URL Kristin had given me, and was shocked to see a real live Web page load, with a polka-dot background and all the dates. The idea that Kristin had created a blog, that my words were out there somewhere—it had never felt real. But then, there was my face, grinning from the top left corner of the page.

"Is that you?" Caleb said.

It was a picture I hadn't seen before. But yeah, it was me. I could tell from what I was wearing that it must have been taken at our last soccer game of the year—the game that had clinched our undefeated season. I had my hair pulled back in a ponytail and this huge smile splayed across my face. I was wearing a bandanna and my arms were around the shoulders of people I couldn't see because Kristin had cropped them out. I looked so . . . clean. And . . . modern. And . . . normal. "Yes, that's me," I said.

"You look so buff," he said. "Are you some kind of jock?"

"I play sports," I started.

"Soccer, right? Aren't you missing camp by being here?"

"Yeah," I affirmed. "Soccer."

"You should talk to Matt," he said. "He's huge into soccer." I blushed. I didn't want to talk to Matt. I wanted to keep talking to Caleb.

"May I?" Caleb said. He took the mouse in his hand and started scrolling down through the entries. He chuckled a little as he read, but then he stopped reading and just started to scroll.

"Gen," he said. "Did you know you're getting a lot of comments?"

"Really?" I said, leaning over to see.

"Yeah. Like, here, you have sixty-three comments. That's pretty huge for a single post."

"Really?" I said again. "Kristin said people in her computer class were forwarding it to their friends. She keeps going on and on about the comments. I think the commenting was part of the assignment."

"How many people were in the class, though?" Caleb asked. "Look, you've got eighty-four comments here. That's no assignment."

"Wow," I said.

"You should get your friend to look up the counter and see how many hits this is getting a day. I think a lot of people are reading it."

"Really? Can I see what they say?"

Caleb clicked on "view comments" but then, just as I was about to start reading the first one, the computer monitor died, the lights went off, and the noise in the room came to an abrupt end. All I could hear was Nora's hoarse stage whisper: "My dad, my dad, he's coming!"

« 18 »

Everybody absolutely panicked. It was hard to see anything in the suddenly dark room, but I could just make out Gavin running into a corner and Katie trying to climb behind the fridge. Matt crouched beneath the window like a cat ready to spring. I froze in the chair until Caleb took both my hands and pulled me down under the desk with him. In the moonlight coming through the windows I could see his grin. Nora quietly locked the door and leaned against it moments before Ron jiggled the handle, trying to get it to turn.

For a second, I don't think any of us even breathed.

The handle rattled again and Ron shook the whole door as if he could break through the latch.

Then we heard his voice. "Who's in here!" He tried the door again. "Betsy?"

The next time he tried the door it felt as if he was going to be able to break it down for sure. There was a collective rustling of bodies as we tried to make ourselves smaller, bracing for the moment when the door would swing open with a bang, the lights would snap on, and Ron would find us squeezed into corners and under tables and behind minifridges that were much too small. Large segments of our bodies were showing—whole arms, tops of heads, a shoe, a skirt. The idea that we could hide in such a small space was a joke. We might as well have stayed right where we were and just covered our own eyes.

"Betsy!" Ron said. We heard him mutter to himself, "I swear the light was on."

It was all I could do not to let out a squeak.

Katie did, actually, squeal, but Matt clamped a hand over her mouth and I don't think anyone who wasn't in the room could have heard.

In the dark, Caleb squeezed my hand, which he was still holding. I squeezed his right back, and even knowing we were about to get busted, I felt a jolt of excitement. This was the second time he'd held my hand, the second time he'd picked me to hide with. Did hand-holding mean something different to him than it did to the rest of the world? He wouldn't hold my hand if he didn't actually like me, would he?

Ron tried the door one more time, and then said, "Hmmph." We heard the crunching of leaves and sticks as he started to walk away.

Just then there was a crash about two inches from my head. Matt had lost his balance and accidentally knocked the keyboard off the desk. Nora leaped across the room, and grabbed the keyboard where it had fallen, as if by putting her hands on it she could somehow reverse time and prevent it from falling in the first place. The receding crunch of footsteps outside stopped, then started up again, this time heading quickly back our way.

Nora was frantically pointing at the window, and I thought she was trying to tell us to crawl out of it, but a) that would have been noisy, and b) I didn't think we could fit. I understood better what she meant when I saw Ron's face pressed up against the glass.

Nora had ducked down right beneath the window. I could see Matt flattened against the wall. For a full minute, we waited. I held myself perfectly still under the table with Caleb. If Ron had had a flashlight and pointed it into the room, we would have been dead meat.

But he didn't. And in another moment his face was gone from the window and we could hear his footsteps retreating once again.

"I think we're safe," Matt whispered after a minute had passed.

"Safe?" Nora repeated. "He's going to be back here with a key in five minutes!" She was talking in a very low voice, but urgently. You could tell that if she hadn't been worried about Ron's overhearing us, she would have been shouting.

"So let's get out of here," Matt said.

"What about the mess?" I said.

"She's right," Nora said, as if she were seeing for the first time the half-drunk bottles of Diet Coke, the iPods tangled up in earbud cords, the random assortment of lip glosses and the sticks of deodorant missing their caps. "But we don't have time."

"Just hurry, everyone," Matt said.

We all set to work, putting the furniture back where it had been, stashing the electronics in burlap sacks, putting caps on bottles and creams and tossing them into the bags they had come from.

"What about the Diet Coke?" Ka said, holding up a half-drunk bottle. "We can't put it back in the fridge half empty, can we?"

"Um . . . ," Nora said.

"We could pour it out outside—," Matt suggested.

"No," Nora said. "He'll smell it."

"He tracks the smell of Diet Coke?" Caleb asked. I think he was the only one who thought any of this was remotely funny.

"We have to drink it," Nora concluded. She lifted a bottle to her mouth and started to chug, but there is only so much Diet Coke you can pour down your throat without the risk of throwing it all up again. So soon the bottles were being passed around between all of us. We stood in a tight circle, as deliberate and serious as jewel thieves, forcing ourselves to finish what by then burned our throats as if we were drinking gasoline.

When the last drop was consumed, Katie let out an enormous belch and we filed out of the shack one by one, fast-walking through the clearing, each finding a different spot to hide in the woods. It reminded me of the night we'd played kick the can and I'd felt like I was in some kind of a slasher movie, running through the woods, being chased, being afraid. No one said "good-bye" or "phew" or "I guess that wasn't so bad after all." And it wasn't until Gavin and I were halfway home, whispering "Bear. Bear. Here bear. Hey bear," that I felt inside my dress pocket and realized that my phone was still back at the shack, plugged into its charger, which was plugged into the power strip, which was plugged into the wall. I'd left the phone on the floor, under the table, lights flashing, sunset morphing into sailboat picture over and over as it filled up with electric juice.

I turned around and ran back just in time to see Ron closing the door behind him and turning the lights on. The phone was on the floor. There was a decent chance Ron wouldn't see it. I waited, thinking he might be quick, but it was cold and damp outside, and after about twenty minutes I went home, muttering, "Shoot, shoot, shoot, shoot, shoot."

As soon as I finished milking Jezebel the next morning, I raced to the shack again. Checking first in the window to make sure no one was inside, I threw open the door, saw that the phone was missing, looked everywhere for it, came up empty, and ran back home in time for breakfast, muttering, "Double shoot, double shoot, double shoot."

This was not good.

<< 19 >>

When Ron came by the next morning to talk to my dad about techniques for harvesting the corn—the cobs were lengthening now and it was almost ready—I was sure he would take me aside and tell me he'd found the phone. I wondered what it would mean if he did. Would he tell my parents? Duh. Would my parents take the phone away for good? Again, a foregone conclusion. What wasn't clear to me was whether or not my family would get kicked out of the camp. Two weeks ago I would have been like, "Okay, bring it on." Now I wasn't so sure I wanted to go home.

Was it just not wanting to face the humiliation of being asked to leave?

Was it the feeling of holding hands with Caleb under the table?

I mean, I didn't like it here.

Or *did* I?

I laughed out loud at the very idea and wished I could text that question to Kristin and Ashley, so they could text something back like "Oh, puh-leez."

"Something funny, Gen?" my dad asked. Ron was talking, and I guess laughing had made me seem crazy, or rude, or both.

"Just life as we know it," I said with a shrug.

Even after he was done talking about the corn, Ron didn't say anything about the phone, or act any different than normal—which is to say he was weird, but not extra weird. I concluded that he hadn't found my phone.

Now I had no idea what was going on. Though I was sure the phone wasn't there I had no better idea than to go back to the shack and look for it again. But it was hard to find an opportunity. My dad had us hauling wood all morning, and in the afternoon, my mom tried ironing again and needed me around for that. Before dinner, she made me sit on the porch shelling peas, which took *forever*. And then at night, she insisted we do a singalong while my dad chopped wood. He joined us only to fall asleep on the porch. I was so tired, I fell asleep fast too, just like my dad.

Friday morning I finally found a window of time when I could sneak away. But when I got there, the electricity shack was locked. I looked in the window and the room looked as it always had—the desk against the wall, the computer on top of it, the minifridge closed up tight. By standing on my tiptoes I could just see down to the power strip on the floor and, just as I'd seen before, there was nothing plugged into it but the computer.

If my phone really wasn't here, and Ron didn't have it, who did?

After lunch, I told my mom I needed to go find Nora. "There's something funny about Jezebel's milk supply," I told her. "I think she'll be able to explain it to me."

"It's nice to see the two of you becoming friends," she said.

Since I couldn't text my mom's comment to Kristin and Ashley, I had to settle for turning my back on my mom and pantomiming gagging myself.

I found Nora in her barn, scraping a bowl of food scraps to their pig. Who was named Pig. There was a cloud of fruit flies swarming the trough.

"Gross," I said.

Nora lifted her head. "Oh, it's you." She gave the dish of scraps a firm bang with the base of her hand, shook it to get out the liquid, and then actually started to walk by me as if she hadn't understood I'd come here to talk.

This wasn't going to be easy.

"Wait," I said, and she stopped. I jogged a step closer to her and looked up into the loft. "Is anyone else here?"

"Come outside." She walked without checking to make sure I was behind her. She always did that, and as always I had no choice but to follow her swinging blond braid that was framed in the upside-down U made by the sides of my sunbonnet. I don't know how a braid could look smug, but it did. Nora stopped at the edge of the woods. "Never say anything important in a barn," she said, as if this was something I should have already known. "Stand out in the open where you can see if anyone's listening."

"Okay," I said, grinding my teeth to keep from saying something rude.

"What do you want?" she said.

"I want my phone back," I said.

"Your phone?" she said. She truly looked like she had no idea what I was talking about, but still, I didn't believe her.

"I left it in the shack the other night. When we were cleaning up. I forgot to grab it. And when I went back in the morning, it was already gone."

"You just left it there?" she said. "*That* was dumb."

"I know you took it," I said.

"I didn't," she said, and for a second, I believed her. During this interval, the sense of panic was instant.

"Then where is it?" I spat out.

"I don't know," she said, and her voice was so cutting, so "this is not my problem," that I felt anger brewing up inside me—she *was* lying. She sighed and closed her eyes and looked at me only out of the bottoms of them, like the conversation was making her exhausted. How could anyone learn to be this mean without having gone to middle school?

"I left it in *your* electricity shack," I said. I spoke slowly, like she was deaf. Or stupid. "If your dad had found it, he would have said something. I bet you went in first thing in the morning before I got there and found it."

"I didn't," she said. "I went back, that's true, but your phone wasn't there."

It's amazing how hard it is to tell someone you think they are lying. Even when you know they are. "Are you sure?" I said.

"Maybe someone else took it," Nora suggested, but she still looked so intentionally bored, I was convinced it was her.

"Like who?" I said. "Who would take a phone?"

"How about anyone?" she said. "You all hate it here. You all can't wait to get back to your friends and your perfect little lives. Maybe it was Ka. She hates it here even more than you. She's probably dying to get in touch with all her friends. The emo people or whatever."

"She's not emo," I said. "She's goth."

"She hates this place like you do."

"I don't hate it," I said, surprising myself again.

"You act like it."

"Besides, Ka's my friend. She wouldn't do something like this to me."

"And I'm not?"

"Not what?" I said.

"Not your friend?" Nora said.

Was she serious?

Of course she wasn't my friend.

She looked serious.

And then she cracked up. "Oh, boo hoo, my summer's ruined," she said, laughing. "Gen's not my friend."

"You know," I said, "I could have been your friend. If you weren't such a jerk to everyone, maybe people would like you more."

"Gen, I don't want to be your friend," she said, and I felt my face burning bright red.

"Let me know if the phone turns up," I said. Walking down the path, out of her hearing, I elaborated. "Let me know if it turns up, like, under your pillow."

I was so sure she had it I almost wanted to get Kristin or Ashley or someone to call her, and when she picked up, say, "Nora, I know it's you." Except I couldn't get Kristin and Ashley to do anything anymore. If I didn't find my phone, the next time I talked to them would be the day we went home. I hoped by then I would know what had happened to my phone.

As it turned out: I didn't have to wait that long to find out.

As it also turned out: Nora wasn't lying. She didn't have it.

Ron did.

At the next Sunday meeting, once all the families were sitting on our benches—Ka joining my family as usual—our picnic baskets waiting in the shade next to Ron and Betsy's porch, Ron reached into his pocket and pulled out my phone. He held it away from his chest, his arm perfectly straight, as if it were a dangerous lizard that might bite if it could reach its head around to get to Ron's neck.

Without thinking, I yelled out, "That's mine!"

Did I think he'd return it to me? That everyone would pretend they hadn't seen it? That if I grabbed it from Ron fast enough my parents wouldn't know what it was? That maybe they'd think Ron was passing out cell-phone-shaped rocks and sticks?

Yes, I did think that. And I also thought, "The phone is off. For all anyone knows, it's been off all summer. If I can keep Ron from turning it on, my mom and dad won't care that it's here."

The word "stupid" barely covers this, I know. But still. The phone was more than just a piece of plastic with a microchip inside. It was a part of me. It was my connection to my friends. It *was* my friend. It was the only thing I could vent to.

"I know it's yours, Gen," Ron said. His voice was quiet, almost gentle. Or was I imagining that? I started to stand. My mom and dad had turned to look at me with expressions of such open horror I had no choice but to ignore them. I knew what I needed to do. I needed to walk up in front of everyone and get the phone back. Then this would all go away.

But the second I was standing, Ron's voice lost any trace of gentleness it might have contained. "Sit down," he said. He wasn't shouting, but his tone was so stern, he might as well have been giving a command to a dog. I sat.

"Gen?" my mom said. Though her voice was a whisper, I heard all the fear and anger in the way she said my name. I think that was the moment when I understood I wasn't going to get my phone back. "Is that the phone I was going to give you?" She paused. "The phone I was going to give you *when we got back*?"

This was also the moment when I understood that Ron's confiscating my phone might just be the least of my problems. "You brought it with you?" my mom said. "You . . . you snuck it in?"

My dad didn't say anything, but he was looking at me with such a shocked expression, I actually raised my hand to my face to make sure I hadn't grown a second nose.

"She's been using it the whole time she's been here," Ron said. "When I found it, it was on. Her last text message had been sent only hours before."

If he had pulled out a knife, the group reaction could scarcely have been more alarmed. There was a collective gasp. I heard, "Oh my gosh!" and "You have got to be kidding."

"In my opinion," Ron said, his voice soft again, "using this phone in our camp violates the essential nature of the entire experiment. You're all here willingly. This is not a prison. Why do it at all if you're not going to do it right?"

I was looking at my shoes now. And Gavin's shoes that were next to mine. And Ka's, on the other side. I tried not to notice that my mother's shoes—her black leather boots sticking out from the bottom of her skirt—were shaking.

"I've had a few days to think about how to handle this infraction," Ron went on. "And I realized that it's not up to me. It's up to all of us as a community. This whole place won't work if you aren't genuinely interested in it. Maybe you think it's okay to sneak the technology of today into 1890? If so, I'm sorry. Sharing the experience of the frontier—this is Betsy's and my life's work. We're not getting rich off it. In fact, maintaining five small farms for ten months out of the year and training four novice farmers for the remaining two is not easy. I'm not going to add policing the rest of you to that list of jobs. I want our decision on how to handle this to come from all of us. Please—let me hear from you."

I almost groaned out loud when Anders Puchinski was the first to stand up. His brow was furrowed and he'd crossed his arms in front of his chest. "I don't like it," he said. "I don't like it one bit. I came out here to get away from all of that and I thought that was the understanding with everyone. I don't even let my kids have the darned things when we're back home."

"I don't either!" my mom piped up. She was looking right at me. "I've never liked cell phones. I don't think kids should have them. Gen, you clearly shouldn't. I want everyone to know this phone was brought to camp without my knowledge."

"Mom—," I started. But what could I say to her to make her calm down?

"Don't even talk to me right now," she said. Her eyes were beaded up into little slits.

My dad had his head in his hands. His bandaged, blistered hands. Gavin was rubbing his knees with his palms.

"Ron," Caleb's father said. His way of talking extra slow—he drew his words out like honey—calmed everyone down. He could have been a hostage negotiator or the guy sent in to defuse bombs. "We are all loving this experience just as it was meant to be," he said. "We're not all sneaking around using cell phones and checking our e-mail."

"Absolutely," Ka's new stepdad, Clark, agreed, but his crisp boy-band perkiness killed whatever calm Caleb's dad's words had started to disperse. "This is clearly a question of one bad seed." Ka was sitting next to me and she rolled her eyes. But her little gesture of sympathy was powerless to counter Clark's words: a bad seed? Really? Me?

One time, at school, Ashley left a pair of underpants in a gym locker and when our principal, Mr. Weber, had his "fashion show" at the end of the year, holding up all the stuff from the lost and found so kids would come to the front of the auditorium and claim what belonged to them, he'd held up Ashley's underpants, which were red and said "Saturday Night" on the back. She'd thought she could just stay in her seat, anonymous, but then Mr. Weber found one of the name tags Ashley's mom had ironed into all of Ashley's clothes for camp. "Ah, Miss Smith," Mr. Weber had said. "I believe these are yours?" She'd almost died.

This was worse.

"I'd like to say something," Ka's mom, Maureen, began. "The whole challenge is to imagine yourself cut off. To rely on your family. But this is not easy for a teenager. It hasn't been easy for Ka." She shot a look at Clark. "It's not even easy for me. I understand how this can be extra hard for Gen."

"I don't think that it's helpful to teens to make exceptions," Clark rebutted. Were they fighting? "Everyone has to toe the line. Otherwise there's no line. Do you know what I mean?"

Maureen raised a hand in a "Fine" gesture. Wholesome blond freckles aside, I was starting to see that she had the capacity to be angry and sarcastic. Like Ka.

One by one, all the grown-ups weighed in. Caleb's mom, the lawyer, who I'd never heard talk in a meeting, used the words "aforementioned," "previously agreed upon," and "original conveyance of intent." I don't think anyone, including me, had the slightest idea what she was talking about. Anders stood up again. He clearly was angry. Others, like Caleb's dad, were nice. But they all agreed that what I'd done was wrong and that it violated the whole purpose of the experience.

"All right," Ron said when the last person to speak was done. "I'm going to skip the progress assessments for now. Let's take a week to think this through. We'll reconvene next Sunday and decide as a group how we want to deal with an infraction of this kind."

My dad stood up. "I want something to be clear. I am sorry on behalf of our whole family. This is embarrassing for Gen, for Cheryl, and for me."

"I want something to be clear as well," Ron replied. "Asking you and your family to leave will be one of the options on the table."

My dad sat down like he'd been slapped.

After a painful silence, Betsy stood. "We still have to eat!" she said, her smile gushing open and then quickly getting swallowed by the rest of her rosy face.

My mom literally threw the food she'd packed onto the blanket. "Hey, that bounced!" Gavin said as her first attempt at cheese ricocheted off the blanket and rolled to the edge. No one was listening. My dad paced around the outside of the blanket, with his arms crossed, which is what he does when he's on a stressful work conference call on the weekend and is simultaneously watching the Miami Dolphins lose.

"This is so not fair," I whispered. My mom had set the blanket up far away from the others, but if we had spoken loudly they'd have heard.

"Did you have the phone or not?" my dad said. This was a question he knew the answer to already. He just needed to hear me admit to what I'd done.

I looked away, but what I saw was maybe worse than meeting my mom's and dad's accusing gaze. The Drivers, the Meyer-Hincheys, the Puchinskis—they were all looking at me. They were whispering. I could imagine Anders giving Disa a lecture on why their children would never turn out as badly as I had. She was the only woman who hadn't stood up to say anything in the meeting, but I could imagine what she thought. I could imagine Clark telling Ka that she wasn't so bad compared to me. Caleb was probably already explaining to his mom and dad that he didn't even know me very well, that he didn't hang out with me, and that he wasn't planning on starting now that I'd been caught so flagrantly violating camp rules. His dad was probably drawling, "Of course not," while his mom was mumbling, "Any association previously acquired must heretofore cease."

"Answer me," my dad commanded. "When I ask you a question I expect an answer. Did you have the phone or not?"

"Dad," I said. Why couldn't he of all people understand how badly I had not wanted to come here? Why couldn't he see that the phone had been the one thing making any of this bearable? "Mom," I said, because I wanted to explain something, but I wasn't sure exactly what.

"Don't 'Mom' me," she said, crossing her arms over her chest.

"Okay," I said. I stood. And knowing that my family and the whole camp was watching, I turned my back on all of them and walked into the woods toward home.

That night, no one in our family spoke to each other. We didn't eat. I milked Jezebel, Gavin sat for a long time fussing over the chickens, my mom put away the picnic supplies, and my dad walked out into the woods to work on chopping down trees. Eventually my mom joined him, and they went back and forth with a two-man saw until after Gavin and I had gone in to sleep.

"I'm sorry," I said to my mom the next morning, while I was washing dishes and she was mixing bread dough and boiling water for laundry. "I hope we don't get kicked out of the camp."

"I'm surprised you're saying that," she said. "I would have assumed you'd *want* to go home."

"Well," I said.

"I assumed you brought the phone to make sure that would happen."

"Um," I said.

"I'm not going to let it," she said. "It's not fair."

"No," I agreed.

"It's not fair to *me*," she clarified.

I said, "Okay, yeah."

It was a quiet week. A dirge of a week. "Dirge" is a word I learned in music last year. It means slow and depressing and is surprisingly useful to describe life in 1890 when you have been caught sneaking in a cell phone and accused of killing more than twenty other people's historical reenactment buzz.

It was getting toward the end of July, but without seeing the date stamp on my texts I lost track of the days. The corn was growing fatter, the tomatoes were ripening on the vine. I wished I'd been able to at least text Kristin and Ashley one last time to let them know I'd been caught. I wondered if they were worrying about what had happened to me.

Thinking this might be our last week here, I started to notice stuff about the place that I hadn't before. Like the fresh and sharp smell when you rip the greens off a carrot or spread hay that had been baking all day in the loft into Jezebel's stall.

Gavin caught more fish, and though Erik Puchinski and his family didn't come over to eat it with us again, the fish tasted no less delicious. Sitting across the fire from my brother, I thought about how, if we hadn't come here, I would never know what a fishing stud he could be.

I noticed stuff about my family too. One day, it rained, and we spent most of the day inside, drinking tea and watching our stockings steam on the chair backs where we'd hung them to dry. Dad somehow started telling stories about Grandma and even Grandpa, who died before Gavin and I were born. In the afternoon, we all ended up taking naps.

I woke up first and lay for a while next to Gavin, listening to the sounds of him and my mom and dad breathing in their sleep. Here we were, I thought, the four of us. At home we never spent this kind of time together. It wasn't exactly pleasant, but it made me notice.

During that week, I think it was Tuesday morning, I was out in the field checking the corn—the silks were starting to brown—when I heard my name. It was Ka calling, from the edge of the woods.

"I snuck over here as soon as I could," she said, still breathless when I met up with her at the edge of the field. "I got stuck yesterday—my whole family had to help the Puchinskis raise the walls for the mill they're building next to the Drivers' dam. It's going to have a water wheel to turn the grindstone. Hey— are you okay?"

"I'm fine," I said, but I wasn't fine. I was thinking about how Caleb had said he wanted to take me swimming once the dam was constructed. They must have finished it. Would I even get a chance to go now? "Do you think my family's going to get kicked out?" I asked.

"Matt's sure you are, you lucky thing," Ka answered. She was casual and glib—how could I explain that this wasn't how I wanted things to go? "Clark and my mom got in this big fight over you. He said it wasn't okay for teens to act out, and my mom said you had to look at what they were going through. As I told Matt and Katie—really, duh, they were talking about me. Matt thinks maybe they'll make you leave in the middle of the night before the next meeting and just pretend you're not there."

"They can't do that," I said, but the same idea had occurred to me too. "Your mom and Clark are fighting for real?"

She shrugged. "I know," she said. "It kind of makes me feel bad. But it's better than the public displays of affection they were all about before."

Ka changed the subject. "It's weird that Ron never said anything about the shack," she mused.

"What do you mean?" I said.

"He must have found your phone there, right? You left it plugged in when we were all cleaning up and trying to get out of there before he got back."

"Yeah."

"So . . . ," she said, as if I should be following her logic. I wasn't.

"So what?" I said.

"Don't you see? He didn't say anything about where he found it because he was worried everyone would find out."

"I still don't see why anyone would care. I mean, why shouldn't Ron and Betsy take a break from 1890 once in a while to play around on the Internet and drink a Diet Coke?"

"Spoken by the girl who thinks it's okay to sneak a cell phone into history camp," Ka said—a you're-not-getting-this tone in her voice. "For people like Anders and Ron, the *total* experience is important. Look," she tried again. "I live in San Francisco, okay? Half my class doesn't eat meat. And the other half? They don't eat meat . . . or milk, or eggs. I've seen what happens when the cafeteria accidentally puts chicken broth in the vegetarian vegetable soup. Kids threaten to make themselves puke. Parents call in. People get fired."

"Really?" I said.

"Yeah," she answered. "This is the same kind of thing. Anders, Ron—anyone crazy enough to want to come here—they're purists."

I put my head in my hands. "They must hate me so much."

"If it's any consolation," Ka said, "I don't think *everyone* hates you."

"Gee," I said. "Thanks?"

"Seriously," she said. "What you did is not bad. Matt said Caleb said your blog was actually famous or something."

"Yeah," I said. But I wasn't thinking about the blog. I was thinking about how everyone was talking about me. How I'd ruined camp not just for my family, but for everyone's. I wasn't a regular kid anymore. I was a bad seed. I was the chicken broth in the vegetarian vegetable soup.

My parents were not at all in touch with the fact that at the end of the week, we were going to be asked to leave. Family dinners were quiet, with my dad breaking twenty minutes of silent eating with gems of conversation starters such as: "Next week for sure we're going to need the kids out in the cornfield, so any work you need done in the garden should be done now."

"You really do sound like a farmer now," I said after he regaled us with an account of how many trees he'd cut down a day since he changed the way he was holding the ax. I thought it was a pretty funny comment, but no one laughed. Gavin rolled his eyes and my mom and dad stared blankly at the dirty walls.

Every time I thought my mom was done talking to me about

the phone, she would turn to me out of the blue and say, "What in the world possessed you to take that out of the box I'd left it in and bring it out here?"

One time I came back in from the woods early to get some water and found my mom holding Pumpkin under her arm, her fingers wrapped around his neck. She was trying to maneuver him onto an old tree stump that had a hatchet propped up against its side—it didn't take a genius to figure out what she had in mind. Or that she was doing it wrong. Pumpkin could still flail and he was moving his left wing in a way that made me think he might break it.

"Stop it!" I shouted. "What are you doing?"

She jumped like I'd slammed a door in a room she thought was empty, gave a little scream, and dropped Pumpkin on the ground. A cloud of feathers floated down around Mom's hair and shoulders and arms. Pumpkin limped away.

"You can't kill Pumpkin," I said. "Think about all that blood."

"I *am* thinking about it," said my mom. She started to cry. "But if we don't kill Pumpkin, it's just one more sign we're not serious about this place."

She pulled a handkerchief out of her pocket, blew her nose into it, and put it back in. Ew. "It's not even the chicken that's making me cry," my mom said. "I don't even know why I'm crying exactly. It's—it's all this work. It's, well, it's just everything!"

"Everything?" I said.

"Yes!" she answered, and it was like she was even more angry now, angry at me for not understanding instantly. "That phone, I still don't know what you were thinking. But it's more than that too. I know you're only thirteen, Genevieve, but you do have eyes in your head and I think you'd be able to use them to see how miserable this whole thing has been for me."

"But—," I started to say. "I thought—" I wanted to tell her that I thought this was her dream, but she didn't let me finish.

"I wanted this *not* to be miserable," she said. "I wanted it to work. But of course you thought of nothing more than how much you hate it here. Did you ever think for a minute that it would be hard for me to enjoy myself knowing how determined you were to be miserable? Did you think that maybe your attitude would affect anyone besides yourself?"

"My attitude?" I said. "What are you talking about?"

She gave me a look that could only be described as "duh." And I was like, "Okay," because she was right. "Maybe I have been a little negative."

She cracked a big sarcastic smile and said, "A little," which made me laugh, I don't know why, except that I guess for a second, she was acting like me. She was being honest. And funny too. I mean, it *was* funny. Wasn't it?

It was. She was laughing now. Or maybe she was laughing the way crazy people laugh—for no apparent reason—but I chose to believe that we were having the kind of moment of mutual understanding that had been sorely lacking between us since, well, since she first announced that we were all going to be spending our summer at Camp Frontier.

While she wiped away her tears, I wondered if I should rub her back or say something to make her feel better. It's weird to see your mom cry. I just stood there, watching, and wishing I were someplace else.

The next morning, while we were weeding in the garden, Gavin said, "Gen, do you ever get scared?"

"Scared?" I said. "Of what? Bears?"

"Not bears," he said. "Scared of, you know—" But I didn't know. So I raised my eyebrows, and he continued. "Do you ever get scared about Mom and Dad?"

"No," I said, because honestly I had no idea what he was talking about.

He used a stick to dig out a particularly entrenched weed next to a tomato plant. "They never talk to each other. They talk to each other less here than they did at home, and they almost never talk to each other at home."

I put my head down. He was right. But I'd always just assumed that's how everyone's parents were.

"You haven't noticed?" he said.

"When we get back home, you'll see," I said, even though I had a feeling he wouldn't see anything differently than he did now. "They'll be fine. It will be like we were never here."

On Thursday, my mom sent me out to this box my dad had built in the stream to keep things cold—it was kind of like a refrigerator, except it wasn't actually all that cold. You had to use the milk in twenty-four hours or it started to go bad. After dropping off the butter my mom had asked me to put in, I decided I would follow the path to Caleb's house and see if he was around.

I don't know what I had in mind exactly. The two of us sitting next to a stream in dappled sunlight? Taking a walk through the woods, him holding back the branches so they wouldn't scrape my delicate skin?

When I got to his house, his mom was in the middle of doing laundry and Caleb was helping her. They were both red in the face and dripping wet. Susan was scrubbing a petticoat against the washboard while Caleb was wringing out one of his sister's dresses—he'd tied the sleeves to one of the porch columns, and was twisting the dress from the skirt end.

"Genius!" I muttered, but then Caleb looked up from his work—almost as if he could see me where I was still hidden by the trees growing close to their yard, and I caught my breath. He was gazing up into the sky, kind of squinting, and he looked serious. I'd never seen him look like that before.

Caleb was always mischievous. Everything I'd ever heard him say was lighthearted. So now I was rocked by this sudden understanding that he had a whole other life here—a house that looked exactly like ours except that it was tucked into the shade, new techniques for doing laundry, thoughts that were serious and real and not meant to be shared in the way all his jokes usually were. I had a sudden overwhelming desire to run.

I was certain that if Caleb saw me, if he understood that I'd walked clear across our land to his, he'd know that the only reason I had come was to find out if he liked me. And what if he didn't? What if I'd only imagined anything between us? What if I said, "I came to say good-bye," and he was like, "Okay, bye," as if my leaving was the same as anyone else's? I knew I should run.

But I didn't run. I just stood there watching, until some movement I made—a stick breaking under my foot? the sound of my breathing?—alerted Caleb to my presence. "Is someone there?" he said.

I stepped out, as if I'd been walking straight down the path the whole time.

"Gen!" Susan said, sounding surprised but not totally displeased to see me.

Caleb smiled broadly. His hair was getting long, and he'd pulled it back from his tanned (or dirty) face and tucked it behind his ears. "A guest!" he said, and I waved, as in, "That's me. Gen P. Guest at your service."

"My mother wants to know if she could borrow an egg," I lied.

"An egg," Susan said. "Well, let me see." Carefully putting the garment she was scrubbing down on top of the washboard, she climbed the porch steps and disappeared into the house.

Caleb was instantly at my side. "Did you get in trouble?" he said. "Ka told Matt you were in serious trouble."

"Yeah," I said. "I guess I am. Though what are they going to do, take away TV? Keep me from going to the movies?"

"Yeah," he said, and laughed. "I guess I've never thought of it that way."

"My family's probably getting kicked out, though," I said. "That's what they can do."

"What are all those people reading your blog going to do without you?" he said.

"I think they'll live," I said. I was dying to say: "But what about you? Will you miss me?" Maybe I could have said it if it had been dark out. Or if his mom hadn't been just two steps away. I thought it, though. I thought the question really hard.

And the way Caleb looked at me, straight in the eye and

puzzled, not letting go of my gaze—I was pretty sure he knew I was thinking something, and just couldn't tell exactly what.

Then his mom was on the porch again, the egg wrapped in a cloth. She placed it carefully in my hands and I turned to go, not a whole lot more satisfied than I would have been if I'd turned around while I was hidden in the woods, and run home.

But still, seeing Caleb, something changed. I didn't feel our chances of staying were better, but I did understand that we hadn't been kicked out yet. We were still part of things.

Later that evening, when Gavin and I were out looking for blackberries to pick for dessert—my dad had seen some in the woods and told us where to look for them—I turned to hold a branch back for Gavin, and I looked at him, right into his eyes. The fact that he had been the one to worry about Mom and Dad told me he was aware of more than I gave him credit for. "Gavin," I said, "there's something you need to know. Mom needs to kill Pumpkin. She thinks it's the only way for us to really belong here. I'm telling you because I think you have the right to know. Okay?"

Gavin's face twisted up into an expression that was half about to cry and half "what are you talking about?"

"You know I'm right," I said.

I couldn't bear to look at him then. I looked out into the trees, noticing how they weren't all straight up and down like they should have been. Some had fallen over and were leaning and others were growing through a mass of tangled brush.

The next time my mom brought up the subject of the phone, I said, "Do you even know where my phone was when Ron found it?"

"No," she said.

"It was in Ron and Betsy's secret shed where they have a solar panel," I said.

My mom's head jerked and suddenly she was facing me. "A solar panel?" she repeated.

"Oh, yeah," I went on. "And a computer. Where I found Nora going online. She goes online all the time in there. They all do. Ron plays solitaire and surfs organic-farming chat rooms. Betsy e-mails her sisters."

My mom clenched her fists. "You're kidding," she said.

"No," I answered. "They have a minifridge there too. Where Betsy keeps a stash of Diet Coke."

"Diet *Coke*?" said my mom. Have I mentioned that she is on a parent committee at Gavin's elementary school that petitioned to have all the soda machines taken off of school grounds? She is.

"That's unbelievable," she said.

"Ka said it's like putting chicken broth in vegetarian vegetable soup."

"You know something?" my mom said. "I think Ka hit the nail on the head."

« 21 »

The next day, we trudged over to Ron and Betsy's, I was sure for the last time. I half expected Ron to tell us to pack our bags before the meeting even began.

But he didn't. He shook my dad's hand as we settled onto our regular bench. He nodded to my mom. He looked like someone who hasn't slept in several days. Betsy was pale and drawn as well.

"Now that we've had time to reflect, does anyone have anything more to say about Genevieve and her cell phone?" Ron began.

Surprisingly, it was Disa Puchinski who first stood to speak. "Before we judge Gen too harshly," she said, "I have something I want to confess to. It is bad—none of you suspected it, even my husband." I was looking at her now. She smiled nervously at Anders, then pinched the bridge of her nose as if a headache were starting to form. "I snuck a layer of Crisco into the false bottom of my great-grandmother's old-fashioned hat box, which Betsy said was okay to bring."

"Your *piecrust*," said Betsy in horror.

"I haven't used it all," Disa rushed to explain. "I just wanted to be sure I had an option. This may sound silly, but a frontier cabin without a woman turning out delicious baked goods—it just doesn't seem authentic to me. I was afraid that I wouldn't be able to get the same results working with lard."

"The muffins you made on the first day?" Clark said.

Disa nodded mournfully. "I'm telling you about this now, because I think before we decide what should happen to Gen, you should all know that she is not the only one who broke the rules."

For a second there was silence. Then suddenly everyone was talking.

"I *never* would have thought . . ."

"Of all the—," someone else began.

"If you want to see a frontier cabin where no one's making delicious baked goods, come to our place," Caleb's mom shouted above the rest. "And here I've been feeling like I'm inadequate and you're using Crisco." Then she smiled. "Though I'm such a noncook I don't think I even really know what Crisco is."

"It's—" Disa looked around and realized this probably wasn't the time or the place to explain.

Maureen stood up next. Out of her pocket came something that looked like a pen. "This," she said, holding it up for everyone to see, "is mascara. I have worn it so long that my lashes are simply gone if I don't." She paused in her matter-of-fact way and sighed. She seemed sad and I wondered for a second if she was sad about Ka. "Because I'm not using any real makeup remover and this is a very good, waterproof essential, I'm only applying it a few times a week. I didn't sneak in anything else."

She sat down, slipping the mascara back into her pocket.

"I brought in the last Harry Potter book," Cara Hinchey said in a voice so soft I could hardly hear it. "I'd finished the sixth one just before we left and I really wanted to see what happened. I ripped off the covers and hid it inside my allergy pillow."

Matt admitted to a deck of cards. Caleb stood to show off his leather necklace. "It wasn't really sneaking since you all can see it," he said. "But I don't think guys wore necklaces in 1890."

"Indians did," Erik suggested.

"Leather would have been available," Betsy said.

Caleb's father stood. "This one's really bad," he said, and he pulled from his pocket a flat, gray box.

"Is that another cell phone?" Ron asked.

"No," Peter drawled. "It's a handy little device that lets me follow the game."

"The game?" said Ron.

"Baseball," Peter explained. "I can't believe that none of y'all know that I'm a huge Braves fan." Suddenly he'd flipped the top up and was demonstrating how the box worked. "You see here, when the Braves are playing, this little square comes on. It's box scores, basically, but it's updated by satellite. I figured it was okay because you could get box scores in the newspaper in 1890. This would just be a little faster of a delivery method."

"How'd you get it in?" Ron asked.

"My sleeves," he said. "While I was changing from my regular shirt into my 1890 one, I slipped it from one sleeve into the other."

At this point, the gasping and whispering had subsided. In fact, Peter's smile was so broad, Maureen and Susan laughed.

Anders Puchinski stood up, and I wondered what he could possibly confess to. It seemed incredible to me that he had snuck in anything at all.

He hadn't. "Peter, if you don't mind my interrupting your fascinating demonstration, I want to say that I don't find any of this funny." He glared at his wife. "I came out here because I don't need modern life. I don't want it. Disa—I thought you felt the same way. I thought all of you felt the same way." He crossed his arms. "But now it seems that Ron and Betsy and I are the only ones who haven't been cheating."

Disa hung her head in shame. Peter Driver looked sheepish and shrugged. Clark and Maureen pursed their lips.

It was then that Ron stepped forward, and I think we all shared a silent sigh of relief. Anders would stop making us all feel guilty.

Ron raised his hands, palms forward, like a priest about to begin a Sunday sermon, his gesture a promise of mercy and understanding.

But before he had a chance to say anything, my mom rose from her seat.

"Actually, Anders," she said. "The only ones not cheating are Susan, Doug, Clark, me, and you."

Ron and Betsy turned to face her, their faces frozen in identical midthought spasm—like when you pause a movie to go to the bathroom and the actor is left with his mouth twisted and one eye half squinted.

My mom continued, as if she were addressing Anders alone. "I take it you haven't heard anything about the 'electricity shack'?"

Anders shook his head, but his eyes did not leave my mother's face.

My mom paused, making sure she had everyone's attention, and then explained about the electricity shack, and what was inside it.

"There's a computer?" Anders asked when she was finished. He shook his head, like he was chasing away a sneeze, then looked from my mom to Ron and then back again, like he was hoping one of them would explain that it was some kind of legitimate 1890s device that just happened to be called a computer. An early typewriter? An abacus?

"Campers aren't supposed to go in there," Betsy wailed. "It has nothing to do with Gen's phone."

"Of course it does," my mom said. "Where do you think Gen's been charging the darn thing? That's where she left it."

"No, the phone fell out of her pocket," Ron said, raising his voice over my mom's and Betsy's. "When she was in our barn the other day."

"What?" I said.

"Nora found it," Betsy explained. "Right after you came over last week. She said it must have slipped out of your pocket when you were in our barn."

"Nora *found* it?" I said. I was standing now, looking for her. The one thing I needed to see was her face, and when I located her, I saw she had the good sense to look like she was about to throw up. Found it, had she? More like grabbed it before Ron had a chance to see it, then used it to have me nailed to the wall.

It made me sick, to think that Nora was behind all the misery of the last week. That my family was embarrassed and on the verge of getting kicked out of camp not because I had accidentally left my phone behind, but because Nora had willfully turned it in. I felt steam rising inside my head. Heat coming into my face. I was an engine without an exhaust system. I didn't know what else to do but roar. "That's a lie!" I shouted. "I *knew* you were lying."

"Are you calling my daughter a liar after you've been lying this whole summer?" Ron wasn't being quiet and gentle now. His voice was booming.

My dad stood. "She's calling anyone a liar she needs to."

Anders pointed a finger at my dad. "You people," he said. "You're the problem. You shouldn't even be here. You don't want to be here."

"Oh, it would be better if we were Diet Coke addicts?" my mom said. "That's what passes for good frontier behavior these days?"

"Let's calm down, everyone," Peter said, standing.

"Yes, please. Arguing isn't going to get us anywhere," Maureen begged.

But Anders wasn't listening. "They don't even have the backbone to kill a chicken, let alone control their own children."

Ron jumped in with, "Do not tell me they haven't killed that bird yet."

Then my mom: "Oh, for the love of Pete, can we leave this issue alone? Gavin's a ten-year-old boy! Pumpkin is like his pet."

Then Nora to her mom: "I told you they'd wreck it." She pointed a finger right at me. "You're the problem here. You're ruining it for everyone."

I yelled back at her: "Me ruining it? Me? This is outrageous is what it is," I said. "That you can stand up in front of everyone and tell such total lies! Everyone saw me plug the phone in at the electricity shack." I knew I shouldn't talk anymore—when you're as mad as I was, you can only get yourself into trouble. But I kept talking anyway. I couldn't let Nora get away with lying.

I met Ka's eyes. "You were there," I said. "You saw me plug my phone in." To Erik: "Remember when we were cleaning up after Ron came by and Nora locked him out? That's when I forgot to grab my phone." Matt and Katie and Erik were nodding, but their faces were pale. "You guys remember, right?" I looked at Gavin. "You saw it too." And to Caleb: "It was plugged in next to all those iPods. You were playing that Green Day song, and then we went online just before Nora told us all to hide from Ron."

Why was everyone suddenly looking so much more horrified than before?

"Um . . . Gen?" Gavin said, tugging at my sleeve. "Ixnay elling-tay oh-nay everyone-way." (Translation: You are a bone-head.)

But the damage was already done.

"You—," Anders said. He was staring at Erik.

Ron had Nora fixed in a tractor beam of a gaze.

Matt, Katie, and Ka had their heads down, and Caleb was looking at his mom, a puppy-dog expression of supplication on his face.

"I think you just got everyone in a whole lot of trouble," Gavin said.

Still staring at his daughter, Ron's face went from its usual gray white pallor to red. His eyes were bright with anger. "I can't believe what you have done," he said. "You betrayed your mother and me. You have stepped on everything we have given our lives to build."

He stopped for a second and in his silence we could hear Betsy crying. "We did this for you," she said, addressing Nora through her tears. "And you've made a mockery of it, using what you know would be dreadfully embarrassing to us to entertain—and corrupt—your friends."

"I'm not sure a few songs on an iPod qualifies as corruption," my mom said.

"Don't tell us what qualifies as corruption," Ron said. Betsy nodded, blinking back tears. "You clearly don't have the slightest idea."

"Now, that's not fair," my mom began.

"I want you to know something," Ron said, cutting my mom off. "I was planning to forgive the phone.

"Look!" he said, pulling out a crumpled piece of paper from his pocket. "This is covered with notes. I've been thinking hard about all of this, reading some of the histories we keep about the frontier. Something that I keep coming back to is that only about twenty percent of families survived out here. In 1850, in Oregon territory, forty-four families are listed on the U.S. Census. Ten years later, only nine of them remain. They died, they went home, they starved, they left family heirlooms behind, and sometimes abandoned even their children. There are stories of families getting through a winter by digging a hole in the ground and living in it for months, like animals. They were desperate to be here and did desperate things to hold on to their claims.

"I was going to share this with you and tell you my conclusion, which is that what really separates our time from back then is community. People back then knew their neighbors and helped them—helped them to survive—and forgave them, which I was planning to do as well.

"But after today, I just want you gone. All of you. This—the way we live here—is luxury compared to the old frontier. We're dishonoring the original frontier people by even having the kind of conversation we're having now. They would have been thrilled to have milk cows and chickens and a variety of vegetables growing in their gardens. And yet you—you people—," he spat. "And even my own daughter. You can't live for eight weeks without your iPods and your cell phones and God knows what else."

"I—," I started. Somehow this was all my fault.

"No," he said. "Don't even try to explain yourself. I'm ashamed of you, all of you. I'm ashamed of myself. You're right, Anders. We don't need the electricity shack. We don't need a computer or Diet Coke. I don't want to be like you people. That's why we left the modern world. I thought bringing you out here would teach you something, but I can see now that I was wrong. So go home," he almost whispered. His anger, his booming voice, even his calm sense of resolve was gone like air from a leaking balloon. "All of you. Back to your cabins. I don't want to see you and your . . . children anymore right now."

"Let's take another week?" Betsy said, her hands wrapped in her apron as if she were going to tear the fabric of it in two.

Ron turned without answering her and walked into his barn. The rest of us gathered into our family groups without speaking. It would have felt like a parade—all of us in our costumes wandering down the path into the woods in a line—if it hadn't also felt like a funeral.

"If we had to spend a winter living like animals in a hole in the ground," Gavin said on the walk home, "we would totally have died."

My mom, dad, and I nodded in silent, grim agreement.

And then my dad added, "Not that we did much better out here."

« 22 »

That night, over a fresh pot of beans, we were silent. You could hear forks scraping the tin plates as we poked and stirred. Then more silence. Finally my dad said, "I think we need to leave."

"Leave?" echoed my mom, and she choked out a fake laugh.

"Yes," said my dad.

Mom started to sputter. "But—," she said. "Ron's crazy. He'll calm down. It's not just us."

"I don't care about the others, who snuck in what, who corrupted whose children. It's not working for *us*. And I'm starting to—" He put his head in his hands. "I'm starting, I think, to lose my mind." He raised his head and smiled helplessly, and for a second he was my old dad again. The dad who would see a joke in everything, who would be able to place the whole idea of our having to leave early—the quadruple humiliation of it all—as just one more detail in the absurd tapestry of life.

But his smile faded quickly. That funny, easy dad was not hungry, sick, and exhausted. That dad was not well on his way to cutting down two hundred trees by hand.

My mom shook her head, stood as if she could pretend that the meal—and thus the conversation—was over. She laid her plate, which still had a bunch of beans on it, in the basin. She took my plate and put it in the basin as well. I wasn't finished, but I didn't say anything. I was too scared of whatever was happening between my parents. But when Mom tried to take Gavin's plate too, he protested. "Hey," he said. "I'm not done."

My mom sighed and sat back down at the table. My father took another bite. I took a bean off Gavin's plate and popped it into my mouth. Then Mom looked up at my dad and there were tears in her eyes.

"Okay," she said. "Okay, this is maybe—probably—not exactly what we all imagined it would be."

"At the least," Dad said. "I know this makes you sad, but you have to admit it goes deeper than being different from what we imagined." My mom didn't say anything. "Come on," he said. "Admit it. This was a mistake. You're the only one who wanted to come and even you are miserable."

My mother sniffed, looked around for something to dry her eyes on, and found nothing. My dad fumbled for a moment in his pocket, pulled out a bandanna handkerchief, and passed it across the table to her. "It will be hard to go back home and tell everyone we failed," he said. "It will be hard to admit to Ron and Betsy that we're the first family in the history of the camp to give up. But we can go home, and we'll be fine. We'll get some rest. I'm still on vacation. We can plan a trip. We could even just rent a car here and do some sightseeing on the way back. We're probably not far from some national park or something."

"It's nice to see you're finally taking some interest in vacation planning," my mom said, a sob escaping even as she cracked this joke. Or sort of joke. It also sounded like she was mad.

"I'm sorry," my dad said. "I know I should be more involved with our vacation planning. With everything. And I promise I will be. Look, we'll get past this. It's a bump."

"Is it?" my mom said. "Is it really just a bump?" It was strange how one little question coming from her could sink us deeper into the hole my dad was trying so valiantly to climb out of. "I don't think it will be a bump for me." She swallowed, and if I could have stuffed the bandanna into her mouth to keep her from saying what came next, I would have. "I think for me this will be a failure," she said. "I think this is about us working together as a family, and if we can't do it, I don't know . . ." She let her voice drift away. "I don't know what to say."

"Okay," my dad said, his head now in his hands. He looked up. "Then let me put it this way," he said. "I'm going to finish that clearing. I said I would clear those trees, and I will. But after that I am leaving. If Gen and Gavin want to come with me, they are welcome to. You should feel free to stay."

He stood up from the table and pushed back his chair, leaving his food on his plate. He lifted his hat from a hook on the wall and held it in his hands. He opened his mouth to speak, and then closed it again.

No one knew where he was going when he left the cabin, and after the door had swung shut behind him my mom continued to stare as if the back of the door might contain the answer to a puzzle she was desperate to figure out. After a few minutes, she stood. She poured boiling water over the basin of dishes, and I picked up a rag and a wooden spoon to begin trying to work off the grease. Before long, we could hear the sound of chopping. As usual. How much longer would he be out there? How many more days did we have left? I put down the dish I was scrubbing and stood in the open door of the cabin, looking out in the direction of the woods. "Is he trying to finish all those trees off tonight?" I said.

My mom sighed. "I don't know," she said. "I just don't know."

I felt like I could taste how it would be for us to rent a mini-van and drive to the Grand Canyon. I thought about eating at Denny's and IHOP on the road, and my mouth began to water. Wouldn't that be better?

But what about Ka? What about Caleb? And Nora—I hated thinking of her satisfied smirk on finding out that I had quit.

What if my mom didn't quit with us?

She couldn't stay here—no one could do the farm by themselves. Could they? If she tried, I'd be left sleeping in some hotel room, sharing a bed next to the bathroom with Gavin while my dad slept all by himself in the bed by the window. I shuddered. I squeezed my eyes and pushed the vision away.

This was all my fault. I should never have brought my phone. And yet, all I wanted right then was to have it back, to be able to tell my friends what was wrong.

I don't know how long I was standing on the porch staring out at the trees, listening to the sounds of chopping, feeling stupid and sorry for myself and wishing things had been different. I do know that that's where I was standing—on the porch, looking out toward the woods—when the screaming began.

« 23 »

It was a horrible sound. It was the word "Help! Help!" but I didn't recognize it as a word at first. It was more of a shriek. Something in pain. An animal?

But then a figure broke into the clearing from the direction of the Puchinskis'. It was Erik's little sister Bryn—the one Gavin's age. She was running so hard her skirt was flying from side to side with each step. Her arms were raised in panic.

My mom came tearing out of the house and my dad was there, just in time for Bryn to take in a gasp of breath. "The mill!" she said. "It's on fire! All the wheat. It could go. My dad sent me."

She didn't have to say anything more. My dad shouted to Gavin, "Get buckets!"

"Anja went to get Ron," Bryn continued in a second gasp of air. "Erik's helping my mom and dad. They're trying to dig a trench around the mill to keep the fire from spreading."

My mom said, "Blankets—Gen—help!"

I remember standing next to the table inside the cabin as my mom threw the blankets down from the loft. She gathered them up into balls to drop them over the side, but they unfurled in the air and floated gracefully down through the open space.

Then we were following Bryn, running so hard my heart felt like a stone pounding inside the hollow box of my rib cage. We cut through the path in the woods, veered off where it went by the Puchinskis', and headed toward the river where Anders had built his mill.

We smelled the fire before we saw it. In the first breath I thought the smell was coming from the trees, that there was something wrong with them. The acrid air burned the inside of my nose.

My mom and dad ran faster than Gavin and me even though they were carrying blankets and buckets. My mom looked over her shoulder right before the bend in the river and shouted, "Gavin and Gen, don't come with us. It could be dangerous for you." We kept running just the same.

The air was thicker now with smoke. My eyes hurt from it and I pulled up my skirt to cover my mouth. Gavin pulled his shirt up over his. The last thing I remember before we actually saw the flames was a poplar tree by the river, its leaves rustling in the heat like this paper Santa we have at home where you light a candle underneath him and the flame makes him spin.

As we turned the corner we could see the mill—or the fire where the mill once stood. Everything else was smoke roiling over the top of the yellow wheat growing up against the mill. I could see why Anders was worried it would go.

Again my mother turned, but instead of speaking, she did something that I couldn't believe and still feel weird thinking about. She bodychecked me—literally. I was running and she pushed her chest out and slammed her body into mine. I fell to my knees. She pushed me down the rest of the way and said, "Stay there. Don't move. Don't stand up. Breathe the air down here." She pushed Gavin down as well. We were scared enough, we didn't get up.

I could see, though, and I watched what happened next. It was really fast.

Erik was there. His face was streaked with soot. He was shouting at my father, but the fire was so loud I couldn't hear what they were saying. My mother took Bryn by the arm and dragged her away from the smoke. Anders and Disa were nowhere to be seen.

My dad ran from the fire to the stream and came out carrying two wet blankets. He could barely run under their weight. He wrapped one around himself and carried the other and walked—stooping—into the smoke cloud. My mom followed him first to the water and then into the smoke with a wet blanket draped around her head and shoulders too.

When I say this went fast, I don't mean the part where both my parents were gone. That part felt like it took hours. Erik crawled over to where Gavin and I were lying on the ground. "My mom and dad are in there," he said. He sounded like he was reading from the telephone book. His eyes were big and round and his pupils were pricks of black. "They were trying to clear an area around the mill so the fire wouldn't spread and then I couldn't see them anymore."

"Whoa," Gavin said. I was silent. The roof of the mill—which was black and dancing with moving red snakes of heat—lifted up off of what remained of the building's frame, hung in the air like it was light enough to fly, and then slid over the side and crumbled. The mill no longer looked like a building but a mound.

A black cloud of smoke shifted shape until I could see that it wasn't a billow of smoke, but something moving deliberately—it was figures covered in blankets. They were coming toward us, and then they collapsed. A figure pulled a blanket off its head—it was my mother. "Gen!" she called out. "Come here." Then she and the other blanketed figure, who must have been my dad, turned back into the smoke.

Erik, Gavin, and I ran forward to the body that was on the ground. It was Disa. She wasn't unconscious, but she looked confused. Her face was black with smoke and her dress was singed in parts and browned in others, like the skin of a toasted marshmallow.

"Put your arm around me," I said, wedging my shoulder under her armpit so I could help her stand. Gavin took her other side and we walked her down to the stream. Just then, Ron was there. His face was white and he was out of breath from running. He held Disa by the shoulders so he could look at her. He shouted, "Betsy!" Betsy came running behind him, and Nora was there too.

"Tell me," Ron said, looking right at me like he trusted me and knew I would tell him the exact shortest and most helpful thing he needed to hear, and I tried. He was putting on a fire helmet, goggles, a face mask, and fire jacket and pants as I spoke—all of which he'd gotten from a red nylon backpack that looked like something you would buy at a camping store.

I said, "My mom and dad went in for Disa. They went back for Anders. They're in there now."

He pointed to Nora, who was wearing a bright blue and yellow pack inside of which was a long coil of flat fire hose. "Help Nora," he said. "She will explain." And then he was gone.

I remember that Nora looked scared. Her freckles were standing out across her nose and cheeks, and her jaw was kind of sucked in. For once, she didn't look mean.

"What do I do?" I said. Betsy was leaning over Disa. She had her breathing from a tank with a plastic mask at the end. She was taking her blood pressure while also instructing Gavin on how to use a satellite phone. He was holding it up to his ear and I could see that he was talking.

"Take this," Nora said, handing me the end of the hose. "Stick it in the water. Make sure it's really in there, and somewhere deep." I ran. I found a good spot, ramming the hose nozzle in between some rocks. I rejoined Nora, who had assembled a plastic black box that turned out to be a generator pump. It came to life with a loud roar and suddenly the hose went rigid. "Make sure it stays in the water," Nora said, and unwound the hose as far as it would go—about twenty-five feet. She must have turned something on the end of the hose, because water began to shoot out of it into the mill fire.

Just then, Ron came out carrying Anders over his shoulders, my mom and dad behind them. Anders's left arm was draped across the front of Ron, swinging languidly. My dad was leaning on my mom, and they were all staggering. Betsy rushed to them and helped bring them out of the smoke to the place where she had Disa lying down under a tree. She passed the oxygen tank immediately over to Anders, who was not unconscious as I'd thought, and could raise his head to make sure

Disa was okay. They were both coughing, and Betsy made them lie back down. I wanted to run to my own parents to see if they were okay but every time Nora moved, the back of the hose became dislodged, so I had to keep resituating it to make sure the water was flowing in.

She was starting to get the flames under control when Ron took over the spraying. He sprayed the wheat—really soaking it as the mill continued to burn. Nora joined me down at the stream. "I can do that if you want to go see your parents," she said.

I ran up the bank to where they lay. I heard the beating of a helicopter in the air above us, and then it was impossibly windy.

"We're evacuating you!" Betsy shouted down at the Puchinskis and my mom and dad. "You need to get to a hospital. I'll keep the children here and Ron will meet you in the hospital." The Puchinskis nodded vaguely. My mom looked at me—she was afraid still, I think, and I remembered how it felt when she knocked me to the ground to keep me safe. My back hurt, and I thought there was going to be a bruise from where I fell.

The smoke and steam coming off the fire now was blown into the woods by the helicopter. Two medics jumped out while it was still running. One immediately ran over to where my mom and dad and the Puchinskis were lying. He asked Anders questions and started ripping open bags and pouches and sterilized packages that came from his blue duffel bag. The other medic started to work on Disa. My mom and dad were sitting up on their own now, but the medics insisted they lie back and they carried all four bodies on stretchers into the helicopter, one after another. It was like a movie, except the paramedics didn't look like movie stars—one had a lot of chest hair sticking out of his paramedic shirt, and the other one was a woman who was chewing gum and had a leopard-print bandanna in her hair. Also, the helicopter looked old. Some of the paint on the body near the door was chipping off.

Ron turned off the generator and started to beat at the pile of soaking wet black embers with a flat paddle that looked a little bit like a shovel. By the time the helicopter had lifted off I'd gotten used to the noise of it, and then when it was gone, it felt like the world was echoing and empty and I didn't know what we were supposed to do, only that it was well past dusk now—it was getting dark. Betsy packed up her equipment, Nora rolled up the hose, and Ron stripped off his firefighting gear and put it away into the pack it came in.

"Come, children," Betsy said, looking very modern with her first aid kit strapped to her back but also very motherly and warm and inviting in her big dress. "You'll sleep at our house tonight." And so Bryn, Anja, Erik, Gavin, and I followed Ron, Betsy, and Nora into the woods to their house, where Ron washed his hands and face, changed his clothes, and then backed the white van out of the barn and drove off on the dirt road into the woods to make sure everything in the hospital was okay.

« 24 »

Betsy made us hot milk and put out some cookies, but I couldn't eat them. I felt sick, and not just about my mom and dad being in the hospital. "You must have breathed some smoke in too," Nora said, passing me a cup of water. "Drink this. You'll feel better in a minute."

She was right. By the time I'd reached the bottom of the cup, the cookie was looking pretty tasty, and when I did manage to choke it down I quickly took two more and drank the milk also. Gavin, I noticed, was on his fourth cookie. Caleb's mom came by, taking Anja, Bryn, and Erik to spend the night at the Drivers'.

"You children did a fine job helping to fight that fire and get everyone out safe," Betsy said. "Gen, you really kept your head, and Gavin, you knew more about operating that satellite phone than I did! Nora, tomorrow we'll have to dry out the hose and put everything away properly, but that was a good idea you had to order it."

I took a fourth cookie. It really was very, very good. And it was hard in Betsy's warm kitchen not to feel that everything was going to be okay, just as it was hard when talking to Betsy not to return her smile.

"The fire stuff was your idea?" I said to Nora. My mouth was full and she rolled her eyes.

"Yes," she said.

"It's time for bed with you now," Betsy said. "You children are up awfully late!" The clock up on their mantel showed ten thirty.

Betsy had told me where we were going to sleep when we first got to her house, but the reality of the situation didn't sink in until I'd started to recover. Because he was the only boy, Gavin got to sleep by himself downstairs on a mattress Betsy laid out in front of the fire. I was sentenced to a night in bed with Nora. It was not the slightly larger than usual bed that Gavin and I had been sharing in our cabin for the last three weeks. It was a regular twin-size bed that as an only child Nora usually got to have all to herself. After we'd changed into our nightgowns and crawled under the covers, our faces were only about two inches apart on the pillow.

Up close, I couldn't help but be impressed by how long, thick, and curly Nora's hair was. It spilled out over the pillow and even down over her side of the bed when she propped her head up on her hand so she could look down at me where I was lying.

I knew I should still be angry at her. After all, she'd been the one to turn the whole camp upside down by taking my phone out of the electricity shack and giving it to her dad. But after the fire, after working with her to pump water onto the blaze, I didn't feel mad. Maybe, finally, I thought, we could be friends.

At first, it seemed she was thinking that too.

"This stinks, doesn't it?" she whispered.

"Huh?" I said. I was grateful to be lying down, and I could have drifted off to sleep in seconds.

She whispered again, her blue eyes narrowed. "It stinks that I have to share a room with my parents."

I nodded my head. My space was just exactly as wide as my body, but I was deeply, deeply tired. I could feel myself starting to fade when Nora was whispering again. "I bet at your house you have your own room. I bet it's huge, right? I bet it's larger than our whole upstairs."

I nodded again, and sleepily conceded, "It has a trundle bed so when I have sleepovers we each get our own space to sleep."

"Do you have sleepovers a lot?" Nora said.

"Well, not anymore. Not the regular kind. But Ashley and Kristin—my best friends—we sleep over each other's houses all the time."

"They're your friends?" she said. "Do they live right in your town?"

"Of course," I explained. "Ashley lives on my street and Kristin's not too far—I can ride my bike." I was almost too sleepy to notice the tone of envy in Nora's voice, but I did notice it, and the idea that she was jealous kind of woke me up.

She moved down to the pillow now, lying on her back and staring up into the rafters of the attic room.

"Kids who come here," I said. "For the summer. Do they ever come back?"

"Sometimes, but not this year. This year, it's all new kids."

"Do you get lonely?" I asked. I think I would have been too scared to ask this question if I had been looking directly at Nora. And I would have been right to be scared. At the word "lonely" she lifted her head and turned the force of her angry eyes on me. She was so close it was worse than usual. "Lonely?" she said. I inched my head back on the pillow as far as I could go without worrying about falling off the bed. "You want to know so you can feel sorry for me? Well, don't, because no, I'm not lonely. Go back to your fancy house and your car and your friends and your perfect life and think, 'Oh poor Nora, it must stink to be her,' but if you really want to know, I am just fine."

"Whoa," I said. By now I'd propped my head up on my elbow too and was fully awake. "I just asked a question." I'd meant to whisper, but I was so sick of her being angry at me, I forgot. "Why are you so mean to me?" I said, whispering again. "What good does it do you?"

"Because what's the point," she said, and turned away from me on the pillow. "You hate it here. Everyone hates it here. The grown-ups think they are going to love it and end up hating every minute until the end when they talk about how it's changed them, blah blah blah. But you know. You and Caleb, Matt, Ka, you know that finding out how hard it was to live on the frontier is just a stupid waste of time. You can't wait to get out of here and when you do, you'll never look back. And you're right to. This whole place is stupid."

"It must be awf—," I started to say, but she cut me off.

"You don't know anything about it." She turned onto her side so she could face me. "You and Caleb, Matt, Ka, Katie, all of you, you think you're suffering. You think you're totally deprived, but you don't know the first thing about deprived. Think about what it's like to have every kid in the entire country growing up normal except for you. Try to imagine what it's like to go all winter with no one your age to talk to, then every summer meeting a new group of kids who don't understand you. Even if you do make friends with them, you know after the summer you'll never see them again. Think about that for two seconds and then you'll understand why it is I don't want you here."

"Some parts of this are pretty cool, actually," I said.

"Oh, yeah?" she said, suspicious.

"Milking a cow is kind of cool," I said.

"You like milking a cow?" she said. "I thought you hated it."

"Yeah, that first day I did," I said. "But now that I know what I'm doing, it's kind of neat. And getting to know the other kids, that's cool too. At home you kind of have to stick in your group—it's not like you can go up to someone you don't know at all and have nothing in common with and be friends with them. Out here everyone's kind of forced to mix together."

She rolled her eyes.

"It's pretty out here too," I said. "At first I didn't notice it, but now I'm kind of thinking I might even miss the mountains and stuff when I go home."

"Hmph," Nora said. She didn't sound convinced. Then she laughed. "I guess there is one good part of this summer, though."

"What's that?" I was yawning now, feeling like I could be asleep in two seconds.

"You don't know?"

"Um, no," I said.

"Caleb," she whispered. Her face was inches from mine, and I swear she was watching me closely to see how I would react. I kind of held my breath, knowing she was watching, letting her words travel down through my ears and into my stomach, which immediately contracted around them, trying to block them from traveling to my brain. But they flew up there anyway.

Before, when I'd wondered if Caleb and Nora were a couple, I thought that finding out might be the worst thing that could happen. But it wasn't. Finding out with Nora watching—this was worse. Now I had no chance of being able to control my face, to keep from showing how I felt.

"I'm not allowed to have a boyfriend until I'm eighteen," Nora went on, "so . . . you know."

"Oh," I said. I thought back to how they'd been partners for kick the can. I thought back to when Nora had booted me out of the electricity shack and Caleb had barely defended me. I thought about how thin and straggly my hair looked compared to hers flowing off the edge of the bed, other times bursting in silky curls out of the braids that tried to contain it. I thought about the sight of my plain fat face in Betsy's mirror. If I turned over, if I blinked too long, if I so much as pursed my lips or took a deep breath, I would give myself away, so I just stared straight ahead, letting my eyes pool up with tears.

"He's your secret boyfriend?" I eventually managed to choke out. Maybe Caleb had been thinking about Nora the other day, when I'd watched him squinting up into the sky. "He's been your boyfriend all along?" I was trying to say something that wouldn't reveal that I felt like the floor was dropping out of the room, and I was about to slip into a deep, dark hole.

"Uh-huh!" Nora said. She turned her back to me, took the only pillow, balled it up under her head, and, as far as I could tell, fell asleep.

Five minutes or so later, I said, "Um, Nora?" and she didn't answer.

I didn't have it in me to try again. In fact, for a while, I was pretty sure I was going to throw up. Only I didn't throw up. I didn't move. I just lay there staring up at the ceiling, listening as Nora's breath became soft and even.

My parents were in the hospital now. I wondered if they were having X-rays taken. I'd only ever had them at the dentist, but I remembered how it felt to be under the lead blanket, sharp pieces of cardboard wedged into the soft places of my mouth.

I imagined Nora and Caleb walking away from me arm in arm, turning to say, "Are you *following* us?" I heard Caleb's voice saying, "Please, Gen—Nora and I never get to be alone." What had I been thinking? I'd thought he liked me. I must have misunderstood. Why had I let myself like him? Did he know I did? He probably did know, I thought, and thinking about that made me want to thrash and twist in the bed. Instead, I lay still as a stone so as not to wake Nora.

Just then, more than anything in the world, I wanted Ashley and Kristin nearby. I wanted to have my phone back.

I don't remember falling asleep, only Betsy shaking me awake in the morning. "Time for chores, my dear," she said. "Jezebel needs milking."

"Are my mom and dad okay?" I asked.

"Ron got in just after dawn," she said. "They're doing okay. Anders and Disa too."

Dressing next to Nora, everything she'd told me, everything that had happened, came back fresh. My hands shook so much I could barely get the buttons closed on my dress.

I walked back to our cabin through the woods, calling out "Hey bear" a few times and then "Stupid bear," and "Stupid, stupid bear" and "You dumb miserable bear, what were you thinking?" As I milked Jezebel, I lay my head against her side, and she kind of grunted. It was comforting, if you can believe that. I nuzzled her a little with my cheek (I knew better than to stop milking; she wouldn't like that very well), and I said to her, "You understand how much my life stinks, don't you, you big old girl?"

And then I thought, "Okay. I am talking to a cow."

And then I thought, "That would be pretty funny to text to Kristin and Ashley."

For a second, I wondered about the blog I'd seen so briefly. I thought about the eighty-four comments. What did all those people have to say? Did any of them understand how much all of this stank? I started trudging back to Ron and Betsy's. "Bear," I called, but I didn't have it in me to shout. "Bear," I whispered. "Bear. Bear." It didn't matter. The woods were empty. The people reading the blog Kristin made weren't real to me in any way that mattered. I was totally alone. Once I realized this, that no one cared where I went or what I did right then, I turned around and went home. I climbed the steps to the sleeping loft in our cabin, slid under the quilt, and fell back asleep.

For the next few days, while my mom and dad were in the hospital, Gavin and I elected to stay in the cabin by ourselves—with one of us running over to Betsy and Ron's house in the morning to get the latest report on our parents. We told Ron and Betsy it was easier that way to get to the corn, which was ready for picking, but really, it wasn't because of that. I had thought sleeping with Gavin was the worst thing that could ever happen to me, but now I knew that sleeping with Nora was even more horrific.

"Don't you want to see your friends?" Gavin said one night as he headed out to fish with Erik. "Ka or Caleb are probably just hanging around bored like you are."

I felt sick to my stomach at the very mention of Caleb, and Ka was not much better. What if she asked me about him?

"No thanks," I said, adding, "And I don't need social planning advice from my ten-year-old brother, either."

Mostly, what Gavin and I did together was deal with the corn.

The corn! It was ready. We ate corn every single night. First we ate it raw. It just seemed so much easier than figuring out how to light a fire in the stove and boil water and all that. We drank warm milk right out of the pail and crunched away on raw corn on the cob.

The next morning, we ate more corn and also some of the tomatoes. Ka came by with cheese her mom had made and a loaf of bread. We had bread and cheese for lunch, and then for dinner decided it was time to cook. Instead of boiling, we tried soaking ears of corn in water without shucking them and then putting the ears on the top of the hot stove. It wasn't very good but it was easy, and better than raw.

All day, we brought burlap sacks out to the cornfield and picked corn. Once the sacks got too heavy to carry, we brought them to the end of the row, and at the end of the day while I experimented with ways to cook corn, Gavin used the wheelbarrow to haul all the sacks over to a small silo next to the barn. It was starting to fill up.

Ron went back and forth to Laramie to visit my mom and dad and the Puchinskis in the hospital. He said they were doing better, but that they were taking steroids to help repair their lungs, which had received smoke damage.

Betsy stopped by to drop off some food and mentioned that in order to keep up with the daily trips to town, Ron had been up until two in the morning, working by moonlight in the field—and Betsy had been doing half his work on top of her own. After that, when Ron offered to bring us to see them, I said no. I knew he really couldn't spare the time, not to mention that Betsy or Nora would have to come over to our place to feed the chickens, milk Jezebel and clean out the stall—I didn't want them to have to do that either.

"If this was 1890 for real," Gavin asked, "would they have died?"

Ron had just had a haircut and you could see his bare, red scalp through the short spiky parts of his hair in the front. He sighed. He looked up at the sky—I knew he was trying to decide whether or not to be honest.

"Anders would probably be dead," he said. "And Disa, your mom, and your dad would have had respiratory problems for life. They might not have been able to work. Which back in 1890—before disability laws, Medicare, Social Security— would have meant you kids would have been put to work, or farmed out to relatives, or sent to live in an institution, and your parents would have had excruciatingly difficult times of it too."

"Wow," Gavin said.

Gavin was quiet a lot after that. When we were working together in the field, I wondered if he was thinking about what it would be like to have Anders die—or to have Mom and Dad not be able to breathe.

Friday afternoon, I was napping in the loft when I was woken by the sound of the van dropping my parents off. I could see them through a chink in the wall. (Chink in the wall? No wonder the bugs were bad.)

My mom stepped out and opened the door for my dad, who was in the front seat. I didn't realize until I saw the two of them that I'd been kind of holding my breath while they were gone.

Once they were inside the cabin, I could tell by the sounds they were making that they were unpacking stuff, which must have included some pills, because my mom said, "You'll need to make a chart or something to keep track of when you take all of these."

"Look," my dad said. "Someone washed all the dishes. Do you think it was Genevieve?"

"Somehow I doubt that," Mom said. That's when I leaned my head all the way over the edge of the loft, "I'm up here, you know," I said. "And I did wash them."

My dad was sitting down, a tin cup of water in front of him. He looked pale and there were about a half-dozen orange prescription bottles laid out in front of him on the table. My mom barely looked any better, but I didn't focus on her for very long because mostly I was staring at what she was pulling out of a plastic bag.

"*What is that?*" I asked as a breath of something I could not believe wafted up into the loft. Call me crazy, but I could have sworn I was smelling my favorite chipotle steak and cheese sandwich. From Quiznos. Quiznos is what we always get for takeout after my soccer games at home.

"It's food from town," my mom said.

I said, "Oh." And then, "Oh!" And then, "Do we get to *eat* it?"

It felt like this must be some kind of a trick. My mom passed Dad a bag of potato chips. He said, "This wasn't my idea."

"Okay," I said. "Mom?"

And then I was standing on the porch, calling, "Gavin! Gavin! Get in here!" and a few minutes later he came running, and he was like, "What?" until he saw Mom and Dad and then the bags on the table. My dad handed him a chip.

"How did you sneak it on the van past Ron?" Gavin asked.

"Ron knows," my mom said. She smiled a little, but then got serious again. "I told him we needed to visit the present day. And that we had to have a talk."

"A talk," I said. I hated to have talks. And I wasn't sure I could concentrate. The food smelled too good.

My mom raised her eyebrows at me. "Start eating," she said. "By all means. But once we're full, we need to decide for real whether we're going to stay here or leave. It won't be one person making the decision this time around. We're going to take a vote. And then at the next town meeting we'll tell everyone what our decision is going to be."

"Wow," I said, taking my first bite of sandwich. All I could think about was how delicious it was. The bread squished down to nothing. The meat was chewy and tender. And it was so . . .

so . . . salty! It was *totally* salty. Maybe almost too salty. But not quite. By the third bite, the salt was no longer even registering. I was back in heaven.

"I hope you take this decision seriously," my mom warned, but I couldn't answer her. My mouth was too full.

« 25 »

After the Quiznos meal—and our family vote—Gavin and I showed my mom and dad all the corn we'd brought in. We ate tomatoes out of the garden like they were apples.

"We should be preserving these," my mom said. "You get points for putting up preserves."

"Who cares?" my dad said. Mom shrugged.

The next morning, after chores and breakfast, we changed into our good clothes and left for the Sunday picnic. It was cold. The leaves were still full in the trees, but up on a mountain, I'd seen a tree with a swath of red where green should be. At first I thought there was something wrong with the tree—it couldn't possibly have changed color in the first week of August unless it was sick—but then I remembered how high up we were. This was a place where fall and winter came early. I'd once heard Nora say they could expect their first snowfall before October 15.

We ran into the Puchinskis on the path to Betsy and Ron's.

Anders was walking with a cane and stopping every now and then to take a breath out of an inhaler. Disa was walking slowly too. My mom told us that the doctors couldn't believe that Anders was going back to the farm after what he'd been through, but he'd insisted.

"Kids," Disa said to Gavin and me. "I've talked to your parents about this already but I especially want to thank you both as well. You all saved Anders's and my life. Gen—I heard what you did with the fire hose, and Gavin calling in on the sat phone. That was tremendous. Thank you."

Anders looked chagrined. "Gen," he said. "I'm especially sorry about all the things I said about you earlier. It's not really my place to judge."

It was so embarrassing to have him talk directly to us like that, all I could do was say, "Sure, no problem." Gavin put his head down.

Erik fell into step with Gavin as Ka came down the path to greet us.

"Your hair!" I said to Ka.

She put her hand up to her head. "Matt cut it."

"Why would you let him?"

"I lost a bet."

"It's so . . . so blond." It was short and spiky too. She looked great. And also a little bit like a boy. Like Matt.

"I'll dye it again when I move to Southern California so no one thinks I chose to become a soulless android," Ka said.

"Does your mom like it?"

"She likes that Matt cut it. She thinks it means we're bonding."

I knew better than to ask if they were.

"Do you think we're going to lose points because of the fire?" Erik asked us. He looked a little shell-shocked still. "My dad heard that the insurance guy said it was caused by improper cooling of the grindstone. He feels really horrible, like that makes it his fault."

"I don't think it's exactly a point earner," Ka said.

Erik laughed uncomfortably.

"We'll probably have to talk about it," Gavin said as gently as he could manage.

I didn't say what I really thought, which is that once my family announced the result of our vote to stay or go, the meeting would be all about that.

"Remember the first meeting?" Gavin said.

"I had to pee the whole time," I confessed. "But I didn't know how."

Gavin said, "I was still looking for the swimming pool."

"You thought there was going to be a *pool*?" Ka laughed.

Gavin shrugged. "There's always a pool when we go on vacation."

Erik whispered, "My dad thought we were going to be able to hunt."

"Like, with a gun?" I said.

"That's what they did on the real frontier. They ate a lot of meat."

"Wow," I said, looking sideways at Anders.

"I guess you guys wouldn't have been up for that," Erik said. "You won't even kill Pumpkin."

"That's right," Gavin said, and he looked kind of smug about the whole thing. "We won't."

. . .

As we walked into Ron and Betsy's yard, all thoughts of the fire, or Pumpkin, or our first meeting, or our family's decision flew from our minds, because here's what Ron and Betsy had in store for us: blinding, searing light.

The light was coming from three poles that looked like something you'd find at one of Gavin's Little League night games—bright shining panels filled with halogen bulbs whose rays you could see bugs swarming into. It was daytime now, but still, the lights cast an eerie glow over everything, like an alien spaceship about to suck Ron and Betsy's house into its tractor beam. We stood at the end of the benches shielding our eyes. Anders took a puff off his inhaler and my mom rocked back on her heels like she had been knocked off balance.

Betsy rushed over, holding her hands up at shoulder level and shaking them—in elementary school, our teachers made us do that instead of clapping. They called it "silent applause."

"Oh, dear, oh, dear," Betsy said, rolling her eyes. "This is so much more—big—than I'd imagined. I'm so sorry. Please try to ignore them. Just find a seat, find a seat. Behave normally."

My mom and dad, Anders, and Disa just stared at Betsy, like they didn't understand who she was. They were on a lot of medication, that was true—and feelings of confusion are a side effect. But I wasn't taking anything and I had no idea what was going on either.

"Betsy!" my mom exclaimed. "What is all this?" Anders was leaning in behind her.

"Oh, dear," Betsy repeated. "I'm so sorry. You see, we had to. We couldn't give up the chance."

"The chance for what?" my mom said.

"It's TV," Betsy whispered, as if she was telling us that a

friend was dying. "You see, they paid us a call just two days ago and said they wanted to do a story. They're amazing, these people, at coming in and setting up, there's practically a little village of vehicles behind the barn and they have all sorts of satellite dishes and . . . and . . . equipment." She laughed. "I can't believe I used to watch this show. I can't believe we're going to be on it."

"On what?" my mom said.

"Oh, of course, how silly of me not to say so right away." Betsy gave a little giggle, and then a squeal. "*The Happy Morning Show*," she said. "*The Happy Morning Show* wants to do a segment on us. Can you imagine? Something this huge?"

"*The Happy Morning Show*?" my mom said. "The news thing?"

"This is more of a lifestyle piece, I think," Betsy said. "Apparently someone on their staff found out about us and they want to do a profile of the camp as part of their summer vacation destination special." Betsy paused, bit her lip, and then smiled hopefully. "I suppose we are fairly unique." Anders's and my mom's silence was clearly making Betsy nervous. "You do know *The Happy Morning Show*, don't you?" she asked. "I used to watch it all the time."

My mom frowned. "I don't watch TV in the mornings," she said. "It's so obnoxious. Even in the hospital I had to make them turn it off in my room." I believed this. My mom is such a culture-phobe. I remember once when she asked me in front of a bunch of my friends, "Who is Justin Timberland?" Totally embarrassing.

"We don't even have it in the house," Anders grumbled. "And I had to make quite an effort to avoid TV in the hospital myself. I was trying to keep in the spirit of 1890 as best I could."

"I can't believe I'm telling *you* then." Betsy giggled. "But it's one of the highest-rated shows on television and they're *here*. I hate to intrude by bringing the present into our midst, but it's only one day, and it will be *such* great publicity. It's a chance for us to get the word out about what we're doing."

"You want the camp to be on TV?" Anders said. If Betsy had said she was planning to sell Nora into slavery, he could not have sounded more shocked.

Betsy giggled, nervous still, and smiled again. "Well, the whole thing has gone so fast! We just found out two days ago they were coming. They have some kind of humor angle—something about vacations turned upside down. They wanted to make sure that all the teenagers were going to be on hand, I remember that much."

"The teenagers?" my mother said.

"Oh, yes," Betsy said. "They asked very specifically for the names of all our teens—of Matt and Caleb and Nora and, well, you too, Gen. They asked specifically about you. Even Erik, Katie, and Ka," Betsy added.

For a second, I had a sense of foreboding. Maybe I knew what was going to happen, or guessed it in the part of my brain that is always working on worst-case scenarios, but doesn't necessarily get listened to by the part of my brain that keeps everything else under control.

"Of course we're hoping none of you will mention Gen's phone, or any of that unpleasantness."

"Of course," my mom said. Anders nodded.

"And one other little thing," Betsy added, leaning in specifically to my mom. "They seem to be asking a lot of questions about animals—they wanted to film someone slaughtering a chicken and show something cooked with chicken. It seems to be a bit of an obsession with them. Chicken this, chicken that. So I'm wondering, if you don't mind—well—" Betsy cleared her throat.

"What?" said my mom.

"Well," Betsy said. "If you could just not mention your views on Pumpkin. It would make it smoother for everyone. I don't want it to look like the experience—well—isn't entirely authentic. We want to really come off as genuine."

"You want us to lie?" Gavin said.

"No, no, of course not!" Betsy gasped in horror. Then she whispered an aside to my mother. "I mostly don't want it to seem as if we put any pressure on you to kill the bird. We didn't pressure you, did we?"

My mom raised her eyebrows.

"Okay, then," Betsy concluded. "Let's say we just don't bring it up."

I could see my mom put a vise grip on Gavin's shoulder. "Of course," she said. "We'd be happy to."

Gavin shook off her hand, and muttered to me, "I'll tell them I killed Pumpkin with my bare hands. I'll tell them I bit his head off with my own teeth. Would that make her happy?" Still squinting under the bright lights, he and I followed my mom and dad to our bench.

But before I sat down, I couldn't resist running over to Ka, who was sitting with her family. "*The Happy Morning Show*?" I said.

She pointed. "Look." And it was crazy: a woman in a miniskirt and thigh-high boots was applying powder to Ron's face with a brush just a little smaller than a feather duster.

Caleb leaned back from his seat in front of the Meyer-Hincheys. This was the first time I'd seen him since Nora told me he was her secret boyfriend. "This is so not 1890," he said, and it was like nothing had changed—he was still smiling and looking right at me, except now I understood what that look meant. It meant nothing.

He must have known that Nora told me about them. I wondered—did she tell him I had acted like it was no big deal? Or did she say, "She looked sick. And I don't think she slept at all the rest of the night." I felt my face burning just thinking about this, and I had to look down.

"Listen to this," he said. "The segment they're taping for is 'vacations turned upside down.'"

"I know," I said. "It's supposed to be funny. Instead of relaxing, people will pay to work."

"Gen?" he said, like there was something I wasn't getting. "Did you hear that they were asking specifically about the teenagers?"

"Yeah," I said.

"This means nothing to you?"

I have to admit, I was hardly listening to him. I couldn't stand to look up into his face. Even looking down, I could see his rolled-up cuffs on his shirt, his big hands, the tanned and strong muscles of his forearms.

I felt his hand on my shoulder. He used his forefinger and thumb of his other hand to lift my chin up and I had to stare into his almond-shaped eyes—full of mischief as always. Was I just part of his mischief? Did he enjoy making me like him— was that some kind of sick I'm-bored-at-Camp-Frontier trick? Suddenly I was angry. "Hey," he said. "Are you okay?"

It was so horrible to feel him touching me, because it felt so right and so good and I had to keep from hurling myself at him and punching him in the face. I had never really believed I would feel this way about anyone—this mad and glad—and now that I was feeling it, I didn't like it. I liked his hand on my arm, but I knew he could keep it there only so long before I put my hand on his arm too. What would he do then? Explain gently that he didn't like me? That he and Nora were finally admitting to their secret relationship? Ugh. I didn't think I could stand it.

But then he started in on what had to be that speech anyway. "Gen," he said. "It's better if you know now. I just want to make sure it doesn't take you by surprise. That might be really hard."

No surprise could be worse than what he was about to say. "I—," I started. All that mattered was I interrupt him. "I already know all about it."

"You already know?" he said. "Really? And you didn't tell me?" He dropped his hand. I hoped at once that he'd put it right back, and also that he would leave me alone. I hoped both those things at the same time, which is totally insane, but there you have it. I didn't feel like I was making sense anymore, just trying not to do something incredibly dumb. I had to walk away from him even as, inexplicably, he was saying, "Aren't you going to give me the details of how you heard?" What did he want, I thought, an outline describing how much it hurt to learn that he and Nora had been a secret couple all summer while I'd been thinking he liked me?

I wished, looking back, that I had understood what he really meant. But I just walked to my family's bench and sat down.

Ron started the meeting, and except for the makeup and the lights, it felt almost normal. The TV people stood behind their cameras and so close to the lights, it hurt to look at them, and that made it feel almost like they weren't there. After a while I stopped paying attention to where they were or what they were doing.

"First things first," Ron began. "Betsy and I wanted to celebrate Anders, Disa, Doug, and Cheryl's homecoming. They are all recovering nicely, and I think it's a testament to the strength of what we're doing here that they have returned to camp." There was applause.

In his makeup, Ron looked like the kids in the school play who come out from backstage at the end of the production so they can go for ice cream with their parents, the boys still in eyeliner and the girls with huge lips and pancake makeup on their foreheads.

"I think we should also note their heroism. Anders and Disa could have left the mill to burn but selflessly they did everything they could to keep the fire from spreading. Wildfires were serious business on the frontier in 1890 and they are serious business now. The fire service loses men and equipment fighting blazes every year. By clearing a ring around the mill, Anders and Disa were able to keep the fire at bay long enough for us to get the hose. Thank you for your good show." Anders and Disa bowed their heads. There was more applause.

"But of course by now we all know the story of what happened, how both Anders and Disa collapsed and might have been seriously harmed if not for the intervention of their closest neighbors, Cheryl and Doug, who without a doubt saved Anders's and Disa's lives by pulling them to safety—at great personal risk to themselves."

Again, there was applause, and now it was time for my mom and dad to modestly hang their heads. "One thing that the frontier teaches us is self-reliance," Ron went on. "We do things here that we—none of us—came out here thinking we could do. We live without modern conveniences. We adjust our diet and what we expect of our children.

"But something else happens to us out on the frontier. We come to rely more on each other," Ron continued. "We see a fire and we know that if the people who are stuck inside the burning building are going to get out of it, we will need to help them. Even children know this.

"Before the fire, I think our camp had hit a low point. We had lost our way. Instead of giving ourselves over to the experience of the frontier, we were fighting it. It's an interesting contrast, isn't it, that we were so afraid of the experience of the frontier that we were willing to do anything to get away from it, but when it comes to something that should truly strike fear into our hearts, such as running into a burning building—our fear is gone, and we find the strength to become heroes?"

I elbowed Gavin. When a grown-up says "We find the strength to become heroes," there's always going to be a part of me that wants to say, "Um . . . gag me?"

Across the aisle, Nora was sitting on her hands and rocking slightly. I couldn't see her face because the sides of her bonnet were blocking it, but I remember what she'd said the other night, about how it feels to think that you are growing up in a bubble and you don't know anything about the real world. Would Caleb send her e-mails over the winter? Would she find a way to break into the locked-up electricity shack so they could IM? Would he visit her here? In the snow?

"In another order of business," Ron went on, "I want to introduce you to Rebecca Cheney, who is here with *The Happy Morning Show*, producing a segment about our camp. Do you all know *The Happy Morning Show*?" Everyone nodded their heads. "Yes," Ron said. "Rebecca told me you all would know it."

A woman I hadn't seen yet stepped out from behind the lights. She was wearing a pencil skirt, high-heeled shoes, and a white starched shirt open at the collar. Her hair was blow-dried into almost impossibly casual perfection—it swooped over her ears, hugged her neck, then flared out again at her shoulders. When she smiled at us, the two-bazillion-watt stadium lights shining down on us were nothing compared to her inner glow. Her smile made you feel not that she must have been a cheer-leader in high school, but like you *yourself* were a cheerleader in high school. Even if, like me, you haven't even started high school. Then she stopped smiling and it was like the lights dimmed and the air cleared, and I was left thinking, "What just *happened* to me?"

"They're giving us some really wonderful publicity," Ron went on. His tone was hesitant, more hopeful than credulous. "They're showing off all the hard work you do, and the amazing transfor-mation that takes place while you are here. The crew arrived yes-terday. We hope that you will welcome them, answer Rebecca's questions, but also that you will ignore them and go about your business." He grimaced at this point, glancing back at the sta-dium lights. "Well," he added, "as much as you can."

Rebecca waved at us, smiled again, and I noticed her dimples. I touched my own face, wondering idly if there was surgery or exercises that could make dimples grow on my cheeks too. "I'm so glad to be here," she said. Her voice was deep and serious, but you had the feeling that if she needed to, she could sing you to sleep, there was so much sweetness lurking behind it.

Then my dad was suddenly standing and I forgot about Rebecca. "Yes, Doug?" Ron said.

"Before we start in on the show, I wanted to say that my family has been having discussions and there is something we want to say to the group," he began.

"Okay," said Ron.

Betsy fluttered her hands at shoulder height—nervous again. "Just remember, cameras are rolling," she said.

My dad nodded. "What we want to say, first of all, is thanks to Ron and Betsy for helping our family out over the last few days. Ron has been back and forth to the hospital. They both have been checking on the kids, making sure they have enough to eat."

Everyone was looking at my dad, except me. I was watching Rebecca Cheney where she stood behind the lights. I could see the cameras on either side of her too, their lenses closing and opening and moving at her slightest signal. She directed them with her hands—using different motions to show when she wanted a close-up, a pan, a shot of the group that pulled out wide.

"I have to admit—," my dad went on. I glanced at my mom. She was staring at my dad as if she was concentrating really hard. I don't think she was even aware that I was watching her. "—this whole experience has been exhausting," he said. "I've been pushed past my limit mentally, physically—" He looked down at my mom. "Emotionally." She lifted her hand up and he grasped it. "I have to tell you all that on the night of the fire, I was ready to leave. Some members of our family were at that point before we even arrived." He laid a hand on my shoulder. "And as you all know, we've had our ups and downs." He chuckled. That was the old dad. "I guess mostly you've seen the downs." There was an appreciative laugh. "I won't go into detail. But I want to let you all know that we sat down as a family and reevaluated our commitment to this place. We don't want to be here if we're only going through the motions. Not anymore."

My mom nodded her head. "That's right," she agreed.

"But before I tell you what we've decided to do, I just want to say that as much as I may have felt alone out here, after the fire I realized I was not. And to me, that is a good thing. Thank you."

I think it was Anders Puchinski who started to clap. Or maybe it was Caleb's mom, Susan, who didn't look any less haggard than she had in previous weeks. But pretty soon they— we—were all clapping, while Ron and Betsy were beaming up front. Ron had eyes only for my dad, like he was his prize pupil. I caught Ka's attention and she grimaced at the Goody Two-Shoes-ness of the moment. Betsy, on the other hand, lived for Goody Two-Shoes moments and she was smiling with customary exuberance.

Rebecca Cheney alone was not clapping or smiling. She was standing perfectly still, the warmth in her expression gone. Her sharp eyes were moving from the cameras to my dad's face, to Ron's, to Betsy's, and then strangely, they kept coming back to me.

My mom's back had become straighter. Gavin was sitting

stock-still. I was waiting too—what would happen when my dad announced our decision? Would there be cheers? Boos?

I wasn't going to find out. Because before my dad could speak, before the applause had fully died, Rebecca Cheney made her move. Looking at her watch and then raising her eyebrows as if she wasn't thrilled with how late it was, she said to Ron, "If we're going to have enough time, I think I'd better get started."

"Oh, of course," said Ron, looking flustered. "Doug, hold that thought—"

While Dad looked confused, Rebecca signaled her crew to direct the cameras at her. She opened her mouth into an O shape, rubbed her forefinger and thumb in the corners of her lips to remove any collected lipstick, raised a microphone to her chin, nodded at the camera, and began.

"I'm standing right now at a much-talked-about vacation destination—one that several weeks ago no one had heard of. Those of you who have been getting the e-mail forwards, who have joined social network groups, who have participated in our online search will know what I am talking about. In fact, I think it would be safe to say that the only people in the country who have no idea how famous this place is are the people here—cut off as they are out here in the middle of Wyoming, a satellite dish or an Internet connection not to be found."

I couldn't help but smirk, wondering what Rebecca would say if she knew half the children had been listening to music on their iPods two weeks before.

"Yes, you may have guessed by now, but I'll give you a few clues," Rebecca went on. "I'm standing, well, not exactly up to my knees in mud"—the ground was bone dry—"but in a barnyard for sure. I've seen cows being milked, butter being churned . . . all the while seeking the answer to the question of the hour, which is, 'Where is Gen?'"

For a second, I didn't remember that Gen was my name. I know this sounds dumb, but it's true. I looked around like maybe I'd see whatever Rebecca meant by the word "Gen," and she could be done.

But then, on a level below consciousness, I started to panic. I could feel the cameras fixing on me. *Gen,* I remember thinking. This might have something to do with me.

Meanwhile, Rebecca was still talking. "Our favorite blogger who has milked and weeded her way into the hearts of thousands has, in the last two weeks—even as her blog has gone viral—completely disappeared. Her fans are going crazy, and some are starting to wonder about the nature of the camp. " I watched in stunned silence as Rebecca made a big deal out of checking an index card she was holding in her hand. "Maybe—some fans have speculated—the jokes were actually more serious than Gen could have known. We've been warned to be on the lookout for . . ." She was reading now. "Physical therapists turned identity thieves, aspiring cult leaders, grizzly-bear wrestlers, foreign spies, unemployable morticians, government workers from Area 51." Putting the list away, she laughed. "This is good stuff." She walked across the grass at a clip, careful not to let her heels sink into the ground. She smiled at me like I'd just won the lottery. "But here we are, and here, without further ado, is Gen. Gen?" she said.

With her microphone pointed directly into my face, it was impossible not to understand that she was talking to me. "What do you think, Gen?" she said. She was standing so close, I could see the line where her makeup ended and her neck began. "Do you like surprises?"

I stared and said nothing. "Because, darling, you're famous! And the question the entire country is asking is, 'Are you okay?'"

"Um," I said, shielding my eyes from the lights that were now shining directly at me. Green squares floated in my vision, and for a second I worried I was going to pass out. I was very, very warm. "I'm fine?" I said.

The truth is, I don't like surprises. In fact, I kind of hate them. "Um," I said again, still squinting. This felt like being called on in class when you don't know the answer—but a million times worse. "I think I'm okay," I tried again.

But I wasn't okay. And I wouldn't be until Rebecca turned the lights and the cameras off. What could I possibly do to make all of this go away?

« 26 »

Nothing. I could do nothing to make all of this go away. No matter how determined I was to ignore her, Rebecca was still there, talking into her microphone, pretending that she was telling me a story, but really speaking to all the people who were theoretically going to watch the show.

"The company that hosts the blog keeps track of how many people visit your site each day," she was explaining. "The first day your blog was up three people visited it. A week after that, it was regularly visited by about fifty. The day before you stopped updating it, there were twenty thousand visits, and last week, after we ran a brief piece on it, it hit five hundred thousand. Everyone wants to know where you are."

"Wow," I said. I rubbed my eyes to make the green spots go away.

Rebecca again pulled out the piece of paper from her pocket. "Listen to this, Gen," she said, smiling and shaking her head. "There are nineteen thousand registered members of the Facebook group 'Save Pumpkin.'"

"What?" I said.

Rebecca's eyebrows shot up. "The rooster?" she confirmed. I nodded. "There's been a lot of discussion on your blog about whether you ought to be killing and eating him. Nineteen thousand say no. Isn't that fun?"

"Nineteen thousand?" I said. I wasn't taking it in.

"They all know about Pumpkin because of your blog," Rebecca said again.

"Her what?" Betsy said. "Her frog?" I could see her now, beyond the lights. Her hands were flapping on either side of her face, double time. She looked like someone at a revival meeting.

"It's not even my blog," I said. "My friend Kristin made it. It was a project for her computer class. She used my texts."

"Well, Gen, I'm telling you, people love it," Rebecca said.

Okay, I thought, but I didn't get much further than that. Okay, I thought again. "Are you sure there hasn't been some kind of a mistake?" I said.

I looked behind me, but the only people I saw were the familiar faces of the Camp Frontier families. Could they help me? What did they know about blogs? As I looked around, though, it dawned on me that they were all *in* the blog. The Meyer-Hincheys, with their sibling dynamic issues now made public. Susan Driver—I'd compared her to a dog just back from the groomer's. I'd mocked Peter Driver's s-l-o-w Southern accent. And the Puchinskis! Good Lord. They could now thank me that five hundred thousand people knew Anders had burned like a lobster and Disa's muffins had made everyone think she was a mutant brownnoser from day one.

As these thoughts were twisting and percolating in my head,

other thoughts must have been twisting and percolating in Betsy's. "So that's . . . ," she said slowly, stepping toward Rebecca like she was finally figuring out how two mental-puzzle pieces fit together. "That's why *The Happy Morning Show* is so interested in stories about animals at the camp?" She looked at me. "It was because of Pumpkin? And everything you wrote about this camp? And I suppose you were unhappy here, so you were—" She paused for a second to separate herself from the word she was about to use. "You were venting?"

Her eyes grew wide with horror as the cameras zoomed in on her. She was oblivious to them. "Oh, gosh, Gen," she nearly wailed. "What did you say?" She turned to Rebecca. "You must think we are terrible fools! This isn't going to be any kind of publicity we want. This is going to be public humiliation on TV." She paused for a second, then gasped for air like someone who has been brought back from drowning. "My mother watches *The Happy Morning Show*. My sisters. Oh, no, no, no."

Everyone started talking at once. Ron was comforting Betsy. Anders was shouting at Rebecca, "Turn those darn cameras off!" Susan Driver was demanding to know whether anyone had signed a release allowing themselves to be filmed for television. Ka was looking right at me, her eyes open wide, slowly shaking her head in sympathy. My mom was hissing, "Gen, this was a project? This was something Kristin did for her computer class?" And my dad was saying, "If she can put it up there, she can take it off. This isn't right. You need to get her to take it down."

Nora was storming across the benches toward me, yelling, "You did it again, Gen!"

"This isn't my fault!" I shouted back. "You blame me for

everything. And it's just because you're the one who hates it here. All I'm doing is saying what you're thinking, and instead of admitting it, you try to turn everyone against me. And I'm sick of it."

"Girls, girls," Rebecca interrupted, raising two fingers to her crew in a gesture I realized later was a signal to turn the cameras off. "This is not good. We're not taping for Dr. Phil." She laughed.

"Do you know what I would love to see from you two though? I wonder if you could reenact the cow-milking incident. You know, Gen, when you pretend you know how to milk a cow? Nora, do you think you could do that for me? I'd love to get both of you in makeup first, of course. And I wonder, do you girls have any clothes that are a little cleaner . . . I suppose we should be grateful viewers can't smell you through the TV." She laughed her I-go-out-to-dinner-in-New-York-City laugh, which made it just so much worse that I probably smelled like pee and had bean stains on the front of my dress.

"Are there really five hundred thousand people reading my blog?" I asked. "They like it?"

"Like it?" Rebecca said. "They love it. Young lady, there are going to be book publishers falling all over themselves to get you into print, maybe even a movie. If you have anywhere near decent grades, this will be your ticket to Harvard. Yale. Whatever you like. You're a writer, my dear, and a famous one at that. All before your fourteenth birthday.

"After this, with your parents' permission I'll whisk you away for some interviews and meetings with literary agents and the like."

"Will we—" I hardly wanted to name it because it was too

good to be true. "Will we stay in a hotel? With room service and indoor plumbing?"

Rebecca nodded vigorously and smiled at whatever expression had appeared on my face.

I had an image of me, standing in Times Square, which I have only ever seen on TV. In the image, I was wearing a big fancy hat and signing autographs. I thought about what it would feel like to have my English teacher stop in the middle of a lesson to say, "Gen? What does our very own real-life author have to say about this book?" I imagined myself in a pencil skirt like Rebecca's. A good feeling had begun to creep into my body slowly, like sleep when you're lying in bed, tired, waiting for it.

Nora interrupted my reverie. "There's no way you're filming me, and I'm not doing anything else to help Gen Welsh become a celebrity," she said. "She doesn't know the first thing about this place. She's a huge fake and has wanted nothing but to ruin it the whole time she'd been here."

"And what about you?" Rebecca said, turning to Nora now, signaling for the cameras to turn back on. "Don't you hate it even more? Didn't you say that if you had your choice, you'd put pesticide in the drinking water? Didn't you say that time and place is important and you are missing out on the life you're supposed to have?"

"Nora!" Betsy said, pain drawing her voice down to a whisper.

"You said those things?" Ron choked out.

Nora blanched. Then her face turned gray. I felt an absurd kind of sympathy for her, understanding what it felt like to cause my own parents pain.

But then Nora looked at me, her steely blue eyes snapping,

and my sympathy vanished in the face of her anger. "Thank you," she spat out. "Thank you for ruining everything in a way I hadn't even imagined you could. The first time I met you, you made fun of me for helping my mother make dolls," she went on. "You tried to turn my friends here against me. You lied to me. You accused me of things I didn't do. It was your phone that got all of us in trouble and nearly wrecked the whole camp. And now you've hurt my parents by putting something I shared with you in confidence into your blog. You're nothing but a chicken-loving phony. Go home, why don't you. Or off to some fancy hotel. No one wants you here."

"That's not fair—," I began, but even as I tried to think of why, I knew that some of what she had said was right. Before I could figure out what that part was, I heard a voice ringing out somewhere behind me. When I turned, Gavin was standing on a bench, trying to get everyone to look at him.

His little face was almost pointy with worry. "Listen!" he shouted. "I have something to say!"

Rebecca made a gesture to the cameras, which turned on him—everyone's gaze followed. "You wanted to know about Pumpkin," he announced, and it was hard not to see that he had become a different person from the time we got here to now. Also, that he was trying to be solemn and not to smile, but it was basically impossible. "I will tell you right now we cannot kill Pumpkin," he said. "Pumpkin . . ." He paused. "We kill roosters because they can't lay eggs. But Pumpkin is not a rooster." He waited for that information to sink in. "He has never been a rooster. Pumpkin is a hen. And he—I mean she—is about to become a mom."

There was absolute silence.

I could do nothing but stare. At Gavin. Where in the world did he get the presence of mind to speak up to the whole world, in front of the TV cameras and lights, no less?

And then I was thinking, "What is he talking about? How has he changed Pumpkin from a rooster into a hen?"

Rebecca Cheney's face was alive with interest. She fast walked over to Gavin, still careful about her heels, sticking the microphone in his face now.

"What happened?" she said. The stationary TV cameras moved in to get a close-up.

"Well," Gavin said, puffing up with pride, not unlike a rooster himself. "It's just that there's a long time after they're born when you can't tell if a chicken is a rooster or a hen, and I think Ron and Betsy had thought Pumpkin was turning into a rooster—I read online that in the beginning it's pretty easy to be wrong. Betsy hadn't really seen much of him. He was living all by himself at our place before we even got here."

"But you knew?" Rebecca said. "You did rooster research before you got here?"

"No," Gavin said. "I didn't care about chickens at all before I arrived. I was only interested when I was looking for a way to save Pumpkin's life. I had a suspicion he—I mean she—wasn't really a rooster," he said. "In fact, I was pretty sure she was laying. We were getting too many eggs for it to have been Daisy alone. I remember Betsy saying that if you want to get a hen to sit on her eggs, you can put fake ones in the place where she likes to lay and she might take the hint. So I whittled fake eggs from wood and stuck them in Pumpkin's box and it worked."

"A broody rooster," said Nora, shaking her head in disbelief.

"When?" said Betsy. "When did she start sitting?"

"It wasn't too long after we got here. Maybe it was the day after the first town meeting? Or that night. I did everything at night when I could sneak into the barn."

"You're lucky," Betsy said, shaking her head at the coincidence. "You can only move eggs under a broody hen at night. Did you candle the eggs?"

"Yes," said Gavin, nodding his head dutifully. What the heck was candling? I wondered. "I read about that online."

"Good," Betsy said, and she put her hands together in a single clap. "Then you'll have chicks!" She counted backward, under her breath. "Any day now. Are you hearing peeping?"

"Yes," said Gavin. "It's crazy peeping."

"That means they're almost ready," Betsy said.

"See?" Gavin said. "See why you should have listened to me about killing her?"

"But . . . ," Betsy sputtered. "I didn't know . . ." And suddenly Gavin's face fell a little. I guess it wasn't as fun to make your point with a dramatic flourish when the enemy you're vanquishing is somebody's bubbly mother who fed you cookies when your parents were in the hospital, and is also maybe the only person in the world as into raising chickens as you are.

"Why did you wait so long to tell us?" my mom asked.

"Because if you knew," he said, "it just would have been another chicken who had to die—Daisy or Romeo or one of the others." And suddenly my mom was hugging Gavin, and Betsy's face twisted into a look of such happiness and pain, I didn't know what to think anymore.

Rebecca did, though. Her fingers were flying—she was signaling one of the cameras up onto Gavin and my mom, another to circle the crowd. Rebecca herself moved in with her microphone. "What do you mean, Gavin, when you say you went online?" Her voice was sly.

Gavin's face contorted immediately into an expression of panic. He looked all around, as if seeking help from the trees, from Erik, from Mom and Dad. Eventually, his eyes rested on Betsy.

"I'm sorry," he said. "I looked up all the information when Nora let us into the electricity shack that time."

"The electricity shack?"

"Now, I don't know—," Betsy started.

"Don't bother," I said. "I wrote about it in the blog."

She looked at me hard. "What exactly did you write?"

. There was no point in trying to cover it up. She could read it for herself. So I told her. About finding Nora listening to my iPod and surfing the web. About how we drank Diet Coke and passed around deodorant and lip gloss and looked through everyone's bag of contraband modernity.

"I knew we should have torn that place down," Ron said. "I knew it would get us into trouble, just like that time I used Roundup."

"You used Roundup?" Anders asked, able to communicate his shock in spite of his smoke-damaged larynx and lungs.

"Actually, I wrote about that too," I said.

"And the whole world knows?" Betsy said. "The whole world knows this already?" Betsy took a deep breath. She held it for a minute, during which everyone in camp was perfectly still. Then she broke down. "We're going to be ruined!" she said. "This is terrible!" She pulled out a lacy white handkerchief and blew her nose. Ron put an arm around her back with all the tenderness he would have used in laying a hand on a table or a chair. I had to wonder, at what point would he break down and give the woman a real hug?

"Sorry," Betsy said. "It's just that with the bills and the taxes and Nora going to college soon, I don't see how we're going to make it out here without something good happening and I'd so hoped that being on *The Happy Morning Show* would be the good thing we need."

How was it that I, an ordinary thirteen-year-old girl from the suburbs looking for nothing more than a summer spent shuttling between soccer camp and the rec-center pool—how had I done something this enormously terrible? Nora was right. I had ruined everything—everyone's vacation, her family's livelihood, and now, apparently, her chance at a college education.

I remembered what it felt like to want to hang Robby Brainerd by his ankles after I caught him throwing frogs at the slide in fourth grade. I'd known even then that for the rest of my life I'd be remembered as the girl who hung Robby by his ankles—and I have been—but at the time, I felt I had no choice but to save the frogs. Now heat was rising into my face, my fists were clenching of their own accord. I could feel it coming over me, the feeling that I had to take action. I was powerless to stop myself.

I tried to call to mind the image of myself in Times Square, signing autographs in a fancy hat, but it was already fading. I fantasized about what it would be like to walk through the doors of my school and have everyone know I was famous. I'd be a hero. But even that felt unreal. And wrong.

Then an idea came to me instantly. It was so obvious and also so simple, I knew I'd found the right answer.

"Susan?" I said to Caleb's mom. "They can't use any of the footage from today if I say no, can they?"

"Not unless you've signed a release," she said. "If they release the footage without your authorization you would have standing to seek an injunction and damages in a court of appropriate jurisdiction."

"You're saying they can't do it?"

"Basically, yes."

I turned to face Rebecca, though this was scary and a hard thing to do. "I won't be on your show," I said. "I won't go back to New York with you. And I'm going to make Kristin take the blog down."

It was amazing, when you are only thirteen years old, to have this kind of reach, to be strong and good when only moments before you'd felt yourself buried under a slag heap of everyone else's collective scorn.

"Nora's right," I said. "The blog is a lie. In spite of everything I wrote, I don't hate it here. In fact, I think I've come to like it. At home, we go around in our own separate worlds. My mom takes care of us, I play soccer, Gavin does who knows what, and my dad goes to work. Here, we were forced to be together and though it wasn't always fun, we got to know each other. At home, I won't let my little brother into my room, but out here, he's kind of been my best friend.

"I don't know very many thirteen-year-old girls who go a

whole day—or even a whole hour—without checking them-selves out in the mirror, but I've been pretty much mirror-free for a month and a half. I know I look disgusting. I know I smell kind of funky, and that you can tell what I ate for dinner in the past week just by looking at my dress. But I have a better sense of who I am right now than I do any day of the week back home.

"Okay, I really can't stand doing the dishes. It still grosses me out every single time. I may never be able to pull another weed again after those first few weeks we spent in the corn. I still haven't gotten used to the outhouse and I don't think at this point that I will. My reunion with indoor plumbing is going to be a happy one, let me tell you.

"But you know? Before you interrupted him, my dad was going to make an announcement. He was going to share the results of our family's vote on whether we should stay here at the camp or go. And not that it matters now, but I want you all to know that we voted to stay.

"Because Ron is right. You feel strong here. You do things you didn't know you could. And it's beautiful. Nora, you have no idea how ugly the rest of the world is compared to this place—there's nothing uplifting about neighborhoods filled with minivans and houses and families and their dogs.

"What I was saying before, about how this place makes you stronger. That's true. I am stronger for coming here. I am strong enough that I know that I want to finish what I set out to do.

"It is not fair that Ron and Betsy and Nora should have their lives wrecked. The blog, *Happy Morning*—it just isn't right."

I took a deep breath. I noticed that everyone had been listen-ing. Some people, like Caleb's mom, Susan, and Disa Puchinski, were looking me right in the eye. Others, like Anders and Ka's stepdad, Clark, stared at the ground.

I don't know exactly what I expected to happen now that I was done talking. Applause? Cheering? I'd talked longer just then than I ever had before in my life, including the time in fifth grade when Kristin and I had traded stanzas reciting "The Midnight Ride of Paul Revere" for our elementary school's poetry festival.

But there was nothing. Just silence. I had the panicky sensation that no one had heard me, or if they had, they'd not understood. Maybe I'd spoken in tongues? What had I even said? I couldn't remember. Something about strength. I think I'd mentioned Gavin. Had the cameras been on the whole time?

"Turn off the camera," I said to Rebecca. She signaled to the crew and they moved away from the machines, covering the lenses.

"And the lights." At another signal, they went dark.

Rebecca put her hand out and I shook it. "I respect your decision," she said. "We got a lot of great footage, so if you change your mind, let me know."

"I'm not changing my mind," I said.

It wasn't until she was walking away that I realized what I had done. And I know this goes against everything I'd just said about strength and resolve, but I wanted badly for a second to call her back, to tell her I'd only been kidding.

Had I really just given up the chance to stay in a hotel with a real bed and bathroom where everything was completely clean? I'd chosen an outhouse and a smelly cabin, weeks more of my mother's beans? Watching Nora and Caleb be secret boy- and girlfriend while I hauled corncobs from the field to the barn every single day?

I watched as Rebecca walked over to Ron and Betsy. I assumed that she was going to apologize. Or say good-bye. I wasn't actually listening, and then, all of a sudden, I was. Because the words coming out of her mouth didn't sound like an apology or a good-bye. They sounded, in fact, like quite the opposite.

"I have great news for you," she was saying. "And also great publicity, if that's what you're looking for. You see, we were really excited about Gen's story. It's already rocked the country and has a great fan base, but even before she made it clear she wasn't interested in being on TV, I was pitching another idea—not for *Happy Morning*. Something bigger and cooler than that—something I thought the network might like for prime time."

It wouldn't be honest for me not to admit right then and there that I was kind of annoyed. I mean, I'd turned down being on TV. I'd made the ultimate sacrifice. What more was out there?

"From the beginning," Rebecca went on, "reading Gen's blog, we knew we had a fantastic profile on our hands. And it has borne out—we have not been disappointed. I mean, reluctant girl on family vacation at frontier fantasy camp? Yes, that plays well. But reluctant girl *living* at frontier fantasy camp? Sneaking out of the house to listen to strangers' iPods? Looking up new technology on the web so she can find out how the rest of the world lives? That's pathos. That's fascinating. That . . ." She paused, and for a second I felt like she was actually expressing something that belonged to her, something she cared about, not just something she was trying to trick into betraying itself on camera. "That is Nora. That," she repeated, "is good TV."

All eyes were turned on Nora now. Her parents looked as horrified as they had when I was confessing about the blog. Or more horrified—if that was possible.

Nora, however, looked as if the hand of an angel had passed across her face. Her seemingly permanent scowl lifted, replaced by an expression of wonder and joy so obvious, one might have thought her incapable of experiencing anything but those two emotions.

"In fact," Rebecca went on, "it goes beyond a segment on this show. From the beginning, I've been pitching the network a couple of ideas. The lazy, obvious one would be about Gen and the blog. But the other is for a show for Nora alone.

"What's great about the Nora idea is that it would be playing out in real time. So much of what Gen's blog tells us has already happened, but with Nora, we could build a show around some kind of ongoing project. Perhaps it would be introducing this girl to the real world? Helping her realize her dream of going to college? I got the approval just before our taping began this morning. Starting today, with Nora's permission, I'll be producer and host of my very own reality show based on a year in Nora's life."

"Me?" Nora squealed. I didn't know she had such a girly squeal in her. "I'm going to be on TV?"

"Yes, you," Rebecca said, flashing Nora a brilliant smile. "We were going to speak to your parents—and you—later this afternoon. Basically, our offer is this, and of course you don't have to accept if you feel the publicity would be too damaging for you or your family's business. But we'd like to profile your family life here—the good, the bad, and the ugly—and then whisk you away for a week on the town in New York, capturing your reaction to big, glitzy city life and well, frankly, all of modernity in a show we are sure our viewers will love. We have this idea to structure the show as a college tour road trip—each episode will feature some of your life here and college visits across the country. But more than college too. There will be parties, career shadowing, shopping sprees, massages. Don't answer now. Talk to your parents and let me know."

I was glad no one was looking at me anymore because, like Nora, I could no longer hide how I felt. I had refused the TV and I'd meant it. I didn't want to be part of it. But to have Nora be on the show instead of me? To have her be so clearly delighted by the prospect of one more thing she had stolen from me? I mean, did she have to have everything?

Without thinking about it too much, I found myself glancing at Caleb. He was looking at Nora in openmouthed amazement.

And Nora? Did she appreciate how great it was to have Caleb's undivided attention? Was she staring back at him, sharing the absurdity of this moment? Did she even understand that it was absurd?

She wasn't. She didn't. She had eyes for Rebecca and Rebecca only—for the twenty-first century, the future, her new and improved life.

"You want this?" Ron asked, his voice cracking.

"New York City is awful," Betsy warned. "The crowds. Everyone pushing. The buildings are so tall, you can't see the sun. And you'll be homesick."

It was obvious, though, what Nora's answer would be. Her cheeks were flushed red now, her eyes opened wide with delight and surprise. "Are you kidding?" she said. "Just tell me where to sign."

"Come on," my dad said, putting a protective arm around me and one around my mom. "I think it's time we all went home." Strange to believe that by home, he meant a closet-size cabin filled with mosquitoes and smelling of mildew where we had not yet—except for the Quiznos—enjoyed a single satisfying soup to nuts meal.

As we were leaving, Caleb touched my elbow and slipped something into my hand. It was my phone. "How did you get this?" I said.

"Before the meeting I asked Nora if I could use it to make a call."

"That's it?" I said. "You just asked?"

"She knew where Ron was keeping it."

"Wow," I said.

And while my mom was gathering up the picnic basket I whipped behind a tree and wrote the first thing that came into my mind.

```
Week 8 - Sunday
11:17 am
I'm alive! Erase the blog, k? Will explain
later.
What's with 500,000 readers? XXOO Gen.
```

I could still hear Nora squealing with delight.

« 27 »

As if by silent agreement, none of us mentioned what had happened with the blog and TV and the meeting when we got back to the cabin. We sat down at the table with the picnic basket and we all ate. My dad took some pills. My mom boiled water. And then Gavin slunk away, who knew where, until he came running back red faced and shouting for us to come see.

"It's starting!" he shouted. "One of Pumpkin's chicks! It's starting to hatch!"

"Really?" my mom said.

Forgetting the meeting and the TV show, we all ran.

And when we got to the barn, there indeed, in a box tucked away in a corner of an unused stall, was Pumpkin, sitting on a pile of eggs sunk down into the straw. She'd sort of shifted her body off some of them, and one of the exposed eggs was rocking slightly. It was also cracked along one side. The crack was wide enough that you could see a kind of rubbery, almost clothlike second layer inside. I'd always thought a chick used its beak to poke through the shell, but it was pushing against the egg in random directions with every part of its body. It seemed like it was panicking, struggling out of fear more than out of any sense that it needed to break through something. It was chirping a lot too, and I wondered if that was a baby chick's way of screaming for help.

"It's freaking," I said.

"Shush," said Gavin, but he sounded like he was talking to the chick, not me.

"What do we do next?" my mom said. "When it comes out? I think it's important for them to stay warm, right?"

"I don't know," said Gavin. "I didn't think that far ahead."

"Here," I said, pulling the phone out of my pocket and passing it to my mom. She looked scared.

"You can use it to go online," I prompted, and she took it in her hand.

"You've been going online?" she said.

"No," I said. "It costs extra, and I knew you'd see the charges."

My mom shook her head, and started to press buttons. Then she handed the phone right back. "I don't even know how to turn this on," she said. "Can you just get me to Google?"

I figured it out, but first I had to stare at the chick, because it had gotten its head out of the shell now. Or maybe that was its rear end. "I thought they were supposed to be yellow," I said, passing my mom the phone again.

"Me too," said Gavin.

"Me three," said my dad. "Maybe they just don't put the brown sticky ones on the Easter decorations."

"Is its leg supposed to look like that?" I asked. It was folded up and kind of flattened against the chick's body in a way that made me think it must be broken, but I could tell that part of it was supposed to be the foot. "Something's wrong with it," I said.

Gavin looked up at us wild-eyed. I thought he was going to cry. "I'm going to get Betsy," he said, as if he was daring us to say he couldn't. "She's going to know what to do." None of us told him not to, and he took off. At a sprint.

While he was gone, the chicken managed to straighten out its leg and stand up on it. I never in a million years would have thought that spindly twig would be able to hold the chick upright, but it did. Next a blob emerged from part of the amorphous body, which I probably wouldn't have recognized as its head if I hadn't seen the tiny beak.

"I can't find anything on what you do after they're born," my mom said. "It's all about what you do if you have an incubator, but we don't have an incubator."

"What did people used to do?" my dad asked.

"I don't know," my mom said. "I can't find that anywhere."

Then my dad was staring at the phone. "Can I use it to check my e-mail?" he said. My mom and I looked at him for a few beats before we realized he was joking. Joking! My dad! It had been a while.

The chick was wobbling around on its legs now, and then as if it was no big deal, Pumpkin lifted her wing, and the chick disappeared underneath it. "Is that good or bad?" I said.

"She's probably keeping it warm," my mom guessed.

"Or suffocating it," I said. "Shouldn't someone be sponging it off?"

"I don't know," my mom said. "Do you think we should try?"

None of us moved. There weren't any other eggs cracking, and yet we didn't want to leave. My mom was still clicking the buttons on my phone, while my dad and I watched Pumpkin and her eggs as if we had to keep our eyes on them or they would disappear.

"I found something," my mom finally said. "It's a Web site kept by a family in Vermont who raise chickens using broody hens. How do you scroll down?"

I showed her and then she scanned quickly until she stopped. "It doesn't really say anything besides that the mother hen takes care of everything if she's there."

"But what does 'everything' mean?" I asked. "What's the mom supposed to be doing?"

Just then, Betsy rushed in. She was moving as quickly as I'd ever seen her, holding her skirts up. Gavin came running in behind her.

My dad quietly pulled the phone from my mom's hands so Betsy wouldn't see it. He slipped out of the barn.

"Is it born yet?" Gavin asked, out of breath. "Is it okay?"

We explained what had happened, and Betsy told us that that was normal. "Pumpkin will take it from here," she said. She looked at the hen long and hard. "You sly girl," she said. "Here you were getting broody on us and we took it to mean you were just a rooster!"

Then Gavin said, "Look!" We followed his pointing finger to see another shell cracking and another chick rolling and rocking, peeping madly like he'd just woken up from a bad dream to find himself buried alive.

And after that one emerged from the shell, two more hatched.

I can't describe what was so cool about it except to say that with each one I was certain it would never be strong enough to break through the shell, and then when it did, I thought it would never be able to untangle its deformed legs and pop out its sticky, slime-coated head. But they did. Every single time.

While we were watching the eggs hatch, we could hear my dad laughing somewhere outside the barn. I assumed he was talking to someone—or was it the medication he was taking? I didn't think that much of it.

But then he came in and touched my mom on the shoulder. She left the barn with him, and soon they were both laughing in a way I hadn't heard in a long time. At one point, Mom was clearly having a hard time breathing.

They came back into the barn just as the fifth chick hatched and Betsy was getting ready to leave. From another stall I could hear Jezebel making impatient noises and I knew it was milking time.

"Well," said Betsy. She stood up and rubbed her hands down the front of her apron, smoothing it. I think it was only then, as we all looked at each other, that we remembered everything that had happened earlier in the day: the lights, the cameras, Rebecca Cheney, my blog, Nora's new career as a reality-TV star. "Oh, my," Besty said, and the rest of us just looked down.

My mom stepped forward, her face flushed, her hair disturbed. My dad had his good hand on her shoulder. "We should talk," she said.

"Now?" said Betsy, and I could tell that the idea terrified her.

"No," my dad said. "We'll come back with you. We want to talk to Ron as well."

And so the three of them trailed off, leaving Gavin to watch even more of Pumpkin's chicks get born. I milked Jezebel, and then Gavin and I drank most of the milk right out of the pail, as we'd done on the days when we were alone.

I sat on the garden fence and looked out at the view—the ragged clearing littered with stumps, the edge of the woods, the cornfield on the opposite side, the mountains looming above it all. I was going to miss it, the feeling of space out here.

Friday morning, after we'd finished eating our Quiznos, we had written our votes on pieces of paper—S for stay or G for go. All summer I'd wanted nothing more than to rock that G for go into action—and trust me, being able to get away from the whole Caleb and Nora situation definitely increased that option's appeal. But somehow, the letter S snaked out of the tip of the pencil instead of the G I'd been expecting to see.

But now, I knew we couldn't stay. Not after everyone had found out about the blog and all the things I'd said. I was sure that was why my parents had gone to talk to Ron and Betsy. They must be making arrangements for packing and getting us to the airport now.

I wondered where I would find the same good feeling I got from looking out at the mountains across the top of the cornfield. Not at soccer camp. Not at the pool.

I could hear the wind blowing through the tops of the trees. The sun was warm on my arm, though it was on its way down into shadow. More corn behind me needed picking—before all the craziness, my dad had been talking to the Meyer-Hincheys about their helping us to get it all in.

I knew I would never live anywhere like this again.

When I saw Caleb coming out of the woods, I assumed he'd come to see the baby chicks, but he walked right past the entrance to the barn. My heart was pounding as he headed in my direction.

"I guess I should be grateful we're leaving," I thought. Otherwise, I might totally humiliate myself, acting like I hadn't given up hope when I knew very well now that Caleb had a girlfriend.

Without even a "hey" or "hello," Caleb climbed up to sit on the fence next to me. We weren't touching, but I couldn't have been more aware of his arm next to mine if we were. Okay, I thought. Get a hold of yourself.

But I didn't get a hold of myself. And even if I knew I should be grateful we were leaving so I wouldn't make it obvious I liked him, I wasn't grateful—not at all. Caleb could have ten girlfriends and it wouldn't change the fact that sitting here on the fence with him together and alone felt perfect.

"Look, Gen," he said. "I just read your blog."

My eyes must have grown wide and round. I could feel myself blushing. Kristin, I guess, hadn't gotten my text.

"How?" I said.

"In the electricity shack. Everyone's been in there, reading it together."

"Really?" I said. I started to laugh. It wasn't that I thought this was funny. I was laughing the way you do when you get caught passing notes about your teacher in class and are paralyzed by fear. But then, when Caleb burst into a smile, something happened inside of me. Instead of laughing, I started to hiccup. Hiccup and cough.

"Gen?" Caleb said.

"So what are they saying after they read the blog?" I hiccupped again. This was embarrassing.

"Are you okay?"

"*Everyone* was reading it?"

"Yes," he said. "That is, everyone who isn't watching Nora lead Rebecca around by the nose on a tour of her life."

"Really?" I said.

"Oh, yeah," he said. "Rebecca asked her to estimate how many hours she's spent shoveling poo, and Nora was like, 'Including what you and I are doing now?'"

I smiled. Faintly. It was obvious how much he liked her.

"Anyway," Caleb said. "I saw your mom and dad talking to Ron and Betsy. Are you guys leaving?"

"Okay," I said back. I know this wasn't an answer.

"I came to say good-bye."

That's when I started to cry. It's embarrassing, but the idea that I would never see Caleb again, that all of it would be gone, and it was my fault, because of the phone, because of the blog. . . . It was too much.

It was a miracle that he didn't look at me. He didn't make me say anything. And he didn't move. He just started to talk. "Look," he said. "When my mom read your blog . . ."

"Yes?" I said, sniffling.

"She said it made her feel like someone actually knew what she was going through. For the first time today she admitted that she hates it here."

I put my head in my hands. "Is your family going to leave too?"

"My mom is one of the most stubborn people ever born," Caleb said. "She'll stay here if it kills her. I think it's actually good, though, that she admitted that she hates it. It's been like this elephant in the room, her pretending that everything's fine. Maybe now that the swimming hole is done, my dad and I can help more with the stuff that my mom is doing. He was already talking about her taking on some of his field work, and his spending time in the kitchen once in a while."

"But what about—?" I could barely stand to say this out loud, it was so embarrassing. "What about all the stuff I put in about your mom's hair? I mean—I basically compared her to a poodle!"

He looked at me so straight I knew he was serious, but still, it was almost impossible to believe him when he said: "She thought it was hilarious."

"That's it?"

"Yeah," he answered. "My mom thinks it's hilarious. Everyone thinks it's hilarious. Even Ron. First time I think I ever saw him laugh."

"Are you kidding?" I was having trouble not shouting. I was having trouble not jumping off the fence. I did jump off the fence.

"Get back up here," Caleb said, and then, when I was sitting: "You don't actually think anyone took that seriously, did you?"

"No," I lied, because suddenly I felt very, very dumb.

"Yes you did," Caleb said. And then he added, "You idiot," and I can't explain why exactly, but if he'd said, "You genius," I couldn't have felt any better.

I looked down at the grass growing up long around the fence poles—the only place Jezebel didn't get to when we let her out to graze. It was yellow and green all at the same time in the ending afternoon light.

I almost didn't understand what Caleb was talking about when he said next, "So you like my necklace?"

I was thinking "Huh?" until I realized that I had texted Kristin and Ashley about it. Once. Or maybe a couple of times. Or maybe a lot.

I felt my whole body flood with extreme and violent waves of shame.

Oh, my God.

I knew I should tell him how sorry I was, how stupid I felt. But mostly, I had to make him stop talking about the blog before any more stuff I'd written about *him* came up!

I glanced at his face. He'd raised his eyebrows. I knew there was nothing I could say that would suck what he had read in my blog out of his brain. I was sure if I tried to speak, I would just choke. He looked so friendly, so kind, so full of humor. Surely, if he was being cruel I would see that in his eyes.

He scooted closer to me on the fence. "I like your necklace too," he said, putting a palm on the side of my neck and running his thumb gently across the hollow of my throat.

"But I don't have a necklace," I think I said. Or maybe whispered. Or maybe I didn't say it at all. It is hard to remember anything beyond the fact that he was looking into my eyes, and he was coming closer and closer.

"Oh, right," he said. "That's too bad." And then his hand slid to the back of my neck, and he pulled me toward him and kissed me. And I can't describe what it was like except to say it made the whole summer—all of it: the mosquito bites and the beans and the twenty-five-pound dress—worth it. I was just thinking "Lucky, lucky, lucky" the whole time.

"But," I said, between kisses. "But, but, but . . ." I wasn't really making sense. I couldn't really breathe.

He kissed me again. Every time, I couldn't help but kiss him back. And I didn't want to stop. But suddenly I had to.

"What about—," I said. I could barely bring myself to ask, "What about Nora?"

"Nora?" he said like he hadn't heard me. Then "Nora?" again, like he now knew what I'd said, but still didn't understand.

"Isn't she—?" I stopped. "She said that you and she—" Nope, I couldn't quite say it out loud.

"What?" he said, and then he understood. "Me and Nora?" he said. "There's nothing."

"Nothing?" I said. "She told me that you liked her, that it was a secret because of her parents."

"She did?" he said. "She said we were going out or something?"

I thought back to my conversation with Nora. "I'm not sure she used that specific term," I admitted. "But I'm pretty sure the term 'secret boyfriend' came up."

"She said I was her *boyfriend*?" He sounded outraged now, and his tone was triggering a tiny twinge of worry on my part. *Had* she said that?

"Actually," I said. "Now that I think about it, she was kind of vague. I think I might have been the one who said the word 'boyfriend' and she let me think that was true without actually confirming it."

"I'm not her boyfriend," Caleb insisted. He was smiling now, as if he'd just solved a problem he'd thought was going to be a lot harder to work out.

"Why would she make me think that then?" I mused.

"Hmm," he said, and he kissed me again. We were in real danger of falling off the fence. "Maybe to make you mad," he said.

"Or maybe because she's bored. At the beginning of the summer, there maybe was a little attraction between us. That is, until I met you. She's so jealous of you it would take a blind person not to see it."

"Because of you?" He was starting to sound a little conceited.

"No," he corrected. "She doesn't even care about me, except to want to keep you away. I think she'd like to be you."

"You're kidding," I said.

"I'm not," he replied.

"How did she know that I liked you?"

"She's very intelligent," he said, and now I felt myself frowning and blushing at the same time.

"But you're intelligent too," he said. "And a good blog writer. And pretty. And you make me laugh. All the time you make me laugh. Which is important. And also you're just so . . . strong."

"Strong?" I said.

"Yeah," he said. "You've been such a good sport about this place. You made it fun. You certainly kept me going out here. And when I see you in this . . ." He pinched a section of my skirt and let it fall. "It actually makes me understand why people used to think these dresses were sexy." He stopped to kiss me again, and rub his hand along my cheek. I felt an electric current traveling down to my toes and back up, like he had lit a switch when he made contact with my skin. If this was my last night at Camp Frontier, this was all I wanted to be doing, kissing Caleb as new baby chicks were poking out of their shells twenty feet away in the barn.

« 28 »

It was Nora who explained it all to me later. Out of nowhere, she told me she had been reading my blog almost all summer long. She'd found it because she loves blogs—they gave her a window into the real world. "And that's why I was so hard on you. I mean, no wonder! Every time I so much as brought you a chicken or showed you how to feed your livestock, you were going back to your little cell phone and writing down as many nasty things as you could, for all the world to read. I was so mad at you I wanted to spit. But I guess you should be grateful."

"Grateful?" I said.

"Yeah," she answered, like she couldn't believe I was too dumb to understand. She narrowed her eyes, but I knew better than to let that get to me. Under the table, I squeezed Caleb's hand. We were sitting on the benches in Ron and Betsy's back-yard, at a long table groaning with food. It was August 30, the last day of Camp Frontier. We'd just exhausted ourselves square-dancing and now it was time for our last meal. Soccer and

September and school were about to start, although they felt as far away and unreal as Camp Frontier once had when I was fuming over the brochures before we came.

We were eating a potluck meal. My mom brought beans with salt pork and boiled corn on the cob. The Puchinskis shared their amazing biscuits that split open at the touch of a knife—no one asked Disa what was in them and no one turned them down. The Drivers contributed potato salad. The Meyer-Hincheys made fried chicken (and it was so delicious we all suspended our understanding that we were eating something that had the capacity to be someone's pet). Betsy had used up a lot of the fruit that was just starting to ripen to bake four pies: blackberry, apple, peach, and raisin/pear.

Yes, we had stayed at Camp Frontier. At the end of that very long "chick birthday day," my mom and dad came back from talking to Betsy and Ron, and told us what had happened. First: while Gavin and I were watching the baby chicks being born my mom and dad were standing outside the barn using the phone to read my blog. Maybe it was the accumulated tension of the past few days—or of the whole summer—but apparently they could not keep the stony aspect of parental disapproval on their faces as they read it. Initially it was my dad, all by himself, so it was easier for him to chortle and assume that no one would know. But when he'd gotten a few entries in, he brought my mother to join him. "Really," he said. "Gen, I was so proud."

"You were proud?" I'd said. He told me all of this back at the kitchen table in our cabin, right after they'd returned from their conversation with Ron and Betsy, and after Caleb had gone home.

"Gen," my mom said, "of course we were proud. We know you disobeyed us, and that wasn't right, but you're such a good writer! We want you to be good at things. We want you to be happy. And the cow!" She burst out laughing again. She put a fist on the table. "I had no idea that day you came rushing in for a bucket that you were about to fly solo milking a cow."

That night, after they told Gavin and me that Ron and Betsy were not going to make us leave, we voted again just to make sure our decision remained the same—and though last time there had been three S votes and only one G from my mom, now we were unanimous. We counted out four votes to stay.

"You want to keep trying?" my mom gushed. "I'm so proud of you."

"We made it a condition with Ron and Betsy, however," my dad explained, "that you are allowed to continue updating your blog. You will only have access to the phone for an hour every day in the evenings, but we think this is an excellent project for you, and we don't want to cut it off."

"Really?" I said. "You want me to keep doing this? I'm not going to be punished?"

"No," my mom said. "But if you lie to us like this again, hide things, or even simply act like we aren't thinking of your best interest, I'm taking the phone away."

"Yes," I said. "Yes, yes, yes." My mom was laughing.

So we'd made it through the last weeks, and had nearly reached the end—this was our last meal, and tomorrow we'd all be going home.

"Grateful?" I said across the table to Nora now, still fuming at the idea that she'd been reading my blog all summer long.

"Why should I be grateful that you spent the whole summer hating me?"

If she'd noticed my obvious agitation and surprise, she gave no sign. Except maybe there was a bit of something, some knowing look in her eye? Was it possible she was kidding? "You're lucky I didn't read the blog for the first time when everyone else was," she said. "Think how much madder I would have been if the nasty things you wrote about me had come as a surprise."

"Oh," I said.

"You weren't kind," she went on.

"You weren't either," I said.

"At least I wasn't stupid, though," she answered back. "You should be more careful. I mean, who doesn't know that something you put in a text could end up going somewhere you didn't mean for it to go?"

I looked down at the table. All during the last weeks of camp, there had been a silent truce between Nora and me. I thought it had gone like this: I had ended up with the guy; she got to be on TV. And the TV turned out to be pretty amazing. After Rebecca Cheney and all the camera guys left the camp, and the rest of us were sweating our way through the final grueling week of harvest—helping the Puchinskis thresh their wheat, cutting and hauling corn, bringing in the Meyer-Hincheys' bean crop, climbing up Ron and Betsy's trees to bring down the first of the fruit—Nora was reviewing her itinerary for the first show. She was going to be flown to New York. They were putting her up at the Plaza Hotel, escorting her to interviews at Columbia and NYU, bringing her to museums and Broadway shows, introducing her to fashion designers, etiquette experts, and even taking her on a shopping spree at the Apple Store on Fifth Avenue. Sure, her parents wouldn't allow her to use any of the cool stuff when she got home, but the idea was to prepare her a little bit for reality—for college and real life after. The lineup of other shows was equally over the top—in the winter, they'd feature her studying with her mom, snowbound for days at a stretch. And then they would take her skiing and shopping and to a spa in Vail, Colorado, stopping by the University of Colorado at Boulder for an interview. You get the idea.

But now . . . now, I was feeling just about done with her. I mean, Nora had been reading my blog all summer and hadn't told me?

"You're outrageous," I said. "You deserve to be spending a long cold winter out here on the farm with no one to talk to but your parents!"

"Oh, baloney," she said, not even the least bit perturbed by my outburst. "I don't have to justify anything to you."

"But, but—," I said.

"But nothing," she answered. "You did what you needed to do and you're all happy and transformed from your summer on the farm. I did what I needed to do and Rebecca's going to help me get a scholarship for college, hopefully in New York."

I let out an angry sigh. "I'm not happy and transformed," I insisted, but she was looking at me with her eyebrows raised. "You don't know everything," I spat out.

"And neither do you," she said, helping herself to a generous forkful of my mom's beans.

I hate Nora, I realized then. Sometimes I really do.

Or at least I thought so.

The next morning, as we were saying good-bye to Betsy over at her house, my mom invited Nora to spend a week with us over one of our school breaks. And in spite of her New York trip and the Vail trip—did I mention Paris? The Sorbonne?—Nora looked like visiting us was something she actually wanted to do.

"Well, it won't be the Plaza," Nora said. "But Genevieve did tell me all about that trundle bed in her room."

And I was like, "Oh, my God, she actually might come."

"See, Gen?" my mom said in the van, traveling back over the dirt road away from Camp Frontier. "You and Nora did become friends. Once you give something a chance, you might be surprised at how things work out."

And I was like—yes. Surprised. A good word.

And then I was like, "What am I going to do with Nora for a whole week at my house?"

Epilogue

A week after Halloween I had just gotten dropped off by Kristin's mom after a soccer game (we won 2–1 and I had scored—I sometimes ask to play offense now) when I ran into Gavin in the kitchen. He had been out at the 4-H club, which he'd joined. He'd brought three of Pumpkin's chicks home with him and the 4-H club was letting him use them to start a flock. We got right down to business. Gavin was in charge of the popcorn and I was mixing up iced tea with a hand blender—one of my all-time favorite snack combinations. We had to hurry.

As the bubbles on the iced tea were achieving maximum foam, we heard my dad's car pull into the garage, and my mom came padding down from the upstairs in her stocking feet. She's studying for a master's in library science now—another dream—and is always locked up reading or writing papers in her bedroom.

But none of us could afford to miss our eight p.m. date with our television. I was still muddy from the soccer field, and we hadn't even had a chance to order pizza, but it didn't matter.

Gavin had the remote in his hand before he'd even put his food down on the coffee table. The opening credits of Nora and Rebecca's show—*Little Hell on the Prairie* they're calling it—had already started to roll.

After imagining what it would be like so many times, it was funny to see it actually come to life on the screen. It didn't feel like it could possibly be real.

And yet there was the opening shot of Rebecca Cheney, smiling coyly at the camera.

And then, boom: there was a satellite image of the world as seen from above. The picture zoomed in in dramatic chops until you could tell you were over the United States, and then the middle of it, getting closer and closer until it focused in on the rooftops of Ron and Betsy's house and barn, and all around, as far as you could see, were woods.

"Oh my God!" we were all shouting.

And then the camera showed the stream rolling by, and a cow walking through the grass, and children playing with rocks or something, and over all this was the theme song to *Little House on the Prairie*.

Then came a noise, like brakes squealing, or someone was scratching a record player needle across a record followed by Rebecca Cheney's voice: "For some, a vacation in the land of *Little House on the Prairie* is a dream come true." There was a shot of a couple dressed in 1890s clothes walking through a sun-streaked field, holding hands—"It's Clark and Maureen!" my mom shouted—and then immediately a cut to Ron and Betsy's cow, Peanut, taking an enormous poo in her stall, followed by a pull back to Nora's squinched-up face groaning, "Yeah, guess who's going to have to clean *that* up," and then Rebecca was talking again. "For others," she said, "life here is more of a nightmare."

The camera showed Nora now, mucking out the stall. "She's fast," Gavin said, and I had to agree. She put the rest of us to shame. Meanwhile, Rebecca was doing a voiceover. "We will trace the life of a girl who has been raised, for all intents and purposes, as if it is the year 1890. She rarely sees other children." A shot of Nora fishing. "She is homeschooled by her mother, and her parents are her only friends." There was a shot of Nora sitting at the table with Betsy, reading a book. "Though she wants to go to college and have a normal life someday, the question must be asked: *can* she? What does she even know of the modern world?"

Suddenly, we were watching an ad for cough medicine. We paused for a second, as if just seeing the world of Camp Frontier had brought us back to it again. Then Gavin shouted, "I can't believe it's on TV!"

"I can't believe it even ever was," said my dad.

"I know," I answered. "I mean, I know we were there. But now that we're back, and everything's the same as it ever was, I kind of don't feel like Camp Frontier ever happened."

My mom gave me this sappy look but not for long.

The show was back on.

Rebecca was interviewing Nora while Nora milked a cow— actually it was Jezebel. "Hi, Jez," Gavin called to the TV.

"Do you ever make friends with the guests who come here during the summer?" Rebecca said to Nora, on screen.

We heard Nora talking about how hard making friends was. We saw her pulling an iPod ("That's mine!" I shouted) out of the burlap bag Betsy kept them in in the electricity shack, and listening to my music—they must have filmed that before we'd left. We saw Nora going online, showing Rebecca the sites she liked to visit, explaining why.

In between all these scenes we saw the family groups gathered for the town meeting, we heard a lot of animal noises isolated for the soundtrack, we heard country music on a banjo like this was that corny old show *Green Acres*, we saw lots of mud, lots of mosquitoes, lots of slop being scraped into the pig's eating trough.

Caleb called during the second set of ads. "You're watching?" I said without even greeting him—I'd seen the caller ID.

"Of course," he said. "It's amazing."

Caleb and I talk on the phone almost every day. I know it sounds dumb, but just before we left camp, he made me promise that we'd keep in touch this way. "No texting," he said. "It would be nice to keep this private. And real."

"No texting," I'd agreed.

But the problem with talking on the phone is that it can make you miss the person even more. "I can't wait to see the part when they go to New York," I said, when what I meant was "I can't wait to see you." How many times can you say something like that without becoming boring?

"I know," he said, and the thing is, I knew he meant exactly the same thing as me.

I had been IMing a lot with Ka. She texted me a picture of her new hair—platinum blond. Plus a picture of herself in her new cheerleader outfit—she'd gone out for the squad.

"Are you okay?" I'd texted her back.

"I'm GREAT," she said. "I'm taking this whole So Cal thing

ON. The uniform will make a killer Halloween costume when I go to college at NYU."

The commercial ended and Caleb and I both shouted "Gotta go!" and hung up fast. We'd just watched Nora catch a fish and now she was in the middle of skillfully bludgeoning it with a rock. This was not to be missed.

When the show was over, Mom, Dad, Gavin, and I were silent—the New York section had been filled with hilarious moments, including Nora talking to the horses that take people on carriage rides through Central Park. But it was the Camp Frontier sections we were all thinking about.

We'd been home for more than two months now—longer than the time we'd been at camp. I no longer had the embarrassing hand and neck tan you get from spending all the day outside in a long-sleeved dress. I no longer thought anything of it when I poured myself a bowl of Cocoa Krispies for breakfast. Even store-bought eggs had stopped tasting strange to me—in the beginning I'd hardly been able to eat them because the ones that were fresh from our own chickens were so much better.

After the show was over, I went up to my room and I did something I hadn't done since we'd gotten home. I read my blog. At first I thought I was just going to glance through it, maybe read the first post or something. But once I started I couldn't stop. It all came flooding back—how hot and sticky it had been during the day, how frigid at night, how cold and damp and boring the cabin had felt after supper. And then as I read, I remembered all the feelings I'd had as the summer moved along. How exciting it had been to be with Caleb. How funny Ka is. Churning butter. The corn Gavin and I ate raw. After I got my phone back, I'd written about getting caught, the fire, TV,

The week we got home, I read through all the comments. It had felt really exciting while I was doing it, and then for a couple of days after, the feeling was like having water stuck in my ear.

Strangers—people I didn't know aside from their e-mail addresses—had seemed to really care about the littlest things! Everything I was thinking or hearing came with an echo and I felt a little bit dizzy. For a few days after reading them, as I struggled to pick an ice cream flavor, or got dropped off by Kristin's mom at tryouts for the high school soccer team, or went shopping with Ashley at the mall, I kept imagining what my blog readers would say.

And then, reality took over and the echoes in my head died away. Mint chocolate chip was the best—no discussion necessary. Kristin could still beat me in suicide sprints—a fact. Going to the mall with Ashley still meant being ignored by the boys who always follow her around. They like her better, even if my picture had been on TV.

This time, reading through the blog, I skipped the comments. They weren't what mattered.

The blog felt private again. Or at least, personal. It helped me, more than *Little Hell on the Prairie* had, to recall the smells and tastes and feel of the summer—the itchy hay up in the loft, the softness of the quilt when I pulled it up to my cheek in the morning to stay warm five more minutes, the feel of Jezebel's solid body against my hand, the whorls of hair on her haunches that I would stare at as I milked her.

As I'd written in the blog, one of the strange things about Camp Frontier was never seeing yourself in the mirror. At home, I have two mirrors in my room, there's one in the bathroom, I pass a fourth next to the front door when I leave to catch the bus, and at school, there's a floor-length window at the entrance to each classroom. I see myself reflected every five seconds as I walk down the hall.

Still, seeing myself in the mirror always comes as a surprise. The person I am inside does not jibe with the girl with the big head who is so much taller than everyone else.

Reading the blog, though, I felt like looking into a true mirror. Finally, I was seeing me. Who I wanted to be. Who I am. And even though I was dressed up in a costume as I wrote those words, pretending it was 1890 when it was not, the blog was real.

After I finished reading it, I wanted to do something to save it forever. Print it or copy it to my hard drive or laminate it—something.

Or maybe I really wanted something even more extreme.

I'm not sure I would say this out loud, or even write it in my new blog (I took Nora's advice and made it restricted) but I wanted to go back.

At the airport, when he dropped us off, Ron had turned to my family and said, "I guess I'll see you next year?"

"Ha!" I'd said, like he was cracking a joke. But then both my parents' faces lit up. Gavin's too. And I knew that we were going to go.

This is totally insane, I'd thought.

And then I'd raised my hand, given Ron an enormous high five, and said in a voice that could have been sarcastic or could have been sincere—I was still trying to figure that out— "Bring. It. On."

Acknowledgments

I wrote this book fast and furiously and could not have managed at that clip without the support, enthusiasm, and guidance of Melanie Cecka. Thank you. George Nicholson has been a bulwark of confidence and advice throughout as well.

The material for this book was years in the making. On a cruise of the Greek Islands with my grandparents, I cracked open *Little House on the Prairie* for the first time—I was eight then, and by my tenth birthday I was knitting blankets, sewing doll clothes, baking my own bread, and making architectural sketches of a camp that would transport visitors to the frontier. Thank you, Laura Ingalls Wilder, for providing me with years of magic.

In researching this book, I read widely beyond the still-beautiful and informative Little House saga—most useful were *Far From Home: Families of the Westward Journey* by Lillian Schlissel, Byrd Gibbens, and Elizabeth Hampsten, and *Pioneer Women: The Lives of Women on the Frontier* by Linda Peavy and

Ursula Smith. I am indebted to PBS's *Frontier House,* and also to docent explanations of old-fashioned artifacts given to me on a lifetime of historic house tours.

I am grateful to my family and friends for their insights, book parties, school invitations, and more—thanks especially to Sophie, Lorri, Theresa, Audrey, and Christine. My mother is unwavering in making time to read and respond thoughtfully, my husband Rick read early and often as well, and even allowed me to overexplain all my jokes—thank you. My nieces and nephews—Jordan, Jacob, Ryan, Ariana, Miriam, Kelsey, Alani, and Rachel—I have been inspired by your lives and what you know about the world. Max and Eliza—you fill me with love and joy every day.

CATHLEEN DAVITT BELL's first book for young readers was *Slipping*. She received her undergraduate degree from Barnard College and her MFA in creative writing from Columbia University. She lives in Brooklyn, New York, with her husband and two children.

www.cathleendavittbell.com

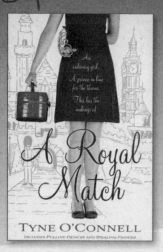
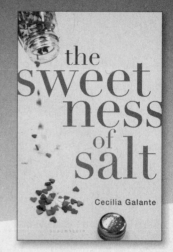